STEPPING STONES

to the City Beautiful

STEPPING STONES
to the City Beautiful

Ellen Carney

PROBITAS PRESS
Los Angeles

Also by Ellen Carney

Ellis Kackley: Best Damn Doctor in the West
Evan Kackley: Carrying on the Tradition
A Biography of Flora Whittemore
The Oregon Trail: Ruts, Rogues & Reminiscences
River of Beaver Stream of Gold
Historic Soda Springs: Oasis on the Oregon Trail
Mavericks in Calico (vol. 1 & 2)
John Gray: Most Spirited of Mountain Men
Edie
Prepared Not Scared
Way Out in Gray's Lake

Co-authored with Elaine S. Johnson:
The Mountain Carriboo and Other Gold Camps in Idaho

**Stepping Stones
To the City Beautiful**
Copyright© 2015 by Ellen Carney

Advance Review Edition
ISBN 978-0-9961850-9-7

If you are interested in reviewing the book
or having Ms. Carney address your group,
contact her publicist at
ymaddox@probitaspress.com or call 800.616.8081
2016 Cummings · Los Angeles, CA 90027

Printed in the United States of America
10987654321

Cover Drawing by Phyllis Cluff
Book Design by Liz Shaw

DEDICATION

To my husband Lewis Nelson's family and my family,
who need to know the stories of their pioneer ancestry

ACKNOWLEDGMENTS

I would like to thank those who have helped in the creation of this book. My aunt, Venice Munro, spent much time critiquing the writing.

I thank all of my family for encouraging me in the work and for putting up with my many hours at the computer, and for their willingness to read and critique the manuscript. I thank Janissa Balcomb for her assistance in formatting and putting the work together and Yvonne Maddox for her help in editing and promoting *Stepping Stones to the City Beautiful*.

About the Author

Ellen Carney, born and raised in a small Idaho town, has visited nearly all the states in the U.S. and lived in most of those in the West. She received a bachelor's degree from the University of Arizona, and a master's from the University of Utah. An award-winning newspaper columnist and author, her 14 books—mostly historical, reflect her deep love of the West. Carney's books have won national and state awards. She originally self-published and distributed her first book *Ellis Kackley: Best Damn Doctor in the West*, selling over 10,000 copies.

Carney's books have twice received honors from the National Federation of Press Women. She was named "Writer of the Year" by the Idaho Writer's League in 1994. Carney has been a newspaper correspondent for the for the *Caribou County Sun* in Soda Springs for the past 33 years and for the *Idaho State Journal* in Pocatello for over 20 years. She served as an officer in the Caribou Historical Society, the Idaho Writer's League, and for three terms on the Caribou County Historic Preservation Commission.

Carney taught elementary, junior and senior high school students for over twenty years. She and her husband Lewis Nelson have eight children (seven living), 24 grandchildren, and 47 great-grandchildren.

Contents

CHAPTER ONE

Richard Harris winced as he stood and straightened his back. The hot sun of late afternoon beat down on him unmercifully and there was not a cloud in the sky. But Richard loved the bustle of life in Buffalo at midday. He bent, and straightened each knee then squared his broad shoulders. He felt stiff from being cramped into the wagon seat all day. He brushed a large, dusty hand across his jaw line, rough with stubble, and made a mental note he must take time to wash and shave. Shaving hadn't been a priority until he met Jenny, but his life had changed dramatically since that time.

New York had been good to him and his freighting business prospered, but lately his thoughts kept turning back to Virginia and the plantation. He had turned his back on his brother and on the responsibility he never wanted in the first place. He had kissed his share in the family fortune good-by, morally, if not legally. Riding off in anger that fateful day when he had become so upset with his brother, Tom, he knew the quarrel had been his fault. Young and hot blooded, he had allowed strong emotions to dictate his behavior—even when the stakes were so high. But inheritance rights were not his concern at this point. He just plain missed the family plantation and Tom.

Richard let his eyes wander across the backs of his team of sturdy draft horses. He had named the mares Daisy and Doll. The familiar aroma of horse sweat assailed his nostrils and caused him to hover briefly on the edge of homesickness. He would have to rub the team down carefully. Richard always made sure his horses received excellent care. His father, Thomas Harris Senior, had installed in Richard a pride in his animals. He remembered how insistent his father had always been that the horses, whether ridden or worked, be cared for promptly and properly.

Richard frowned slightly as his mind wandered back to his boyhood. He and his brother, Thomas, "Tom" they called him, always had more than their share of disagreements. As a boy, Richard had daydreamed a lot. He wondered about justice, freedom and all those other intangible things people seemed to have forgotten or at least weren't talking about.

Richard remembered a time as a young boy, when his father's friend, William, had brought his son to play with him one sultry autumn day while the men talked business. The roguish little eyes of the boy, George, six or seven years of age, glimmered with mischief. "Let's kill the pigs and make bacon," he suggested as they stood beside the pig pen.

Richard had joined George and a couple of the slave children in chasing the young pigs around the pen. They were off like the starting line of a foot race. They planned to slaughter the pigs, just as they had seen done each fall on their plantations and make them into ham and bacon. "My dad will be so proud of us if we get the meat ready for winter all by ourselves," Richard exclaimed.

Richard's father and his friend arrived just in time to rescue one pig with all four boys piled on top of it. He hadn't been pleased. George blamed the little slave children for the escapade, and though Richard insisted George had come up with the original idea, his father, as usual, never listened to him. The results of that prank still haunted Richard. His slave friends would carry for life the stripes across their backs from the terrible whipping they received. Richard and George got off with only a lecture and being confined to the house for a while.

Richard never wanted to play with George again. It reminded him too much of all the pain he had unwittingly caused to his friends and he hated young George for lying and refusing to take responsibility for his actions. He played mostly with the slave children, who he found to be more honest about things. He also played occasionally with the young son of a share cropper on an adjoining plantation. His parents and Tom deplored Richard's choice of friends, even at that young age.

Richard wondered why slaves were subjected to inequity and poor quality of life. His sympathies as he matured were with the abolitionists—a political philosophy which didn't set well in Virginia. His father usually treated his slaves well, but Richard thought no human being should be owned by another. He tried to tell his father how he felt, but the senior Thomas looked as though Richard had no understanding whatsoever of how to run a plantation. He swept his hand across the area of his vast estate, and replied, "Now son, tell me just how you'd propose to run the plantation if we freed all our slaves?" When Richard suggested they could give the slaves a chance to stay there and share crop, his father just laughed.

Tom, the eldest and his father's namesake, seemed to Richard to be the favored son. Tom had no qualms about using slaves to work the fields, and as his father aged, he took over much of the responsibility of the plantation. Steadfast and dependable, his parents had always expected Tom to watch out for Richard and keep him out of trouble.

From his first memory, Richard felt himself nothing but an annoyance to Tom, whose expression seemed to be one perpetual glare of disapproval. "Now what?"Tom would demand, peering down the bridge of his nose at his little brother when Richard tried to talk to him, knowing whatever came next probably wouldn't be to his liking. When Richard accomplished anything, it seemed Tom usually received the credit. Richard drew in his breath; compliments were something he'd never had many of while growing up. He'd hated it when Tom stole his thunder.

Richard resented his brother's interference in his affairs, and things hadn't improved as they reached adolescence. Handsome Tom, towering over his little brother's average-sized frame, soon stole the attention of every girl who showed an interest in Richard.

Richard often stood by the pond and studied his own reflection. He saw his solid frame, his full face with a strong jaw line, and his brown mop of hair which seemed dull compared to Tom's. Richard's brown eyes filled with anger as he cursed fate for giving his brother those striking icy grey eyes and long lashes in a thin, handsome face topped with thick, dark hair which so attracted the girls.

Richard would throw a pebble into the pond and watch its ripples erase his image. He wished it were as simple to erase the conflict between himself and Tom and between his feelings about justice and equality and what transpired at the plantation. Some day he would be able to leave—to go up north where people thought more like he did, and start his own business. A business which would enable him to make his own way in the world, and treat all people with the same justice and equality.

After their parents died, Richard thought since he owned a share of the plantation, he should have some say as to how it would be managed. Tom insisted everything be handled the same way as his father had always handled things. When Richard proposed freeing at least his half of the slaves and giving them the opportunity to share crop the land, Tom fairly hooted, "Where on earth did you come up with that crazy idea? You'd better start watching the company you keep."

Just thinking about the past made all the old pain come flooding back. Richard's full mouth tightened into a line of grimness beyond his twenty-five years as he remembered his consuming frustration at the time. Richard who had a restless spirit anyway, had decided it was time to part company with his brother, whatever the cost. He had ridden north and wandered about for nearly a year, trying one job after another before finally settling in New York in 1825, just as the Erie Canal opened.

The canal stretched from the Hudson River to Lake Erie. New York's building of the canal had been a smart commercial move. The canal enabled horse-drawn barges to make the trip to Albany in eight days instead of twenty. The new canal soon attracted shipping from the Hudson River and other established routes.

It didn't take long for Richard to recognize the advantage of getting into the freighting business. All those goods being shipped to and from the Buffalo area had to be transported to the canal somehow. He started hauling farm products from near Buffalo, but soon expanded into carrying goods manufactured in the city also then bringing freight from the barges back to the area. As business expanded, he hired his wife's brother, Aaron, and three free blacks as additional drivers. It looked as though he would soon have to hire more help.

It hadn't been easy, but he had rapidly made a place for himself in the world. He didn't need to depend on Tom nor the plantation for his livelihood. Richard savored his independence, but felt guilty about it. As he matured, a sense of loss replaced most of the anger he once felt and a strong desire overcame him, almost like an addiction, to have a relationship with his brother.

He knew he should have written, just to let Tom know he was still alive, but his pride kept him from contacting his brother. He and Tom hadn't communicated or set eyes on each other for nearly seven years. He tried to convince himself he didn't care, but he felt an emptiness he couldn't shake. He realized that though they'd been too busy arguing to ever get to know each other well, there had been a bond—one he hadn't realized existed. He raised his arm and wiped the sweat off his brow with the sleeve of his homespun shirt—none too clean after sitting behind a team of horses all day. He took a deep breath and began unloading the freight from his wagon. The hefty proprietor of the store receiving the boxes and barrels came out and gave him a hardy "Ho, Richard, what do you have for me today?"

The mare shook herself, and Richard patted her neck. He felt happy to be back in Buffalo. Jenny would be waiting for him. Jenny, with long, reddish-brown hair always slightly disheveled; sprinkled with freckles all the way to her shoulders; wearing that same warm smile which had first attracted him to her. That smile set her apart, somehow. It came easy, seemed natural and covered her whole face, all the way to her sparkling green eyes. Her parents had named her Genevieve, a name much too long and too formal to fit her, so everyone called her Jenny. Jenny had become the most precious thing in Richard's life.

It seemed hard to believe they had been married almost five years. It had been a good marriage, but both felt disappointed when they had not been able to have a child—the one thing they both felt would have made their marriage perfect. Life had not looked kindly on them in that department. With Richard away so much, the house had become too empty for Jenny to bear. Needing companionship, she started a private school. She loved children and enjoyed working with them, allowing her to almost forget her unhappiness at not having a child of her own. For several years now, she had conducted one of the best private schools in the city. Jenny had an abundance of grit. Since marrying her, Richard had realized how much difference one person could make in the world. She had derailed intractable Richard completely and turned him into a man of accountability.

———————

Thomas Harris looked around him with a sense of awe. He took a deep, delicious breath of the fresh morning air into his lungs. May 30th held promise of being a beautiful day. It felt good to be alive. The sun's sparkling rays on the early morning dew made the earth glisten like a shiny new gold piece. Leaves on the oak trees sparkled as did the grasses, mosses and ferns—all full of life. He gazed at the lush meadow, which stretched toward a small rise.

Tom's tall, lean body sat easy in the saddle, blending with that of Brandy, his bay mare, as though they were one. When he lifted the reins, the horse responded to his touch. This mare, his favorite mount, seemed practically human. He circled the rise and ascended it from the back side, then reined up Brandy and gazed at the panoramic view of wide, green fields before him.

Off to the west he could faintly see the majestic gaps of the Blue Mountains. Across the river and along it curved a high ridge covered with virgin forest where nature existed perpetually at its best. It amazed Tom how quickly new growth could repair the ravage made by man. He wondered if it would always be that way, or would man eventually overrun nature's healing power. Below him, a large, flat area stretched for miles, green and luxuriant, much of the rich soil planted into tobacco. He felt sure God would bless his labors again this year.

A covey of quail whirred up in front of him and a cuckoo called out. One of his favorite times, that of hunting quail with his father burst out of his memory and into his mind. He had always loved to hunt with his father, whether they were trying to bag quail, deer, or other game. He remembered how excited they both felt when he shot his first white-tailed deer—a small event, but still large in his memory.

A tiny smile appeared, softening Tom's angular face. The estate looked just as it had when his father lived. The tobacco crop looked good, his overseer kept the slaves in line, and he would soon be the father of a son. He had no doubt that the baby Christina carried would be a good-sized boy. Why else would her usually flat stomach be so extended?

Tom smiled as he pictured his young wife with her willowy body, her luxurious, dark hair, brown eyes, her lovely features and quick smile. His deep grey eyes sparkled as his heart filled with love and tenderness. Just thinking of Christina warmed Tom through and through. Never before had he felt such overwhelming love for another human being.

Tom's thoughts interrupted by the call of a mocking bird, his mind's image faded away and a shadow crossed his face. He hoped he could be as good a father as his own father, who had affected Tom's life so profoundly. He remembered riding around the plantation with him from the time he was old enough to straddle a horse, and thinking what a wonderfully vast domain his father managed to not only supervise, but constantly improve. Now, it had all become his responsibility and he realized so much more than he had as a child, the accountability connected with a large estate. "How I miss you, Papa," he said aloud, as if his father were within earshot. He missed him terribly, and had for long years now, since he had taken his last breath.

Though Tom's parents took little time for amusements with their children, they imparted their Christian ethics and work-oriented philosophy to them. He seldom remembered seeing his father without a hammer, a shovel or an axe in his hand. Tom's gaze rested on the little family grave yard where they were buried, on the plantation, in the place they loved more than any other spot on earth. Maintaining the plantation, as his father had, seemed to him the most fitting memorial possible to his parents, who had raised him and given him everything he now had. Tom had tried to run the plantation just as his father would have done.

Tom's thoughts turned now to his younger brother, Richard, who hadn't seen things the same way. Their difference in philosophy had led to constant fighting between them. Fighting between the brothers wasn't anything new. Tom remembered when Richard was born, and how his baby brother had invaded his world, turning it upside down. He lost his place in the spotlight and as the only son. The sparkle in his parents' eyes focused on someone else.

Richard seemed to be always tattling on Tom, goading him about the little girl friend who asked him to sit beside her at her birthday party, or causing some other havoc in his life. That was when Tom pushed his brother and he fell out of the tree house, breaking his arm. He refused to tell his parents what had happened, and so his father had torn down the tree house—a place where Tom spent many hours of his time, his favorite place to get away from everything.

Tom and Richard differed in so many ways. Richard had never seemed to care about the plantation or take any responsibility. As a child, he preferred playing with children on slave row rather than making friends with the families of other plantation owners. He wouldn't listen to his father or Tom when they tried to tell him you didn't make friends of the slaves. Later, he had become friends with a group of abolitionists, and picked up their crazy ideas. It seemed almost as if Tom and Richard came from different blood lines.

One cloudy evening after his father's death, his brother had insisted they should free the slaves and let them share crop the land. When he angrily refused to listen to Richard's ideas, Richard packed a few things in his saddle bag and rode off, never to return. Tom wondered what had happened to errant, fun-loving Richard, who came and went as he pleased, refusing to be accountable to anyone for anything. Richard possessed a magnetism about him that strangely drew people to him—sometimes people not considered by Tom as those he would want to call desirable friends. Tom felt sure Richard had met with foul play or a prison yard. If he were alive, surely there would have been some word of him by now.

A mighty wave of sadness mixed with a fair measure of guilt swept over Tom and his grey eyes watered as he thought of his little brother. It wasn't nostalgia for their shared boyhood, a succession of minor battles and trying to outdo each other. He loved Richard and now wished he had shown it more when he had the opportunity. For several years after Richard's disappearance Tom had been filled with deep melancholy. It seldom surfaced now, but still resided deep inside him as if it longed to be released and his feelings resolved.

Christina had dispelled the dark silence of the house and brought happiness back into his life. Christina, so alive, so full of childlike enthusiasm! His smile returned as he thought of her.

Tom rode for hours, checking on his estate. Dampness from rain the night before still lingered in the warm Virginia morning, but the slight breeze was beginning to pick up the fragrance of growing things. At noon he found a grassy knoll and dismounted. He patted Brandy gently and she nuzzled his side. He reached up and scratched behind her right ear, then let her graze while he ate the sandwiches Christina had Mandy pack for him.

It had become a full day's job to check out the plantation. When Tom turned toward home, the sun had already set in the western sky. He stopped in the last patch of woods and picked a wild rose bud for Christina; one just beginning to open. He tucked the stem carefully into his breast pocket with the bud protruding, as the gathering dusk closed in around him.

————————

Icy fingers of pain reached out from Christina's spine and encompassed her. She screamed as she felt immense pressure tearing her insides apart, then the pain receded and she fell back upon her pillow in exhaustion.

"You're doin' fine," Mandy's soothing voice told the new mother to be, but Mandy sounded more cheerful than she felt. "Must be a boy chile," she muttered to herself as she reached up to wipe away a streak of sweat running down her black face, which glistened like newly varnished mahogany.

Christina's whole body tensed and her shrill screams again rent the air as the infant made its appearance into the world and accompanied the entry with a lusty cry.

Mandy had worried about her mistress, Christina, this small wisp of a girl with a slim, straight form, carrying what seemed to be an obviously large baby. She looked at the girl child with amazed wonder. She doubted if it weighed over five pounds.

"It's a girl!" Mandy told the mother, now lying back again on the pillows, breathing heavily, her eyes closed. Mandy wrapped a piece of white string around the umbilical cord and tied it in a square knot. She made another tie farther down the cord and cut between the two. Christina did not show any interest in the baby, but tensed as if she were having another contraction.

"You has a fine baby girl," Mandy reminded her.

Christina didn't even look at the infant. "A girl; Tom will be so disappointed," she said between clenched teeth when she was able to get her breath.

"I'll clean her up so you can hold her."

Christina opened her eyes and looked at the baby for the first time. For a moment the terror that had filled her eyes during the birth was replaced by wonder as she stared at the crying child, then she turned her head away. "I thought they came clean," she said wearily.

Mandy knew Massa Tom had his heart set on a son, but this baby seemed healthy and strong, which should gladden the heart of any new parent. She took the newborn to the small wooden table in the center of the room and began to wash the grayish white film from its skin. Interrupted by another scream from Christina, she quickly placed the infant in the cradle, tucked a blanket around the tiny body, and hurried back to the bed.

"What be it now, Miz Christy?" she asked anxiously as the new mother clenched her fists and began pushing as if to expel another child. "Lawd a mercy," she breathed, "there IS another one coming!"

A small foot reached out toward Mandy. "Lordy, it's breach," Mandy said to herself.

"Don't push," Mandy commanded, but the words hardly penetrated Christina's consciousness. "QUIT PUSHIN'," Mandy almost shouted.

"I can't," Christina breathed.

"YA'ALL HASTO!" insisted Mandy firmly, as she reached inside the mother to align the limbs with the body of the baby. Christina's muscles were taut. Flesh tore as the baby came through the narrow birth canal but at last the second child, another girl, small and wrinkled, appeared.

The way its elbows and knees bent close to its body, the small form somehow reminded Mandy of a large frog. No lusty cry announced the arrival of this little one. Mandy thumped it on the bottom of its feet, and at last a weak wail of protest came from the tiny grey bundle.

"Lawd a mercy," she exclaimed again. "Massa Thomas want a boy chile, not a parcel o' girls. What he say 'bout dis?"

Mandy picked up the piece of white string left from tying the cord of the first babe. She made two more ties and cut the umbilical cord then tucked the second infant into the cradle beside her sister. She could finish cleaning the babies up later, but now Christina needed her. This small one, its wee skeleton covered with wrinkled parchment-like skin, would probably die anyway. Its breath came thinly, as if life hung by a spider's thread. The slender fingers, no bigger than bird claws, balled into a fist barely larger than an oversized grape. How could such a tiny, frail being possibly survive?

As Mandy had feared earlier, Christina was not doing well! She looked like all the strength had drained from her body. Her face seemed as white as the blood-covered sheet she lay upon had once been. Mandy tried to hold back the panic swelling up inside her as she pressed on Christina's stomach to expel the afterbirth, but with it came fresh, bright red blood gushing from her mistress. Mandy pressed her open right hand on the girl's stomach, grabbed hold of the uterus and began to knead it, but the organ, too tired to contract on its own, did not respond. Mandy watched in horror. Christina failed to react as her life blood continued to drain from her body, leaving only silence and death.

Mandy's own daughter had died in childbirth less than a year earlier; now she had lost Christina whom she loved almost as her own. She had done her best to save both of them, but her best wasn't good enough. Her head dropped until her chin rested on her chest. How long she sat engulfed in anguish she did not know, but as reality set in, she began to wail. When Old Hannah, the cook, appeared in the doorway, she joined in Mandy's lament before going to spread the sad news to the slaves.

At last Mandy rose slowly and began to change the bed. She carefully removed the young woman's clothing and gently washed her body. She dressed her in her best gown and fixed her hair, piling it high upon Christina's head as she did when she dressed for plantation parties. She lifted her mistress's limp arms and crossed them over her breast. When she finished, she stepped back and scrutinized the scene. Christina's beautiful form lay on clean, white sheets, looking almost as though she were asleep.

Mandy turned her attention to cleaning and dressing the baby girls. In spite of her small size, the first one was quite lively. She spent extra time with the tiniest one, massaging the little body with warm olive oil.

Tom turned his bay mare into the tree-lined drive toward the big house. He wondered why the usual warm glow at the windows was absent and the curtains remained closed. At the stables he reined Brandy in and she came to a halt. He rubbed the arching neck of the mare affectionately and spoke softly to her before dismounting. Ben, the stable boy, came quickly to take the horse and rub her down. In addition to his other duties, dependable Ben tended the chickens and livestock and kept the barns and watering trough clean.

Tom stood back to admire the fine lines of the mare as he watched her being led away. She had been well worth the price he paid for her. As he turned and walked quickly towards the big house, still enveloped in darkness, he felt a sudden wave of uneasiness. A cold chill swept through his body.

"Christy," he called as he opened the front door—the way he always did when he didn't see her immediately. No answer greeted him—only darkness and silence. Without stopping to light a candle, he took the stairs two at a time. "Where are you, sweetheart? Where are you?"

Mandy appeared in the bedroom doorway. The soft glow from the taper in her hand revealed her puffy face and red eyes. From the recesses of the room a soft wail, like a baby lamb bleating, reached his ears.

"What is it Mandy? Where's Christina? Is she all right?"

"I'se sorry," Mandy stuttered, and began to wail again.

He pushed her aside and burst into the room. Christy's form lay motionless upon the bed. He rushed to take her in his arms, but her body lay lifeless.

"No," he shouted, "No, it can't be." He reached up and tore the fresh rosebud from his breast pocket and threw it onto the floor, then turned and rushed out of the room and out of the house, kicking the front door open instead of turning the knob. He never even glanced at the small bundles lying side by side in the cradle. For him, only death filled the room.

When Tom finally returned to the house, he moved on leaden feet. He forced himself to look at the twin girls, one with its tiny face slightly upturned and innocent eyes wide open, the other with eyes tightly closed as if shutting out the world. He rubbed his hand across his own eyes in a gesture of disbelief. This situation whipped the heart out of him. He should feel something for these babies, but felt only anger— their birth had brought only death and sorrow. He wondered if they could feel the dark silence of the home they had come to, or if they felt the peace and contentment of which their coming had robbed him. Why had God deserted him? Why had He taken his wife when Tom was not even there to tell her goodbye, to hold her in his arms and help bear her pain? Christina's love formed the adhesive which held his world together. Now he had nothing; how could he live without her? New life seemed meaningless without the love that had once filled his heart.

Mandy looked at the tiniest infant and thought of a corn cob doll she once cherished, a forlorn creature without arms or hair. She picked the baby up and held her close. The infant nuzzled her breast. She knew the lives of these babies were in her hands and she felt totally inadequate. She could not nurse these infants; she had no milk for babies. What could she do? She remembered her mother once warming milk and dipping a rag into it to suckle a baby lamb. Mandy warmed a pan of milk and dipped the end of a rag into it. She let it drip into the mouth of one baby then the other, until each seemed at least partially satisfied. The process seemed to take forever. She knew more permanent arrangements must be made for feeding these babies or they would both die.

Mandy held the tiny girls, one on each arm, as she approached Tom. She kept her voice low and steady, making her face a blank so he would not see her worry. "Dey needs t' be fed."

Tom caught the concern in her voice and shook himself from the trance-like state into which he had withdrawn. He glanced quickly at her face, then looked at the babies with detached reluctance. "Do you know of anyone who might be able to wet nurse them?" he finally asked. "Maybe one of the slaves who has recently had a child?"

She took a long, thoughtful look at the babies, then nodded. "Don't know 'bout none here, but Massa William's Eliza have a baby dat just die."

Drawing a slow breath, he rubbed the back of his hand against his lower lip. His eyes looked at empty air beyond her. "I'll send a rider to make arrangements with William," he thought aloud. Then giving Mandy a somber smile, as if a load had been taken from his shoulders, he said, "Get the babies ready to go."

Mandy carefully put a fresh belly band, diaper, undershirt and nightgown on each baby. Christina had hand sewn the little garments with such care, her tiny stitches almost invisible. The sight of them caused a lump in Mandy's throat. She wrapped the babies in tiny quilts, also made by her mistress, and placed them side by side in a basket she had woven for the new baby. It easily held them both.

Mandy waited in the entry until she heard the buggy coming to take them to the adjoining plantation. Young Moses, the driver, stopped and took the basket while she climbed in.

He looked at the two babies. "Tis a shame 'bout Miz Christy," he said. "Massa Thomas sho' seem to be takin' it hard."

"Tis hard t' be takin'," said Mandy.

The June sun shining down upon them and the beauty of the drive, which Mandy usually enjoyed so much, seemed a mockery to her this day. They drove up to Massa William's plantation and to slave row. Eliza, the stout and buxom dark-skinned slave of Massa William, stood in the doorway of her quarters. Mandy brought the basket inside and set it on the table with a little sigh.

Eliza peered at the babies and tears filled her eyes. "They'se so tiny," she said. She reached out a hand and the largest baby's wee white fingers curled around her big black one. She remembered the joy of having her own tiny daughter and holding her in her arms–a daughter, a daughter to love and care for! Rousing herself, she nodded at Mandy with forced cheerfulness.

Mandy's eyes filled also. This wasn't how it should be. A swell of caring rose in her throat which made speech impossible. A kaleidoscope of memories filled her mind. She thought of Christina who never had the opportunity to feel the joy of motherhood and now her babies were left to be cared for by someone else. She thought of her own daughter who had brought her so much joy, of little Sully–her only grandchild. Love stirred within her for these two motherless babies. She skewed her face into a look meant to be reassuring, then with great reluctance, she turned and slowly went out the door and back to the buggy. Her expression betrayed the tension she felt. "They'll be okay," Young Moses reassured her.

For the next few weeks, Mandy went to the plantation of Massa Williams as often as she could get away from the big house. She held the little ones and massaged them with warm oil. They began to fill out and to grow. They were all that was left of Christina and Mandy shared all the love she had for Christina with them as if they were hers.

"Lawsy, you sho' do love dem babies," Eliza said as Mandy watched her matter-of-factly suckling one white child on each large breast. "I expect I'se gettin' as attached to dem as you, but it no good. We'se not expected t' love an' care. Why even our own chillins is sold away from us." She paused and looked down at the two babies. "Carin' only brings us grief. I don't know how de Massas can do violence to dose who grow der crops an' feed 'em, but dey do. You knows most of de massas in Virginia has sucked a black mammy or been raised up by one." She brushed back a strand of black hair.

Mandy knew Eliza was right, but she couldn't help caring about the twins. Clear images of the past still haunted her. She had served Christina since her mistress was a young child and she had helped bring these children into the world. It seemed Tom wanted nothing to do with the twins but somebody had to love them.

Tom eventually named the babies Sarah and Laura, after Tom and Christina's mothers. The stronger baby was named Sarah after Tom's mother. They grew fast and even tiny Laura soon began to fill out. Their eyes and hair turned dark, and accented their small, finely formed facial features; their tiny, delicate hands grew plump and dimpled, cheeks grew fat and legs sturdy. Eliza carried them about, one on each side, with their pudgy little legs straddling her body. She occasionally stopped to settle one or the other more comfortably against her hip.

At two-years-of-age, when they were weaned and ready to come home, Tom accepted the news with a nod, his face impassive and mouth tight. He could hardly believe it had been two years; the wound he had felt from losing Christina had not begun to heal. He hadn't visited the children except when they were christened. He had turned his back on the twins and on the world. The house, now empty of her presence, still bore Christina's imprint. He missed her dreadfully. Tom had put Christina's portrait and all of her tangible, little possessions which constantly reminded him of her into her room, locked the door, and forbid anyone to disturb it. He thought banishing her memories to this room would banish his sorrow, but instead, he felt attracted to the room and spent many hours there, head in hands, before her full length portrait in the beautiful gilded frame. It had been a present from her family on their first Christmas.

Tom knew he had become increasingly despondent, moody and irritable since Christina's death, but his life has lost its luster. He almost envied Richard, dead or alive. Tom had always loved the plantation, but now the chore of running it seemed formidable—like a yoke around his neck. And the twins—how would he ever be able to raise twins properly? He could hardly bear the pain of looking at these miniature replicas of his late wife.

Chapter Two

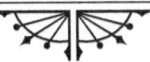

A stiff draft from the west combined with the humidity from off Lake Erie caused a bone-chilling wind. Richard felt thankful for his heavy coat. The wind seemed to go right through you on stormy days. He had just delivered a load of wheat to the wharf to be barged to Albany. With the canal in operation, he had no doubt Buffalo would soon become an even more important grain and livestock market. Richard could hardly believe the changes he had seen in the years he had been freighting here.

He checked his team and noticed one horse had lost a couple of nails out of her shoe. He hated to take the time, but knew he must take care of it before his next load, so he headed through town toward the blacksmith shop. At the first crossroads, he could see a crowd gathered. He pulled over to the side of the road, set the brake and wrapped the horses' lines around it, then walked over to the edge of the group. Several loud and obnoxious men were heckling someone. "What's going on here?" Richard asked a skinny man whose collar bone protruded from an oversized shirt.

The man pointed towards the center of the crowd, where two young men seemed to be getting all the attention, "Say they're missionaries. Say Joe Smith had a vision and saw God," the man continued.

These men must be crazy, Richard thought. Even religious radicals didn't claim to see God. That had ended with the ancient prophets. He ducked as a stone, thrown at the missionaries from the opposite side of the crowd, whizzed past the young men and into the bystanders. "This looks like an explosive situation," Richard said under his breath, "Don't those men know better than to cause a riot? They may be tough, but not tough enough to take on a whole crowd." Just then he heard another stone, this time thudding against the flesh of one of the missionaries.

Mob violence angered Richard. This wasn't a time to sit around and chat. Nine times out of ten you could head off trouble with a good offensive. Richard ran back to his wagon, jumped to the seat and turned his horses into the crowd. A path quickly opened as people jumped out of the way. When he was even with the missionaries, he yelled, "Hop in before you lose your hides."

The young men bounded into the wagon, and Richard applied the whip to the horses' rumps. A couple of rocks thudded against the wagon bed, but the crowd quickly began to disperse. When they were half a block away from the commotion, Richard reined the horses in and looked at the young men. One had a long, thin face in which the piercing blue eyes were the most compelling feature. The other, a blond young man, seemed to have unusually long legs and arms. Their homespun clothing looked threadbare but clean. "I don't know what you said to that bunch, but apparently they didn't like it. You're lucky to be getting away with a whole hide," Richard chided.

The man with piercing blue eyes spoke up. "We thank you for your kindness. Things were starting to get out of hand," he added. "I'm Elder Cox and this is Elder Anderson," gesturing toward his companion whose eyes squinted slightly. "We're missionaries for the Church of Jesus Christ of Latter-day Saints, commonly known as the Mormons."

Richard had heard a time or two of the Mormons. They seemed to be a radical group with strange ideas. "Where you staying? I'd better take you there," he noted.

The men hesitated and looked at each other. Finally, Elder Cox answered slowly with forced cheerfulness, "We just got into town this morning. You see, when we're working for the Lord, we go without purse or scrip, and rely on the Spirit to guide us to those willing to advance His cause."

Richard looked at him levelly. "In other words, you don't have any money or any place to stay? When did you last have something to eat?" He saw the answer in their eyes and knew their hunger.

"We had a lovely meal last night with some people out of town about ten miles," volunteered Elder Anderson with reluctant honesty.

Richard shook his head. Oh, no, here we go again, he thought. He fought the urge to laugh. Jenny often said that if there was a hungry person within twenty miles, Richard would find him and bring him home. After she started her school, he had promised her he would be more careful about who he picked up. You couldn't bring just anyone home when children were there.

He grimaced inwardly. What could he do at this point? The two looked perfectly innocent. "I'll take you home with me for a hot meal and a good night's rest, then you're on your own," he said.

"We are much indebted to you," replied Elder Cox. Richard turned his team toward the blacksmith shop.

———————

Back at the plantation, Tom put Mandy in charge of caring for the twins. As with many young plantation children of the day, Sarah and Laura cut their teeth with the slave children. They had the run of the place. There were few young ones—except Greene, Hannah the cook's son, and Sully—Mandy's granddaughter. The four soon became fast friends.

The twins and their friends romped through the yards, pulled up vegetables in the garden and picked the petunias. In spite of Mandy's efforts to keep them in sight, they occasionally slipped away. They roamed through the barns, the chicken coops, the sheep pens, pig pens and sometimes into the slave-row cabins.

They picked wild flowers, found shiny stones, pine cones and snail shells from along the stream bank. Sometimes they caught a butterfly or frog. These treasures were exhibited to Mandy with great pride.

The gnarled oak tree by the creek on the edge of the woodland, hidden by the upward slope of the grassy bank, became a choice place for adventure and discovery. Mockingbirds sang and flitted about this enchanted woodland. The children would lie on their backs and listen to the water gurgle lazily over the stones in the stream or watch clouds form into mystical shapes. In the spring, they delighted over the fragrance of the dogwood when out in full bloom and the many different flowers which grew along the stream—blue forget-me-nots, pink crow's foot and white daisies. Sometimes they found a bird's nest or frightened up a covey of baby partridges.

In the fall, they played in the corn patch and ran between the stalks that produced the plump ears of yellow corn. Though it was strictly forbidden, they ran between the rows of golden tobacco leaves hanging over poles to dry. They watched when the hogs were killed then cut up and hung over slow fires of hickory to smoke.

They played Massa and slave, played horse and rider—climbing onto each other's backs, played hide-and-seek and played tag. They cooked mud cakes on the foundation of the chimney then trooped into the kitchen covered from head to toe with mud dough. Hannah would close her eyes to hide their rolling, then order the children outside where Mandy could wash them up without bringing all that dirt into the house. She made special treats for them; Hannah had a knack for making food unforgettable. After lunch, the children would all lie down for a nap on a quilt pallet, then go back to their games and mischief. Hannah was square, firm and imperturbable, but she had a tender spot for all children.

The children used a big flat stone in the yard as a place to set their play table. Greene always played the father and Sarah always insisted on being the mother when playing "house." Laura and Sully gave up fighting to be the mother—Sarah always got her way. But it became a running battle who would be the daughter and help in the kitchen and who would be the son and assist Greene on the plantation.

"You be the boy dis time," Laura told Sully one afternoon.

Sully stamped her little foot and shook her black curls. "I don' wanna be de boy; I'se de boy last time!"

She appeared about to cry, so Laura finally gave in.

"So? I'll do it dis time, but ya'all has t' braid me up a grass bracelet." Sully agreed and they began the game.

Sarah pulled out an old kettle, a bowl, some plates and utensils hidden under the back corner of the porch. She dusted the dirt out of the kettle, then let her breath out slowly and commanded, "Son, bring your mudder a kettle o' water."

Laura took the kettle and dutifully marched off toward the small creek behind the house. Ankle-high grass, home of numerous small swamp creatures, bordered the stream. A large frog, hearing her approach, hopped from a rotting log and headed toward the stream bank. Laura dropped the kettle and tried to catch the frog.

As she reached for the frog, it hopped again, barely eluding her grasp and always keeping one jump ahead of her. She soon found herself quite a distance down the stream—where the grass grew taller and the area became swampy—beyond the limits of where they were allowed to play. A raccoon, startled from the bank where he washed his food, rambled off through the foliage. A bull snake slithered off in the grass.

"Son," bellowed Sarah, her hands on her hips. Laura jerked to attention, then ran back towards where she thought she had dropped the kettle. It was nowhere in sight.

"What you doin'?" Greene asked as the others joined Laura.

"I'se lost the kettle," Laura admitted, looking ready to cry.

"You what?" asked Greene. "How you lose de kettle?" He looked around at Sarah for approval, "I think we whip her."

Laura didn't wait for Sarah's reaction. She ran screaming towards the big house and Mandy's protection, with the others right behind her and Greene yelling, "Catch dat girl, don't let her get away."

Laura stumbled over the kettle and fell into the wet grass and they all tumbled on top of her. They rolled off and Laura stood, then bent over and tried to brush the grass stains and mud off her dress and stockings.

Black children were taught to obey—with a willow. Greene looked around and suddenly realized they were too far from the house. He was truly concerned. "Mandy be mad!" he warned.

Laura picked up the kettle. Sarah poked her twin in the ribs with her elbow. "Ya'all hurry up with dat water, 'less you want a hidin'."

Sarah measured a full cup of fine dirt into the bowl for mixing mud cakes. "Get those dishes on the table," she instructed Sully.

When Laura returned, Sarah dipped a half-cup of water and poured it into the bowl, then stirred the mixture well. She patted a dirt cake together and frosted it with white dust before setting it carefully onto the foundation of the chimney to bake.

Meanwhile, Greene and Laura were riding stick horses and plowing the fields with stick plows.

Sully appeared at the edge of the field, and yelled in a voice which sounded much like Mandy. "Yo' want dinner, yo' better get in here," she called.

They sat around the flat rock and talked while they pretended to eat the mud cakes. "Dos niggers up Nawth say dey's gonna be free," said Greene.

Sully shook her head. "How you know dat?"

"My mudder say so," countered Greene.

Sarah dropped her hands in exasperation, "So?"

"When my mudder say so, it's SO, even if it not so," said Greene. He ran the back of his knuckle across his lower lip and frowned.

"Why dey wanna be free?" asked Sarah who was nibbling on a hard piece of grass she had picked. "What's dat mean?"

"Dey don't want nobody tellin' 'em what t' do," explained Greene. "Someday I'se gonna be free."

"Me too," chorused Sully and Laura.

"Don't be silly," Greene said to Laura. "You is free."

"You is one dirty mess," Sully said looking at Laura. "What you gonna do to clean yo'self up before Mandy see you?"

"Ya'all can wash your clothes in de waterin' trough," suggested Greene.

"Papa says we can't play there," said Laura.

"He'll never know," said Sarah, "I heared him tellin' Mandy he'd be gone all day. Help me clean up and we go do de washin'."

Sully began to clap her hands and dance around. They stashed their kitchen gear under the porch and started toward the long watering trough for the riding horses. Sarah and Greene climbed up on the side and looked into the sparkling water. Ben had cleaned and filled the trough that morning.

"Let's play wash day like you said," reminded Sully.

"Take your dress off and we wash it," Sarah said, turning back to look at Laura.

"I don't wanna take my dress off," objected Laura, making a face at her twin sister.

"I know!" said Greene, "jus' climb in and wash yourself without takin' it off."

"Okay," said Laura and she quickly climbed into the trough before anyone could object to this more palatable solution. She started scrubbing the mud and grass stains off her clothes.

"Dat look fun," said Greene as he hopped in beside her. Soon all four children were wading around in the warm water. Greene splashed Sarah in the face, and she shoved him away. He lit on his behind with only his head above water.

"Sarah! Laura! Where you is?"

It was Mandy's voice calling. They all scrambled out of the trough and headed for the yard as fast as a rabbit heads for its hole when a fox appears.

"Ya'all come here!" Mandy shouted.

She was furious when she saw them. She cut a willow switch and whipped Greene and Sully. She bathed Sarah and Laura and banished them to their room.

"Why do Sully and Greene always get whipped?" Laura asked.

Sarah did not reply. She was watching out the upstairs window as her father rode up.

Tom stopped to give Brandy a drink at the trough. The mare smelled the water and snorted. When Tom tried to get her to drink, she strained some water through her lips, bared her huge white teeth, and spat it back out, shaking her head and snorting. Tom looked in the trough and saw the dirty water. He shouted for Ben, the stable boy.

"I clean it dis mornin', Massa Tom, an' fill it from de water barrels," he insisted.

"Then why is the water muddy?" asked Tom.

"I don' know, I don' know," he insisted. "I seed de chillins out here, maybe dey playin' in it."

Tom entered the house and shouted, "Sarah! Laura!"

They fell silent and obediently appeared in the doorway.

"Were you playing in the horse trough today?" he asked.

They looked down at the floor and nodded meekly. "Yassuh."

"Who was playing with you?"

"Greene an' Sully," Sarah stammered.

"If you don't want a good whipping stay away from the horse troughs—and the barns," he said. The twins could tell by his tone of voice and the way his eyes narrowed and darkened that he meant what he said.

"Mandy!" he yelled.

"Yassuh, Massa."

"Sully and Greene are to be whipped for playing in the horse trough."

"They has been, Massa."

"Well, I'm going to do it again. Bring them to me tomorrow morning."

"Yassuh, Massa."

The girls hurried back into their room. Laura looked tearfully at Sarah. "It's not fair! Why's Sully an' Greene always whipped? We'se not."

"I guess it 'cause we'se 'free'," said Sarah.

"I hope Greene and Sully do run away so they'se free," said Laura. The twins fell silent, thinking about their friends being punished so severely and the inequity of it all.

Richard had no idea of the changes in their lives that would come about when he took the missionaries home to dinner. He and Jenny had both been raised by Christian parents, and they often read the Bible in the evenings. They had tried to find a church whose teachings they felt comfortable with, but a lot of questions remained unanswered. Elder Cox and Elder Anderson seemed to have an answer for all the questions which troubled them and the answers made sense.

"What is your church's stand on slavery?" Richard asked.

"Well," replied Elder Cox, "they haven't taken an official 'stand,' but Joseph Smith has advised new members to free their slaves unless they want to remain with them. He says no person should own another."

"That's good enough for me," said Richard, taking a big bite out of one of Jenny's freshly baked biscuits, spread thickly with jam. Jenny had a knack for kneading soft bread dough, and for making biscuits, cookies and cakes. Her talent seemed well appreciated by the hungry missionaries. Over Jenny's delicious hot biscuits and jam, they talked into the wee hours of the night.

Later, in their own bed, Jenny confided, "I have been praying for weeks the Lord would send someone who could answer my questions. I think these young men are an answer to that prayer."

Richard weighed his response, aware Jenny had already detected his hesitation. "Then this Joseph Smith story doesn't sound ridiculous to you? You think God might actually have appeared to him and answered his questions?"

Jenny's slow outward breath came accompanied by a nod in the affirmative. "Let's pray about it," she urged. "I feel that warm feeling inside which confirms the truth. There's some-one there—someone hearing me because someone is answer-ing my prayers. But, Richard, I want so badly for you to also be able to feel it."

She could see his frequent, boyish grin—even in the dark-ness. He opened his arms and she snuggled into their en-chanting masculine warmth. "I'll ask Elder Cox and Elder Anderson if they can stay with us for a while," he said.

The missionaries agreed to stay a few days, and Richard and Jenny invited their friends and family to hear them. Jen-ny's family reacted angrily. Her mother took her aside and instructed, "Don't let that Richard get you into something you'll be sorry for. You know some of his ideas are rather unconventional."

Mrs. Hall, a diminutive Irish lady, trim and outspoken, had a will as strong as iron. She crossed her arms and added,

"Have you thought about what having these Mormons in your home might do to your school and to Richard's business?" Her voice lacked its usual steadiness, which told Jenny how strongly she felt about the situation.

Jenny struggled to keep her face clear of the irritation swelling inside her, but her words sounded more clipped that she meant them to be. "Don't blame Richard. I have a mind of my own, and I'm convinced what these men are saying is the truth."

Her mother shook her head sadly, "I hope you won't do anything foolish which might jeopardize your future," then added, "I knew letting you marry this irresponsible man was a mistake."

Jenny felt furious. Her parents always blamed Richard for anything she did that didn't meet with their approval. The missionaries stayed at the Harris home for two weeks. Richard soon recognized Elder Cox to be a man of great natural intelligence and respected his opinions. The more Richard heard, the more he knew what Jenny had said that first night to be true. As he learned more, Richard was quick to embrace the new religion. By the time the elders left, both Jenny and Richard had been baptized.

Jenny's family tried to get her to renounce the new, unpopular belief on threat of being disinherited. She only became stronger in her convictions. Richard admired her determination. Even though other freighters kept constantly busy, Richard's business started dropping off. As soon as Jenny's patrons found out she was a Mormon—which didn't take long—one after another withdrew their children from her school.

Richard came home one night and entered the kitchen, still fragrant from baking bread. Jenny's face was etched with concern. She tried to sound like it didn't matter, but he knew how deeply she felt about her school. "Mrs. Clifford removed her three children from the school today. She grabbed my hair and pulled it, then yelled at me as she went out the door. She said I wasn't fit to teach anybody's children since I'd been deceived by the Devil."

Richard felt the blood slowly rising to his face. He swore silently. How could anyone treat Jenny in such a despicable way? He wanted to kill the woman. He was amazed Jenny managed to go on living sanely with the things that were happening in their lives. His voice sounded deceptively mild when he finally answered, voicing what had been in his thoughts for many days now, "Jenny, we're going to have to get out of here. Perhaps we should think about joining the Saints in Missouri in the spring."

"We can't leave," she said at first. "We've spent years of backbreaking labor making this place just like we wanted it." But even as she spoke, he saw her eyes get that set look, which showed she had made up her mind to something.

"Let's think about it," suggested Richard giving her a quick hug. "I can see no other choice, unless we want to renounce our beliefs." Jenny knew neither of them could do that.

"We can move; we've done it before," she said with more confidence than she felt. She wanted to cry as she looked at the spot which had been their home ever since their marriage. She knew nothing could be done about it now, she had to face the facts. The time had come for them to move forward.

Once she made up her mind, there was no turning back. Richard took inspiration from her calm courage in the midst of so much uncertainty. They began to make quiet plans to leave New York.

Mandy sat, legs crossed, at the Harris's kitchen table. She worried about Sarah and Laura; it seemed about time someone paid them some attention. They were beautiful children. Each day they looked more like their mother. While they looked alike, their personalities differed greatly. Shy, quiet Laura, when you were able to get her to smile, wrinkled her nose in a funny sort of way—almost like a baby rabbit. Outgoing Sarah, a healthy, precocious child, possessed apple red cheeks, almost naughty little eyes and a ready grin which she used persistently.

Mandy had become deeply attached to the girls but she knew their manners and education were sadly lacking. Even when Massa Tom stayed at home, which wasn't often, the girls ate in the kitchen with the house slaves instead of with their father. Tom, still carrying the burden of his loss, paid little attention to his daughters.

"Massa ain't de same man since Christina die," Mandy mumbled to herself. "He jus' work, work, work and don't seem t' care about nuthin' else."

She rose and walked into the parlor. Her eyes fell upon Christina's large piano, dusted and polished, but sitting unused. She thought of the many times she had marveled at the way Christina filled the house with music. The girls should be able to play simple pieces by now, but there was no one to teach them. They both had Christina's long, slim fingers which tapered at the ends and would make the girls potential pianists, but there remained gray silence where music belonged.

Mandy tried to teach the girls a little cross-stitch, but they became impatient with it and she soon gave up. At their age they should be getting some book learning. Mandy knew she couldn't help; it was considered a crime to even teach a slave their ABCs. If anyone ever found out she could read, she'd be in real trouble.

Christina, a kind and tender hearted woman, had taken a big chance when she secretly taught Mandy how to read and write. Massa Tom had once caught Christina teaching Mandy to write her letters and reprimanded her severely, reminding her it would ruin Mandy as a slave.

"Education and slavery do not go together," he said. "I know Mandy is exceptional, but learning will spoil the best nigger in the world. If you keep this up, she'll become dissatisfied and unmanageable."

His remarks only reinforced Mandy's determination to get an education. She had learned by then that not all blacks were slaves, that some had their freedom. She vowed that someday, she, too, would be free.

A year after Christina's death, free black David Walker had published a pamphlet called *Walker's Appeal* in which he decried the injustice of slavery and called slaves to rise up in arms and overthrow the practice. Southern states, one by one, made it a crime to circulate the *Appeal*. Those who hadn't already done so, made it a crime to teach slaves to read or write. Walker disappeared the following year, but his Appeal went on. The pamphlet was brought secretly to Mandy. She read it at moments when Tom was away and it seemed safe, then told the house slaves about what she had read.

In 1831, just a year after David Walker vanished, Virginia slave Nat Turner led seventy blacks in a revolt that killed fifty-seven white men, women and children in rural Southampton County. Troops rushed in and killed over a hundred slaves, both innocents and insurrectionists. Wild rumors and alarms spread. The slaves discussed these events in hushed whispers around the evening fires, and wondered what would take place next.

Mandy was the only slave on the plantation who had access to information about current events. She kept up on what was going on by secretly reading Massa Tom's newspapers. Her favorite job became the dusting because she could get her hands on some of Massa Tom's books and the Virginia Gazette without engendering suspicion. He had reading materials spread out all over his study, but she had to be extremely careful not to be caught reading them, or even handling his books and papers.

Bondage laws became increasingly harsher. Turner was sent to the gallows at age thirty-one. As slave owners became more and more frightened of slaves receiving an education, Tom's newspapers were no longer left lying around. If caught reading, Mandy knew at best she would get a hidin'; at worst she might be sold down-river or end up as a field hand.

Mandy's mother had been a field hand before Christina's Massa bought her to cook in the big house. Mandy remembered how shocked she had been the first time she had seen the terrible deep scars across her mother's back. Her mother sat her down and explained about the process of planting and growing cotton and the long hours she had spent working in the cotton fields.

"But how you get dem stripes on your back?"

"Durin' hoein' de overseer's on horseback with de whip, his lash a flyin' from mornin' till night. De fastest nigger with a hoe head de lead row. If anybody pass him, de lead slave get a whippin'. If we fall behind, we whipped. We jus' finish one hoein' an' it time to start another."

Mandy could remember being held on her mother's lap while she told her of earlier times. "Chile, if you think hoein' bad, pickin' season were de baddest. You has to be in de field at first light or you get a hidin'. Each of us has a sack, with de strap a goin' over der neck holdin' de mouth of dat sack dis high." She raised her hand to the height of her large breasts.

"You stop at noon jus' long enough to swallow cold bacon an' a corn cake, den back t' work 'till it's too dark t' see. If der's a full moon, sometime we pick 'till de middle of de night."

Mandy sighed, she couldn't imagine living that way. It seemed no better than being a field animal.

"Den," continued her mother, "we has to go home, grind corn, fix supper and make corn cakes for dinner for de next day. When I finally lays my head down on de stick of wood I calls a pillow, I has to worry about not hearin' de horn blown de next mornin' an hour before daylight to get me goin' again. Dat's no life for my chile, dat's why you learn to cook and sew an' do house things."

Mandy was full of questions. "Why some people slaves an' some Massas an' Marsas? Why I a slave?"

The answers she got were not satisfactory. Now, much older and wiser, Mandy dared not let her master know she continued to read everything she could get her hands on. Mandy wondered when, if ever, her people would cease to be abused. It seemed the harder they worked to improve, the more limited their opportunities became. Now the Massas didn't even want slaves to gather together. Mandy had escaped auction blocks and the horrors imposed by slave traders. Born to a kindly master, she had learned house duties well. Christina's father had given Mandy to his daughter when she was very small.

Mandy had married in her late twenties, but two years later her husband died from an accident incurred while trying to stop a runaway horse and wagon. Her daughter had also died young, leaving one grandchild, Sully. Though

Mandy had not suffered extreme abuse, she heard others talk about beatings, desperate escapes and near starvation. Her daughter had been raped by a white man. She hated anyone who took advantage of others, but she had wanted to kill the man who had his way with her daughter.

Chapter Three

Sarah and Laura played in the front yard. They giggled and screamed with delight as they rolled a hoop across the grass, but when they began arguing over it, Mandy stuck her head out the door and yelled, "Put dat up, and you stop dat fightin' or I'll tan both yo' hides."

The girls knew she was just threatening, but they didn't dare cross her or they might be banished to their room again.

"Now see what you did!" Sarah said accusingly. "Now we can't play with the hoop anymore."

She leaned the hoop against the side of the house where she discovered a large spider web. They squatted down closely and watched in horrid fascination as a fly became tangled in the web. "Poor thing," said Laura as the fly struggled, only to become more snarled in the strands.

"Stupid fly," countered Sarah, as she absentmindedly picked an azalea blossom from the flower bed and looked at it a moment, then tossed it onto the ground. "He oughta know better than t' fly into a spider web. She'll eat him up, an' he deserve it."

The rumble of carriage wheels sent them both to the front gate. When the carriage drove up they saw their father, and someone with him—two someones in fact. The slim lady had tons of blond curls cascading onto her shoulders. Her elegant dress made of shiny pink material, matched her pink cheeks and brightly colored lips. The girls stood open-mouthed as their father helped her from the carriage.

Then the boy, slightly larger than the twins, jumped out of the carriage beside her and stole their attention. His brown hair, carefully slicked down, almost hid his sly hazel eyes. His carefully starched short linen pants buttoned onto his shirt. He looked all decked out to go to Sunday meeting. He scrambled toward the front gate, then stopped suddenly, seeing the girls, and surveyed them with aversion.

"Are these your girls, Tom?" the woman asked too sweetly. Accompanying the question, from under her long lashes, came a stare of disapproval only the twins were in position to see.

"This is Sarah and this is Laura," he replied opening the gate for her to sweep through. The woman looked down her long, slim nose and regarded them with icy blue eyes.

"They certainly need a mother," she said.

"I do the best I can with them," Tom replied.

"Oh, darling, I'm sure you do. I didn't mean to criticize. They're sweet children," she said, "but little girls need to be kept clean and neat and taught how to be young ladies."

She turned to the boy and quickly added, "Now Freddy, why don't you play with the girls, but see that you don't get dirty."

Tom opened the porch door and he and the blue-eyed lady disappeared into the house. The twins continued to stare at Freddy without speaking, until he felt compelled to start a conversation.

"Hey,"

"Hey, what?" Sarah questioned.

"Where's your mother?" he asked, curious from the previous comments.

"We don' have a mudder," said Sarah.

"What happened to her?" he asked brushing his hair back to reveal a well-freckled face.

"She die," said Sarah.

"Oh," he said, satisfied on that topic. "My father died. He was a famous soldier." Then rapidly changing the subject he inquired, "How old are you?"

"We'se seven-and-a-half," said Sarah.

"Who's we?" he asked. Then before she could answer he turned to Laura, "What's the matter, can't you talk?"

"I'se seven-and-a-half, too," said Laura, leaning closer to her sister.

"You don't look seven. Are you sisters?"

"We is," said Sarah climbing onto the gate post where she perched to survey him from a higher spot.

"How can you be sisters and both be seven?" he asked, sure they were trying to deceive him.

"We'se twins," they replied in unison.

Freddy looked at them thoughtfully, still wondering if they were being honest with him.

"You talk funny," he observed, shrugging his shoulders, "Don't your daddy make you talk King's English?" He paused a moment and looked at them curiously. "I'm seven too, and I can read," he said smugly. "Can you read?"

"No..." the twins admitted reluctantly.

"Well I can," he said with pride. "I've been reading ever since I was a baby."

"So?" said Sarah. "We don' care."

"I guess you're just not as smart as me," said Freddy, looking superior.

"We'se smarter than ya'all is any day," said Sarah, her anger rising instantly.

"You're both stupid," he said with disgust. "I can tell just by listening to you."

"Take dat back," Sarah insisted as she jumped down from her perch on the gate to confront him. "If you don't, I'll knock your smarts right outta your head."

He gave a short contemptuous snort. "I won't take back anything, Miss Priss!" he said defiantly. "It's true."

Sarah instantly had him in a headlock and before he knew what had happened to him she was rubbing his face in the brown Virginia plantation dirt.

The screams that came from Freddy rose steadily in pitch as his mother appeared. He could probably be heard for a mile.

"Let him go," the woman shouted at Sarah, then retrieved her boy from the dirt, holding him at arm's length to keep from getting herself dirty. "What have these ill-mannered little girls done to you?" she asked, patting him and straightening his clothing. Then looking toward the porch, at Tom just emerging, she said haughtily, "Tom, you'll have to take us home immediately."

"Mandy!" Tom thundered.

Mandy appeared in the doorway in an instant. She recognized the anger in Tom's voice. "Take these girls in and clean them up. They look terrible. Then keep them in their room the rest of the day."

Sarah began to cry. She hated to stay in their room on a sunny day. Mandy took the girls in tow and scurried off toward the kitchen with them.

"What fool thing you go an' do now?" Her eyes wrinkled in fine lines. "Dat boy's your company, and you don' treat company like dat," she whispered angrily. "You's disgracin' your poor father."

"Dat boy said we'se stupid," said Laura, wrinkling her nose in a frown.

"I's just tryin' to make him take it back," said Sarah.

Mandy's eyes narrowed. She had a few choice words to say about the little smartie. Who did he think he was? But she didn't dare even show her displeasure.

She took Sarah and Laura each by a hand and proceeded down the long hall, her voice fading to gentle mumbles of disapproval. She held the great oak door into the kitchen open for them.

"He said he could read," said Sarah, still seething from the insult she felt she had received.

Mandy shook her head, "I can't believe de things dat happen here." Then she looked at Sarah thoughtfully, "Well, Missy, you better learn to get along with de little fellow. He could be your brudder one of dese days."

The girls looked at each other questioningly.

She stared a second at the twins, again shaking her head. "Let's see if Hannah have some warm water for washin' yo' up."

Mandy scrubbed the girls from head to foot in the tin tub, using a rough cloth and a bar of lye soap. When they were dried, she put them in their night clothes.

When the door to their room shut, Sarah looked at Laura with a defiant gleam in her eye. "I'se had enough o' bein' sent to my room. Wanna do some explorin'?"

"Explorin'? What's dat?" asked Laura.

"You know dat room across the hall dat's always locked?" said Sarah.

"Yeah?" questioned Laura.

"I heared Mandy say that room belonged to our mudder. I wonder if she's not dead and our papa has her locked inside there. He goes in der all de time and stays for a long time."

"Ya think so?" breathed Laura.

"Might be," noted Sarah. "I think we'd better rescue her."

"But da room's locked," reasoned Laura.

"It's locked, but I knows where de key is. I saw where Papa put it last time he came outa there. I'll get the key an' we'll find out what's really in dat room," Sarah suggested before quietly slipping out into the hallway.

Laura felt terribly frightened as Sarah put the key into the lock and opened the door. They slipped into the room quietly and shut the door behind them. As their eyes adjusted to the dark room, she felt the presence of someone else beside them. She glanced up and saw the full-sized portrait of a beautiful woman looking down at them. Sarah saw the portrait at the same instant, and they both gasped.

"Who is she?" asked Laura.

"She has to be our mudder," said Sarah. "She looks a little bit like you, Laura."

"I think she looks like you," replied Laura.

The girls stared with open mouths. There stood their mother, the one who had been such a mystery to the girls, imprisoned in a gilded frame. Sarah and Laura, spellbound, looked at her for a long time. "Look how long her fingers are, and how they get smaller at the ends," said Sarah, raising her own hand and looking at her long, slim, tapered fingers. "Mandy said we had long fingers just like our mudder, and they were built for playin' the piano."

Laura raised her hand and looked at her fingers, then sighed. She looked again at the beautiful woman, long dress draped around her figure, holding a hat with a feather plume in one hand. "Look at how pretty she is," she breathed. "I want to grow up to be just like her."

Just then, the voice of their father boomed "Mandy!" from downstairs. The girls quickly slipped out of the room. Sarah fumbled with the key in the lock, but finally turned it and they slipped back into their own room. "I hope Papa don' look for the key before I get it put back," Sarah's voice quivered. But the girls were lucky this time. They could hear Tom talking to Mandy at the bottom of the stairs for a moment, then the outside door open and shut.

That night when the girls were tucked into bed Sarah closed her eyes, then opened them again when Mandy left the room. She sat up and tossed her dark brown hair over her shoulder. "You asleep?" she asked her twin.

"No," said Laura, raising up on her elbow.

"What Mandy mean when she say dat wicked boy might be our brudder?"

Laura bit her lip. "I don't know," she sighed, "but I don't ever want a brudder like him."

"Me either," said Sarah as she stretched and yawned. "I'd scream bloody murder if he was my brudder."

"Me too," said Laura.

Richard flexed his shoulders against the tightness and warmth of his shirt, then slowly began to unbutton it. The humidity high, it seemed unseasonably warm for a May afternoon. No breeze lent a breath of freshness to the air. The sun was hot, even under the canvas canopy which provided shade from its merciless rays. Jenny, not one to complain, looked as though she were about to wilt. Her forehead glistened with sweat and her clothes appeared almost as wet as if she had gone for a swim in the river without removing them. She reached up and wiped the rivulets of sweat from her brow.

No matter how uncomfortably hot the sun, as the wagon rolled along behind the finely matched pair of dapple gray mares, Richard basked in the warmth of being back in familiar Virginia countryside. Night frost had finally disappeared with the advent of warmer weather. Morning breezes stirred the new, still small leaves of the maple. The woods were dense with dogwood and a profusion of wild flowers. Meadowlarks sang. Richard loved the magical days of spring in Virginia, bringing sunshine and warmth to the earth. His keen brown eyes took in everything, but he still felt he couldn't capture enough of the sights and sounds around him. He was coming home!

Jenny's brother, Aaron, had threatened to kill Richard if he took his sister to Missouri. They hadn't dared tell her family they were leaving, but secretly packed the wagon inside the barn, where they wouldn't be seen. Then, leaving most of the family possessions behind, had walked out and driven away one morning after breakfast—never to return. They left food and dishes on the table, as though they had just stepped out for a moment, hoping if Aaron or Jenny's parents came by, they wouldn't realize for at least a few days that they did not plan to return.

Richard, though anxious to join the Saints in Missouri, would make one last trip to the home place and try to make peace with his brother, Tom. It wasn't far out of their way. He just hoped Tom would be agreeable to reconciliation. Richard felt a wave of shame every time he thought of how he angrily rode away from his home and family that night so many years before.

It had been a difficult trip for the team, Daisy and Doll, plodding down red-clay roads treacherous from spring mud which still lingered in places. From Pennsylvania to Cumberland, Maryland, they had followed Braddock's Road—named for an early English general defeated in that region—as it wound through the woods and along the valleys. Some of the narrow, twisting drives seemed hardly smoother than the surrounding countryside. The balance of the trip hadn't been much better, but now they were almost there.

Two vultures, frightened by the approach of the wagon, flapped away from a dead rabbit beside the road. "It's been a long time," Richard mused. "I wonder if Tom will be willing to let old dogs lie."

Jenny's long reddish-brown hair glistened in the sunlight. It fell across the shoulders of her gray-striped calico dress fastened at her throat with a brooch. When Richard looked down at her he could see her hair looked darker in the center and lightened towards the ends from long hours in the sun.

She turned her face toward him. The freckles across her nose and cheeks seemed more prominent than usual. She was a smiling-type of person. She flashed that same warm smile which had first attracted him to her. Richard marveled at her determination, but today, in spite of the smile, her green eyes looked troubled. Richard studied his wife thoughtfully. Her manner and expression, usually pleasant and confident, now showed grave concern. "I think you should have written and told him we were coming," she said nervously.

He turned into the lane of huge old oaks and walnuts and stopped for a moment beneath a stately black walnut tree. It seemed much taller than when he saw it last. The Harris estate pleased the eye. The handsome two-story Victorian house with huge columns holding up the wide veranda hadn't changed much in the last fifty years. It had that look of southern grandeur. Most of the very old, "big houses" in Virginia were built a story-and-a-half high to avoid the additional tax imposed by the King of England on two-story houses, but the Harris home had been built just after the Revolutionary War.

Circular flower patches graced the front yard of the plantation house with vivid colors of spring—bright yellow daffodils, red tulips, shades of purple foxglove and soft blue of bluebells.

New horse barns and corrals looked neat and well kept. The group of small, low, newly whitewashed cabins which constituted the slave quarters sat a quarter of a mile behind the main house. The vast tobacco fields, flanked by rolling countryside and woods, showed obvious prosperity.

"Looks like my brother Tom's doing well," Richard told Jenny. "The place still looks just like it did when Father was alive."

The wide lawn, framed with lilac bushes and extending to the veranda entwined with green vines, caught Jenny's attention. "Oh, look, Richard—lilac bushes!" she said excitedly as she breathed deeply of the lilac scented air.

Richard knew how Jenny had hated to leave the lilacs which she had planted so carefully in their yard in New York. She had dug some lilac roots and carried along with her. Each day she made sure the roots were dampened and protected from the sun.

As Richard remembered their home in New York, he could see and even smell the lilacs there. The tugging of Daisy and Doll on their lines brought him back to the present. He clicked his tongue, flicked the reins and drove up to the front gate.

———————————

Aaron Hale rode up the lane to Jenny and Richard's house in Buffalo, New York. He hadn't had any contact with his sister and brother-in-law for several days now, which was unusual. They were acting strangely since they had taken up with the Mormons.

Jenny had put so much time and energy into fixing up their modest home and yard. Aaron, amazed anew at his sister's ability to make a place homey, dismounted, tied his horse at the hitching rail, and knocked on the door. He heard no answer.

He opened the door and yelled in, "Hey, anybody home?" Again there was no answer. Aaron walked into the kitchen looking for some indication of where they might be. The dishes and leftover food from the last meal were still on the table. They had eaten and left without doing any cleaning up. That seemed odd, Jenny always cleaned up immediately after each meal. He walked over to the table and reached out a finger to touch the small amount of fried potatoes left in the bowl. They felt dry and hard, as did the food scraps on the plates. No one had been here for several days. He swore softly under his breath.

Aaron walked into the sitting room and ran his finger across the fireplace mantle. His finger made lines in the dust. Upstairs beds were made, but again, the furniture looked dusty. When he pulled open a drawer, he found it empty; so was the closet.

Aaron slammed the bedroom door behind him and stomped down the stairs. He felt sure his sister and brother-in-law's absence could be traced to their alliance with the Mormons. He couldn't believe they would take off, just like that, without letting anyone know they were leaving.

Aaron plopped into a chair and put his head in his hands. His hat fell to the floor. Things had been going so well for them in Buffalo until the Mormon missionaries had appeared and started holding meetings in his sister's home. Richard had never been the same since he had first brought those missionaries home to dinner. He had enticed Jenny into letting them stay for a long time—too long a time for Jenny's good. Richard had even expected Aaron to listen to their blasphemy, but Aaron knew he could not believe the implausible stories of "Old Joe Smith" and his golden plates. The man hailed from Palmyra, a little settlement along the canal not too far from Buffalo. Aaron had heard numerous stories about the Mormons and few were complimentary.

Aaron had warned them, but they wouldn't listen. What more could he have done? He couldn't understand why Jenny, when she had the best dame school—as schools taught by women were called—in Buffalo, would join up with a group like the Mormons, and ruin everything. The parents of her students were shocked. He'd been told some had shouted at her and one woman had even attacked Jenny, grabbing her by the long, red hair and yelling obscenities at her.

Jenny didn't deserve that barbarous kind of treatment. Aaron couldn't understand how Richard could be taken in by such a hair-brained scheme. Aaron had tried again and again to reason with him and finally ended up losing his temper and threatening to kill Richard if he even thought of running off with Jenny to join the Mormons. Now he suspected that was exactly what they had done. If so, Aaron vowed he would hunt them down and make good on his threat, then bring his sister back to Buffalo. What else could a brother do? It would be the best thing for Jenny in the long run.

He picked up his hat and jammed it onto his head. As he walked back through the kitchen he thought about how excited Jenny had been when she bought the new china dishes. Here they sat abandoned on the table. He opened the door and stared down the lane. Jenny had planted her lilacs there with care, using a bucket to carry the life-giving water to each bush. He couldn't believe she would just up and leave everything she had unless forced to by her husband. Yes, as her brother, it was his duty to rescue Jenny.

Tom stood looking aimlessly out the front window of the big house. A path of sunshine lay across the floor, but Tom seemed oblivious to it. This particular morning he felt his aloneness a little more keenly than usual. He remembered the sweetness of Christina's laughter. If Christine had just lived, things would be so different—but there was no Christina, and had been no Christina for so many years now. Even after all these years, he would sometimes awaken in the middle of a long night, and expect to find her lying beside him. Then he would realize he was just a lonely man lying by himself in the dark, filled with an utter sense of loss, almost too intense to bear. He expelled a long, angry sigh. This was no time to be letting sentimentality creep in; he was too old to weep and wallow in self-pity.

"Well, I'd better get to work," he said aloud to no one but himself.

Though in his mid-thirties, Tom, still attracted the attention of the local belles who thought him the answer to any ambitious girl's prayers. He stood nearly six feet tall, and broad shouldered but trim. His dark hair and those deep-set gray eyes which characterized the Harris men—except Richard—added to his charm. Women tried to get his attention, but he had little interest in them and no inclination to remarry. If he had been looking for a wife, the twins would probably have scared the woman off, he thought, as he remembered with some embarrassment the incident with Freddy and Sarah. He smiled slightly as he thought of how Sarah had the little dandy yelling for mercy. Freddy's mother had been so indignant she never wanted to see him again.

He wondered what to do about the twins. Mandy was taking good care of them, but they were getting old enough now that they needed some schooling. He would have to look into getting a governess. He wondered why he had been singled out to be the father of twins and to have to raise them without a mate. Somehow he dreaded seeing those faces which were growing to be so much like Christina's. He resented it a little, too, finding it almost unbearable that Christina's looks, her eyes, her dark hair would go on while she lay in the grave. What a strange thing was memory.

Tom stared off into the distance, lost in deep thought—in overwhelming bitterness. Make a good life? It was easy to say, maybe even easy to do when a man had a beautiful wife to share his home. It was not so easy when suddenly left alone.

Tom's eyes widened as they focused on a cloud of dust billowing up toward the far end of the lane, now coming closer and closer. He watched, straining to see what it might be. He could make out a wagon carrying two people, but couldn't tell who they were. He was not expecting anyone today. Tom walked into the yard and watched as the wagon drew up to the front of the house.

A figure climbed down from the driver's seat. Tom sensed something familiar about that form walking toward him with hand outstretched, saying Tom's name. His eyes grew larger as he recognized who was coming toward him. His jaw dropped and he stared in astonishment. "Richard," he gasped.

Richard needn't have worried about how Tom would react. His face broke into a wide grin as he brushed the outstretched hand aside and gathered his brother into a joyful bear hug. After they pounded each other on the back several times, Tom pushed Richard away and held him at arm's length. "Where have you been all these years? I almost didn't recognize you, but your voice gave you away. No one hereabouts ever knew what had happened to you. Never a letter or a message, only rumors of possible foul play..."

"I'm sorry about that, Tom," said Richard, his voice going quiet as he noted the hurt in his brother's eyes. "I was a fool and kept putting things off. I guess I was pretty hot-headed and proud when we were young."

"That's for sure," laughed Tom, shrugging his broad shoulders. "But the past is just that—it's past, and what is important now is that you are here and I know you're alive. What a wonderful surprise!"

Tom's sharp, strong features had always engendered Richard's envy, but as he looked at Tom's face, he quickly noted he appeared not only older, but a bit haggard. He looked weary, as if time had not been good to him. His brother's face had a pallor which was not from plantation dust. Richard felt dismay at the changes he could see and sense in Tom.

"Tom, I want you to meet my wife, Jenny," Richard said remembering his manners, and leading his brother toward the wagon. Tom turned his attention to the pleasingly plump, red-haired girl sitting on the high seat delightedly observing them. Tom thought she looked just the type for his little brother. Richard never had much patience with women in fine gowns who fluttered their eyelashes and handkerchiefs and simpered behind their fans.

"Glad to meet you, Mam," said Tom, looking at her intently.

She felt his eyes examining her and when he smiled, she knew she had passed the test.

"How about getting out of that wagon and coming into the house?" He held out a hand to help her down, a model of gentlemanliness and courtesy.

Jenny looked closely at Tom, a handsome fellow, with deep-set, dark gray eyes that looked as though he had known deep sorrow. He and Richard didn't look much alike. When a smile flashed across his perfect teeth, Jenny breathed a sigh of relief. She hadn't known what to expect when they arrived. She took his hand and climbed down stiffly.

As Jenny reached the ground, her knees half-buckled. She felt like they had jelly in them instead of bones. For a moment she thought her legs would not hold her up. In spite of the wagon seat being suspended on wooden springs to prevent too much shaking, her body felt well shook.

Tom ushered them onto the porch, then through the huge carved doorway into the wide entrance hall. As they entered the sitting room, Jenny felt totally awed by the high papered walls covered with paintings and tapestries, polished hardwood floors covered in spots with area rugs and the lavish mahogany furniture with brightly polished surfaces. She shook her head in wonder, feeling like she had stepped into another world. She had only seen such places in her imagination.

Chapter Four

Richard walked slowly and looked around appreciatively. He stood gazing at the big, tall-ceilinged rooms. Most things were just as he remembered them; the place hadn't changed much. It remained a pretty imposing house.

"Sit down, sit down," said Tom. "We have a lot of catching up to do."

Richard and Jenny sat on the settee. Jenny sat up straight with her hands folded in her lap, clearly ill at ease. Richard slipped his arm around his wife, and she relaxed visibly as she felt the warmth of him. Tom walked over beside the sitting room fireplace and began to ask his brother questions. "Where are you living? How far have you come?"

"We came from Buffalo, New York," answered Richard.

"That's a long ways," said Tom. "How was your trip?"

"Tolerably well except for the mud. On good roads we could travel up to ten, sometimes fifteen miles a day, but there were very few places where the roads were good."

"I'll bet you're exhausted," said Tom.

"It's been tiring. I'm sure Jenny will appreciate a place to rest and clean up. By the way, Tom, haven't you married? You haven't mentioned a wife."

The smile vanished from Tom's face, which momentarily looked like that of a slapped child. He slid heavily into a chair. His throat moved as he swallowed.

"She died in childbirth," Tom said finally in a low, scarcely audible voice, his tone deep and grave. His eyes riveted blankly on Richard and Jenny, as he sat and pondered over steepled fingers.

Richard felt stunned by his brother's naked despair. He could see the scars had not begun to heal. An uncomfortable silence, strong enough to shatter the eardrums, filled the room for what seemed a long time before Richard spoke. "I'm sorry," he stammered. "I hadn't the least inkling..."

Jenny stared at him then moistened her lips with her tongue before speaking, "And the baby?" she asked leaning forward.

A troubled frown lingered on Tom's face. "Not one, but two—twin girls," he responded with a haunting laugh. "If there is a God, I don't know how he thinks I can manage twin girls without a mother for them!"

"Where are the girls and how old are they now?" Richard asked. "Jenny here has been wanting a baby for years. I'll bet she'd love to set eyes on a pair of twins." His words broke the strain for the moment.

Tom smiled, then got up suddenly. "I'll send for them," he said as he rang the bell for Mandy.

Mandy appeared at the top of the steep circular stairway. "Yassuh, Massa?"

"Get the girls, Mandy. My brother Richard and his wife are here and want to see them."

"Lawd a mercy," exclaimed Mandy, "I'll bring them right down." She scurried off mumbling to herself. She had never met Richard, though over the years she had heard guarded remarks about this younger brother. She hoped his appearance would bring Tom happiness, something which had become such a rare sensation he seemed suspicious of it.

Jenny could hardly believe her eyes when the two girls appeared. They stood at the top of the tall, curved staircase beneath the pictures of Harris family progenitors hanging sedately in elaborate carved and gilded frames.

"Meet Sarah and Laura," Tom said with a bitter edge to his voice.

It was love at first sight. One standing straight with her dark head held high looked half a hand taller than the other, who hovered behind her sister. If one hadn't been taller, Jenny would have sworn she was seeing double.

"Come down here," their father commanded.

The twins looked apprehensively at each other, then started down the stairs. Sarah had the bearing of an antelope. She descended the stairs with small, quick steps, wary but curious. She shot a quick, inquisitive look at Jenny from dark brown eyes. Laura, the smaller mouselike one, came with hesitancy and head down, visibly uneasy. Jenny instantly sensed her need for love and attention.

"Come over here," Tom commanded. "Do you know who this is?"

Sarah came closer and peered into Jenny's face. She put her hands behind her and rocked back and forth on the balls of her feet. "Are you my grandmama?" she asked quietly with her head cocked sideways.

Richard and Tom laughed, but Jenny knelt quickly beside the little girls and said softly, "I'm not your grandmama, but I'd love to be your fairy godmother." The eyes of both girls opened wide as they smiled—Sarah a confident warm smile,

Laura a shy small upturn of the corners of her mouth, barely perceptible, but there nonetheless.

Jenny, with a soundless giggle, pulled the girls toward her and gave them a quick hug. Laura, her eyes wide with astonishment, glanced at her sister, who was responding warmly to Jenny's girlish, light-hearted manner. Soon Laura's reserve began to melt. Jenny had always been good with children. Now, in ten minutes time she had the girls both talking and laughing with her. She began to covet Tom's twins—not a small bit, but with great longing.

The twins hadn't found much time to play with Sully and Greene while Richard and Jenny were there, but today all the adults were busy entertaining an assortment of friends and Harris family relatives whose plantations were located within driving distance. The girls slipped out the back door, and found their friends.

"Well, what you been doin' lately?" Greene asked from under a wide brimmed straw hat which almost hid his whole face. "Ain't seed you for ages. Heard your uncle done come home."

"Uncle Richard and Aunt Jenny both come home," said Sarah. "We been havin' school with Aunt Jenny," said Laura. "I can almos' read."

"Well, ain't you smart!" said Greene. He glanced around quickly to see if any adults were near. "What you wanna do?" he asked with a furtive look.

"Let's walk out to de barns," said Sarah. "I hasn't seen de horses in ages. Is de kittens still in de hayloft?" She paused and looked at Laura thoughtfully. "Remember, if Mandy calls, we all run back here fast and don't you answer 'til we'se back in de yard."

"Race you to de barn," said Greene.

They were off in a whirl, with only a streak of dust to show where they had been. They slipped into the horse barn. The air inside the barn felt warm and heavy with the pungent smell of dung. They went from stall to stall speaking to and patting the horses. Brandy, Tom's bay mare, nuzzled Greene's side and he reached up and scratched her neck. A soft-eyed chestnut whinnied as they came up to the stall, putting her face forward for them to rub. Laura petted the white muzzle of Uncle Richard's dapple gray mare called Doll, then the one called Daisy, who had a white streak down her forehead.

They climbed to the hayloft and found the kittens right where they had always been. They each picked up a kitten to cuddle. Sarah held the little black one closely, petting it, crooning to it, and listening to it purr. Laura buried her face in the fur of the gray one.

They stopped at the pig pens where they perched on the fence and held a conversation with the old sow, who grunted enthusiastically at them. They looked at each other and giggled, then broke into a perfect storm of laughter. The chicken coop was next.

"What dat hen keep sittin' on dos eggs for?" asked Sully. "Ain't Sam gatherin' de eggs?"

They chased the hen, clucking in alarm, off the nest and each took a handful of warm eggs. "Hey," said Sarah, "we can use dese eggs t' make mud cakes." She looked around fugitively. "Sully, you run get de dishes from under de porch."

They found a flat rock behind the barn to use as a table, and set the eggs on it. Sully was soon there with the dishes. Sarah dipped some loose dirt into the bowl and handed Laura a cup. "Get some water from de horse trough, son,"

Laura ambled off and Sarah picked up one of the eggs,

looked at it carefully, then started to break it into the bowl. The egg did not come out. It cracked, but the shell held together and slick, damp feathers appeared in the crack. They all gathered around as Sarah began to pick the shell off the baby chicken in the egg. They could see its feathered body move up and down in the shell as its heart beat plaintively. Laura returned and watched intently.

"Wow," said Greene, "What you think it be?"

"It be a chicken, stupid," Sarah said, then laughed with delight. "Hey, I know what let's do! Let's play chicken dinners." She handed out the plates and the eggs. They began cracking eggs and picking the shells off the baby chicks.

"Mmm, dey do look delicious," said Sully as she set the chick, gasping it's last, on her plate and pretended to take a bite.

"Sarah! Laura!" Mandy's voice called from the front yard, "Where you is?"

"You clean up and put the dishes back," Sarah hurriedly told Greene and Sully as they all scrambled to their feet in wild confusion. She and Laura ran quickly around the back of the barn and into the far corner of the big house yard where they skidded to a stop.

"Sarah! Laura!" Mandy called again. Ya'all come here!"

"Here we is," Sarah called out.

"What took you so long to answer?" asked Mandy, suspicion in her voice and in her dark eyes.

"I guess we didn' hear you the first time you called," said Sarah, turning to her sister with an uneasy laugh.

"Who said I called twice? If you heard me the first time, what took you so long to answer?" asked Mandy, "and how ya 'all get so dirty?"

"Just playin'" said Sarah.

Jenny had never seen so much food at one time. She ate 'possum, rabbit, roast pig, turkey and duck. The meats were complemented by mustard greens, squash, okra, black-eyed peas and buttered yams. She ate stew made of peanuts, and for desert—cakes, watermelon and brandied peaches. If they stayed here much longer, she was afraid she would become absolutely fat.

That night after she and Richard retired in the large four-poster bed of the guest room, Jenny lay unable to sleep, thinking of how she might approach the two brothers about her plan. Richard rolled onto his side, facing her.

"You still awake?" he asked, holding out his arms. She snuggled into them, putting her head on his chest. Her auburn hair lay across his neck, light and warm.

She lay there quietly for a long time listening to the moonlight symphony of frogs croaking in the nearby swamp, backed by the steady drumming of Richard's heartbeat.

At last she mustered enough courage to speak of what was on her mind. "Oh, Richard, the twins are so cute. They're absolute dolls."

"I thought you'd feel that way," he mumbled, already near to sleep.

"Do you think Tom would let us take them for a while? I could teach them reading and arithmetic—they really need some education."

Richard sat up abruptly as if a bucket of cold water had been thrown on him and stared toward her in the darkness for a moment while he tried to digest this rash plan.

Jenny knew her request was beyond all reason and almost beyond expectation. She paused, then continued, "I've been playing school with them a bit, and they're really bright little girls. In all my experience, I've never seen children so anxious to learn."

Richard cleared his throat. "You don't take young'uns away from their parents," he said gruffly. "Tom isn't going to let his girls go join the Mormons. Besides, what if your brother, Aaron, catches up with us? You wouldn't want to put the twins in danger, would you?" His voice held a nasty edge.

"I don't think my brother would really hurt us." Jenny's voice trembled. "God will protect us from harm, I know he will." There was silence a moment, then she continued, "I'll bet Tom would be glad to have someone else take the responsibility of raising those two. Can't we at least ask him?" She waited for Richard to answer, but she may as well have saved her breath. He didn't seem to be listening.

Richard didn't want to talk about it; he tried to dismiss the subject. "I love you so very much, Jenny," he said, squeezing her gently. She didn't respond. After a short silence, he tried again, "Listen to the frogs croaking in the swamp. Doesn't it almost lull you to sleep?" When she again refused to answer he turned over and soon she could hear his regular, heavy breathing echoing through the quiet room.

Jenny lay silent, engulfed in melancholy, pretending to sleep but still grappling with her thoughts. She felt angry Richard would dismiss her desires so quickly and then fall right asleep. He had shrugged off her question, but she knew he would do some thinking about it. It still galled her that he had fallen asleep practically during their conversation.

The next day turned cloudy with a nip in the early morning air. Richard's place in bed lay empty when Jenny awoke. A feeling of despair almost overwhelmed her. She climbed out of bed and dressed, but bit her lower lip as she washed in the cold water of the lava bowl. She just had to make Richard see how she felt about the twins and agree to at least ask Tom if they might take them for a while. She had already learned to love them and couldn't bear to think of leaving without them.

When Jenny descended the stairs, the two brothers were already in the dining room talking with animation about those years when they were boys. A fire crackled in the fireplace and firelight danced on their faces. When Jenny entered they turned and Tom greeted her with a cheery "Good Morning." Richard remained silent, his mouth firm, almost to the point of grimness.

Jenny looked in amazement at the breakfast table, filled with canned peaches in heavy cream, grits, scrambled eggs, hickory-smoked fried ham, biscuits, gravy, buttermilk and coffee. The succulent odors of the varied foods filled the room and made Jenny's mouth water.

The girls clattered down the stairs. Jenny looked up and totally forgot all thoughts of food. Sarah came first again—the trim little creature blinking her big brown eyes. Laura gazed at Jenny with that nobody-loves-me expression, then smiled ruefully for a second when Jenny tousled her hair. Richard looked at his wife with obvious concern in his brown eyes. Jenny vowed to herself she would not be parted from these children. Somehow she would be their fairy godmother as she had promised.

———————

When both girls had been scrubbed briskly from head to toe, Mandy stuck Sarah's head in the basin and washed it with lye soap. She filled the basin with fresh water for each rinse. "Ouch," squealed Sarah as Mandy toweled the wet head dry and began to comb out the tangles. When Sarah's hair was properly braided, she did the same to Laura. Mandy wasn't usually quite that rough, but tension was beginning to surface. She finished their hair and sent them out to play.

The plump, red-haired woman called Jenny wanted the children with her every minute of the day. She seemed a kindly person and the twins basked in a warm glow of happiness. Her second day here, she had set up a small area in her bedroom where she held daily school. The girls worked diligently and were apt pupils, but Mandy knew this only temporarily solved the problem.

She wondered how long Jenny would be here. The children were becoming frighteningly attached to this woman. How would they react when she had to leave? Mandy sighed as she opened the door and threw the tub of dirty bath water into the back yard. Something had to be done about these girls, running around like little boys, growing up like slave children with no white friends, and rubbing the faces of little boys in the dirt when they were insulted.

A lump formed in Mandy's throat. She had done all she could to raise up Christina's children, but her household duties left little time for spending with them. What would become of the girls?

It was wash day and Mandy had a busy day coming. She already had clothes soaking in the new wooden tubs one of the slaves had made for that purpose. With the extra wash generated by Richard and Jenny, it would be a long day. But before she started, she wanted to check on her setting hen in one of the small coops.

A short time later, when the twins came into the kitchen they found Mandy in tears. "What's de matter?" asked Laura.

"A mean ol' skunk must of got in wid my settin' hen an' eat all the eggs full of baby chickens—and jus' when dey was 'bout ready t' hatch," sniffled Mandy. "I'se worked so hard t' get those baby chicks, I jus' can't believe it."

Laura and Sarah's eyes met in a moment in a flash of horrified realization at what they had done. They felt like tongueless idiots for a moment with a deep feeling of guilt. Laura tried to talk, but gasped and gave up, then Sarah raised her head. "Dat mean ol' skunk!" she said and they both sat down and started to cry with Mandy.

Richard rose early and slipped outside for a walk before the others awoke. Soft clouds in the eastern sky appeared in harmonious tones of grey and rose, with patches of pastel blue and pink showing here and there. He marveled at God's handiwork and for a moment forgot the problem that kept repeating itself over and over in his mind.

Jenny seemed seized with new energy as her natural passion for children found fulfillment through the twins. Why, he wondered, did these children come to his brother, when their very lives seemed a torment to him? Why couldn't they have come to a home where a loving wife, like Jenny, would dote over them? Did God find him and Jenny unfit to have children? Richard found the twins delightful, but you didn't just ask to take someone else's kids home with you, especially when you were in his and Jenny's situation.

They had been in Virginia a week and had enjoyed a marvelous time. He and Tom discussed the crops, reminisced, fox hunted, and covered the plantation from one boundary to another. They sat and talked for hours as they wished they had been able to talk on those hundreds of evenings they spent together when they were younger.

"Why don't you stay?" Tom asked. "I could use your help running the plantation, little brother, and you know half of it belongs to you. Times are tough right now. I just heard three more banks in the area have failed. It's a bad time to be setting out to seek your fortune. Why would you want to live in some frontier outpost only forty miles from the far boundaries of the United States? This is your home; you grew up here."

His brother had a likeable side Richard was just beginning to recognize. Perhaps their problems of the past had been due to his own immaturity and uncontrolled temper, Richard thought, but he knew he had to go on to Missouri.

When Tom saw he could not change Richard's mind, he spread out surveyor's maps and they went over and over the route to Missouri. They would go northwest on the wagon road across the mountains to Wheeling, then take the Cumberland Road to the Ohio River. There they would take a flatboat down the Ohio, and at Cairo, take a steamboat up the Mississippi to Independence.

When Richard mentioned God, Tom's anger spilled out. "If there were a God in charge, he would never have taken Christina, when she was so desperately needed and loved. At first I cursed Him for doing this to me; then I realized I was fighting a nonexistent being. If there does happen to be a God, if He'll leave me alone, I'll leave Him alone."

Richard tried to tell Tom about his new religion. "Mormons," said Tom, "I never heard of them, and I don't want to hear about them, but I do have to admit you wear your newfound faith well." Richard struggled to keep down negative feelings trying to surface. His brother's attitude about his religion reminded him strongly of earlier days and how Tom had felt about things which were important to him then. They had both put the past aside and their relationship was amiable. Richard didn't want to take a chance of becoming estranged again, though he felt Tom's inner desperation, and knew the Gospel would give him a great deal of comfort if he could only embrace it. But Tom was not yet ready for this newfound faith.

Now they must get on their way. Jenny had determined they should take his brother's children with them. He had tried to convince her of the folly of such an idea, but whenever he started to speak she interrupted him. Her eyes filled with tears and she had that woebegone expression on her face. There was suddenly a wide gulf between them which had never been there before.

When he again tried to explain, she turned red and didn't answer. Richard knew when Jenny was terribly angry she turned red. Topped by her red hair, she was quite a sight as she stood there brushing at her cheeks with the back of her hand. There wasn't any use arguing with Jenny. It was like kicking at a brick wall. He knew she had her mind made up and would take no notice of anyone who tried to get her to think differently.

Frustration mingled with guilt as he recalled the previous evening. Jenny ignored him for hours, and unspoken words hung heavily between them. When she did speak, he felt the determination in her voice, also the disappointment and the hurt. Their voices and tempers rose until he yelled at her when she said she would not be separated from these children. Losing his temper had only seemed to increase her determination.

She turned on him fiercely, her chin firm and her lips set. "I'll not leave without them!" she whispered, and he could see that her resolve had passed the bounds of reason. While usually a sensible woman, she now acted with what he felt to be petty childishness. He retired to another guest room, but slept little.

Richard walked for a long time. It galled him deeply that Jenny would not accept his decision. His mother would never have thought of opposing his father. What were women coming to these days? Next thing you knew they'd be trying to run the country. Some were already clamoring for woman suffrage.

He stifled a sigh as he grudgingly decided he would have to give permission for Jenny to ask Tom if she could take his children.   He was conceding with great reluctance. Surely Tom could convince her of the error of her ways. If Richard loved Jenny one bit less, he would just leave without her, but he couldn't think of facing the days and months of his life without his wife. He walked back to the house and squatted down on the veranda with his back against a post until he heard morning noises inside the house.

————————

Jenny glowed with excitement. Just when she had admitted to herself it was not going to happen, Richard had finally acquiesced to her pleas and had agreed to let her ask Tom about taking the children. It seemed too good to believe. Once Richard made up his mind, he rarely changed it.

She steeled herself for the task, then waited until she found Tom sitting alone reading a book at his desk in the study. She peeked into the room, then stood in the doorway and waited until he looked up.

"Tom."

"Yes, Jenny," he said in a tone which invited her to continue.

She hesitated a moment before speaking, "I've enjoyed your children so much. They are apt pupils and need to be getting some learning..."

"I've been concerned about that for some time," he admitted as he closed the book. "I understand you have a good background in education. What do you suggest?"

Jenny caught her breath as her courage almost faltered. She had to say this just right or she would botch the whole business. Everything depended upon Tom's answer. But when she started talking the words tumbled out non-stop and her words gave her courage to plead for what she so passionately craved. She told him how much she had always wanted children, about teaching in New York, how deeply involved she had become with his children and how she would love to take the girls for a while and give them the education they needed so desperately. She stopped only when she ran out of both words and breath. She took a deep breath, then exhaled slowly.

Tom sat looking both serious and reflective. "What does Richard think about all this?" he asked after a moment.

"He doesn't think you'll consider letting them go, but he said I could ask you."

"Well," Tom said thoughtfully, "I guess I'd be a fool to turn down such an offer. The kids love you, they're happier than I've ever seen them, and you seem well qualified to teach them what they need to know. Do you think we could persuade Richard to stay around a few more days while we get things ready?"

Jenny felt momentarily stunned. A strong sense of unreality swept over her, then suddenly, like she had been hit by lightning, she realized what Tom was saying. Tears of joy began streaming down her face. Turning, she saw Richard standing behind her, looking incredulous. She jumped up and down squealing with delight, and threw her arms around his neck and kissed him. It was the happiest day of her life. In spite of his earlier opposition to the idea, Richard couldn't help but catch some of her enthusiasm.

"Come sit down, and let's talk,"Tom suggested, a serious note in his voice. They sat around the table and chatted about what the children would need. Jenny leaned across the table absorbed in what Tom was saying.

"What would you think of taking Mandy to look after the girls?" Tom asked. "I don't know what I'll do without her; she's become almost a part of the place." He stopped a moment, in thoughtful silence before he continued. "When Christina was a young girl, Mandy became her maid. She has been with us ever since I married Christina. She's practically raised the girls. It would help make the adjustment easier for them, though I've never seen them take to anyone like they have to you."

Richard thought a minute, then nodded in agreement with his brother, though he had some doubts in the back of his mind. Besides his own abhorrence of slavery, the Mormon Church urged members to free their slaves. What would they think of him bringing a slave along with his new family? Through his shipping business contacts Richard had become well aware of the political situation in Missouri. He had been to the thriving little frontier town of St. Louis, on the west bank of the Mississippi River several times. The narrow streets were filled with rats, soot, horse manure and urine. It was a hotbed of prejudice—for slavery and against Mormonism.

Richard couldn't help but feel some foreboding about the situation in Missouri. Aware of the enmity his religious beliefs had aroused, he knew there was more than religion involved here. Richard felt certain the Saints would be in for trouble in Missouri when the residents there realized their political power. They would have a tendency to vote as a block, which strengthened their political position greatly. Already the Mormons were becoming the focus of mounting opposition.

"Another thing," said Tom thoughtfully. "I've never heard of Mormons until you two arrived, but you have to promise me you won't make Mormons out of my girls. When they are old enough to understand religion and make up their own minds, then they can choose whatever church, if any, they want to join."

Richard and Jenny nodded in agreement.

"It's all decided then," Tom said as he rang the bell for Mandy. She appeared at the top of the stairs. "Bring both girls here and stay with them," he instructed.

When the three stood in front of him, he looked down into the girls' upturned faces. "How would you like to go with your Aunt Jenny and Uncle Richard for a while?" he asked.

The twins stared wide-eyed at each other for a brief second, then squealed in amazement and yelled, "Yes, yes," as each hugged one of his legs.

"I mean you, too, Mandy," he said as he noticed the shadow of concern crossing her face.

"Lord a mercy," said Mandy, reacting with surprise and confusion. She glanced from the twins to Jenny, then back to Tom, "I never thought of such a thing."

Everyone smiled except Mandy, who stood in stunned silence. She wondered how she could bear to leave Sully and the plantation. She wondered what Missouri might be like.

CHAPTER FIVE

Richard stood in the yard looking at the wagon, already piled full, and wondered how they'd STILL get five people and their trunks into it. Tom joined him, rubbing his angular chin thoughtfully as he took in the situation.

"You'll have to have another wagon," he said. "I've got one I can let you use, and Mandy can drive it. I'll have the stable boy bring it over so you can begin loading it."

"Thanks, Tom," Richard replied, then tried to search for the right words to tell his brother how much he appreciated his kindness of the past few days and his offer for Richard to stay and help run the plantation. It didn't come out easily. He always had a hard time communicating his feelings to Tom.

"You know I appreciate your asking me to stay, don't you? I probably would if Jenny and I hadn't already made up our minds to join the members of our faith in Missouri."

Tom grinned at Richard, "It's okay, little brother, I understand. Just take good care of my girls."

"I'd give my very life to protect them if needs be," said Richard, then feeling a little embarrassed by the fact they both had moist eyes, he said, "I'd better check on what the women are packing before we need three wagons." He turned and disappeared into the house.

Jenny seemed in fine spirits. The task of packing what would be needed by Mandy and the girls seemed endless. They wanted to take half of the house along. Richard took in the situation and smiled. He would leave the task to Jenny. He wouldn't argue with them this last day, at least not until the second wagon was full.

Mandy folded her dark dress and white shawl carefully and placed them in the trunk underneath the extra clothing for the twins. She took pride in the fact she had a Sunday dress, a luxury few slaves enjoyed. She had made it from cloth Christina had given her shortly before she died.

No one in the Harris house got much sleep that night. Tom hoped he was doing the right thing letting his girls go with Richard and Jenny. He had known it was inevitable from the moment she had set eyes on his children. It would be far better for the girls than living here in a big house, where there were no other white children for miles. He didn't want them to find their friends among the slaves as Richard had done as a child. They needed to associate with people, not slaves. If he had Jenny pegged right, she would soon have another school of her own and his girls would have plenty of other children around as well as plenty of instruction in womanly arts.

Jenny felt prouder than a mare with a new foal, and her mind so busy formulating plans that sleep could find no place with her that night. Richard felt dazed and wondered what he was getting himself in for. The girls became so excited they popped up, under one pretense or another, every time Mandy put them firmly, but gently back into bed.

———————

Mandy could scarcely imagine going clear to Missouri. Her heart sank every time she thought of leaving her granddaughter, possibly never to return again. Now she understood how mothers felt when their children were sold away from them. She felt like she was bursting to ask questions, but unable to do so. What a pity that being a slave she could not even ask the numerous questions now crowding into her mind.

Mandy would miss the others who worked for Massa Tom. She checked daily on the gardener, Sam, talked with Hannah, the cook, and kept an eye on the children, especially Sully. Sully would be well cared for by the others, but Mandy could hardly bear the thoughts of leaving her. She had lost all of the rest of her family to death—now she was to be separated from her granddaughter by a whim of her master. Silent tears rolled down her wrinkled cheeks.

Who would look out for Sam? Sam was getting old, his vitality diminished. He was hardly able to do his work, though he appeared with a hoe each morning in the yard or vegetable garden and did what he could. Many masters would have sold Sam by now, so they didn't have to feed him when he was able to do so little work, but Massa Tom would keep his faithful slaves until they died—unless they were caught breaking his rules.

Hannah threw her arms around Mandy's neck and started wailing when she heard Mandy was leaving. All of the slaves would miss her. She had kept them informed about happenings in the big house and in the world. Information from the occasional newspaper which fell into her hands, conversations she overheard and Massa's comings and goings, were all reported by Mandy to Hannah or the other house slaves who lived in the back room off the big kitchen. They in turn kept in touch with the field hands. Occasionally Mandy joined them after work—when she could get away from the big house. Oh, how she would miss them; they were all like family to her.

Mandy's life had been one of unceasing difficulties, but a slave had to be prepared to work hard and long under adverse conditions. Others had it much worse; Tom was a good master, and kind to his slaves. He gave lighter tasks and some time off for pregnant women and nursing mothers. He provided extra rations at seasons of the heaviest labor and gave two days off at Christmas time. Many slaves had come through the tortures of hell and lived half-crazy with fear of what the future might bring. That had never been the case here.

Her feelings about leaving were mixed, she must break emotional ties with the only life she had ever known. On one hand she was thankful she would not be parted from the twins, but she had no idea what would await her in far off Missouri. She couldn't entirely forget all the horrid tales she had heard about life on the frontier.

She wondered how she would ever get used to sleeping on the ground at night after bouncing around in a wagon all day so that every muscle in her body ached. She had been on wagon trips before, and she wasn't anxious to go clear to Missouri.

Sarah and Laura had never been so excited. "Where's Missouri?" Laura wondered.

"Somewhere at the berry edge of the country, I heared Uncle Richard say so."

"We'se never been away from home." Laura looked out the window thoughtfully. "I wonder what it'll be like. Sarah, do you think dey have houses?"

Surprised by the tone in her sister's voice, Sarah thought a minute before answering. "I don't think so. I heard Daddy say the wagon would be our home. I'm jus' a little scared. Where we gonna sleep?"

"I don' know," said Laura, "I can't eben imagine, but Aunt Jenny will figure out somethin'. She's so nice. I think our mudder was like Aunt Jenny. I know she wasn't like Freddy's mudder. I'd hate to be her kid."

"Me, too. Can you 'magine having dat lady for a mudder?" She paused for a moment, "Everybody keeps talkin' 'bout makin' 'young ladies' out of us. I wonder what dey mean." She laughed nervously, "Til Uncle Richard and Aunt Jenny come, I thought maybe all ladies was like Freddy's mudder. I'd hate to see anybody tryin' t' make a lady out o' me—eben a young one!"

Laura fanned herself with an imaginary fan mimicking Freddy's mother, "Now Freddy, play wid de girls, but don't get dirty."

The twins looked at each other and giggled, but soon Laura looked serious again. "I wonder what it would be like to have a real mudder."

"I don' know," sighed Sarah. "If we had a real mudder, like Aunt Jenny, we could stay here. I'll miss Sully and Greene."

"Me too! Who we play wid?"

Mandy entered the room. "Is ya'all still awake? Now you just settle down and get t' sleep if you want to go anywheres," she said with finality.

———————————

In spite of little sleep, everyone arose at daybreak. The house slaves had come to say goodbye to Mandy long before that, and to put a nourishing breakfast on the table to fortify the travelers for the long trip. Sully and Green showed up at the back door of the plantation house, red-eyed and somber looking. The twins seemed almost too excited to comfort their friends. "We'll be back 'fore long," Sarah assured them.

Tom and Mandy had packed foodstuff—an extra barrel of flour, slabs of salt pork, and a barrel of dried fruits. But in spite of all they were taking, Tom knew Richard could never carry enough to get them to Missouri without relying on his gun and his hunting ability to help keep their stomachs filled. He felt assured knowing Richard had hunted much as a young man on the plantation and had become a crack shot.

When goodbyes had been said, the women and girls climbed into the heavily loaded wagons. Tom put a hand on Richard's shoulder, and squeezed firmly. "Take care of them, little brother," he said for probably the dozenth time.

"I'll do my best," Richard assured him, then hopped into the wagon. With a flick of the reins across the backs of Daisy and Doll they moved off, Richard's wagon in the lead, followed by the wagon Mandy was driving, with a box of chickens tied on the back and the cow named Rosie trailing behind. Mandy's heart pounded as she turned her head to get one quick, last look at the plantation.

Tom stood at the edge of the yard for some time watching them wave goodbye and waving back at them until they disappeared into the trees. He stood, rooted to the spot for a moment longer, listening to the still audible sound of the wagon wheels while staring at his life as it passed through his mind. He started back toward the house, turning briefly at the door for one last look at the spot where his family had vanished from view.

He would miss the girls and Mandy, but under the circumstances, it seemed imperative he do something. He felt good he had found such a fortunate solution to the problem of educating the twins. They were with family, and that meant a lot. He knew Richard and Jenny would love the girls like they were their own.

Though this seemed the best solution for everyone, he wished he had spent more time with his children; they didn't seem the least bit sad about leaving him. Their faces flushed with excitement, they hardly wanted to take time to kiss him goodbye. They seemed terrified they might be left behind. He thought of the times he had used harsh words on them which he knew stung more than a hickory limb and wished he had bit his tongue off instead.

Tom's life for the past few years had been filled with an overwhelming sense of the past. He had grieved for Christina and thought of her constantly as the empty years passed and the emptier ones came. Even Mandy had been a reminder of Christina, whose love had been the joy of his life. Now maybe the wounds would begin to heal. Richard and Jenny had that quiet faith and enthusiasm for life he had lost, and he envied them for it. He would just have to go on living, day by day, doing the best he could. Maybe eventually he would find some joy in the process, and find comfort in the memory of his late wife instead of continuing to mourn her loss.

Tom entered the porch, then paused to look back again. To the side of the porch, the two little slave children sat woefully watching the place in the distance where the wagon had disappeared. He stopped in surprise as he saw a rider coming down the lane. "Now who on earth could that be?" he mumbled as he ran his fingers through his thinning hair. He watched as the man rode up, dismounted and came towards the house.

Tom stepped out and greeted the stranger. The man handed him a letter. "Thank you," said Tom as he paid the rider the postage due. "Won't you come in and take some refreshment?"

"I'm hoping to make Richmond tonight," the man said. "Thank you anyway."

Tom went into his study, sat down at his desk and opened the envelope. The letter came from a man named Aaron—apparently Jenny's brother.

It sounded friendly enough and said that he had lost track of his sister, and would appreciate knowing her whereabouts. For some reason Tom felt a strange wave of foreboding. Jenny hadn't mentioned having a brother; it seemed too bad she had just missed his letter. He thought of Richard and how long they had been out of touch. Families should know the location of other family members. He would answer the letter tomorrow, but now he had to check on the tobacco crop. He rose, put on his hat, and went out the door.

———————

The road, lined by stately oaks and pines, rambled along, then turned sharply to the west toward the river, where it twisted through trees and willows, pushing back the undergrowth so travelers could pass. This first day, the twins thought traveling was fun as they took turns riding beside Jenny. When they stopped for the horses to graze, Jenny played games with them. She pointed out the habits of the birds and animals they saw.

"Look at that cardinal," she would say. "What do you think he is saying?" Then, "Why are the squirrel's cheeks so full?"

When the sun was almost down to the ridge and long fingers of shadow crept into the gullies, Jenny felt exhausted from trying to talk over the shrieks of little girls. The girls had never been on a long wagon trip before or slept out in a tent. Camping was a new adventure.

"I'll make my bed 'neath the wagon," said Mandy when they urged her to sleep inside the tent with the others, "wid de sky full of twinklin' stars as my ceilin', de soft brown dirt as my floor, and de sturdy oaks for walls. De full moon can cast its light down and provide night light for my bedroom."

The girls fussed to sleep out beside her, but Jenny didn't want to take a chance of their catching cold. Jenny felt perfectly grateful for Mandy who sat beside the children's bed until their eye lids became heavy enough to close, then crawled into her cold bed beneath the wagon wrapping herself in a blanket. Mandy felt a need to be by herself and have a place where her thoughts wouldn't feel as crowded as in the wagon or tent. The soft night air seemed a balm to her soul.

Jenny looked at the twins, asleep in their bed in the tent. She had to smile every time she looked at them, though it had been a more difficult day than she had anticipated. Child raising took a lot out of you, she concluded.

Jenny and Richard sat at the camp fire as the sky grew red, and the long June twilight faded. A curtain of night gradually fell about them. They breathed in fragrances carried by the air–flowers, pine needles, others they could not identify. Jenny thought it the sweetest perfume she had ever inhaled.

A faint whir of wings and the squeal of a rodent caught in the grasp of a predator's talons, broke the evening silence. Indistinct sounds filled the twilight–the whispering of the trees, the scurry of small foraging creatures. Occasionally they could hear the distant barking of dogs. They were still sitting at the campfire when the stars came out in their glory and the moon came up like a giant orange ball.

"Are you happy?" Richard asked.

"Ecstatically!" she replied.

He slipped his arm around her and they sat in silence until the embers began to grow dim and an owl hooted from a nearby tree. Jenny felt safe with Richard there beside her and the stars above.

"We'd better get some sleep," Richard said, standing up and pulling her up beside him. "It's been a hard day." His voice took on a humorous, half-bantering tone. "We'd better get used to the idea life isn't easy when you have a family. I don't know what to think about that; it's a little frightening." They stood arm in arm for a moment watching the thin clouds drift over the moon. The moment became magic. He took her in his arms and kissed her longingly, then took her hand in his and led her toward the tent.

Being thoroughly exhausted, everyone slept soundly that night. The next morning dawned cool and clear. Jenny awoke with a start as a mockingbird began to imitate the calls of its other feathered friends. Even the twins were up before the sun rose in the east. Mandy filled the bake oven with biscuit dough, fastened it securely, then covered it with a pile of live coals. Jenny milked the cow while Richard checked the wagons and readied the horses. While the biscuits baked, Mandy helped dress the girls. Creamy gravy over the top of warm biscuits made a perfect breakfast. Jenny put the milk in a pail with a tight fitting lid and hung it onto the wagon.

"What you doin'?" Sarah asked, watching Jenny intently.

"Not doin', but doing," Jenny corrected. "Your language isn't fit to come out of your mouth. You need to learn to talk proper English." Then returning to the child's question, she answered, "Tonight we will have fresh butter, churned by the motion of the wagon."

"Are we ready?" Richard asked, impatient to be on the way. Jenny gave a short, curt nod. They all climbed onto the hard wooden wagon seats and started off, Rosie, the cow, reluctantly bringing up the rear.

The next few days they spent crossing the Piedmont. Some days they made fifteen miles, some only three. In places the land became marshy or they had to creep through bushes. They crossed a number of streams. The girls laughed as the clip clop of the horses' hoofs made a hollow sound going over bridges.

The road became better and more heavily traveled. They met people in homespun shirts and trousers traveling on foot, others riding on horseback, and some leading pack horses or driving cattle. They traveled with caravans of wagons or singly. Most wagons, like theirs, were loaded with goods. Animals grazed among the rocks, men cut wood for fires and branches to build temporary shelters.

A friendly couple with two little boys invited Richard's family to sit around the campfire with them one moonlit night. They sang their favorite songs over and over and the adults seemed to enjoy the welcome respite as much as the children.

In the distance beyond the broad sweep of country before them, they could see the pale gray outlines of the Blue Ridge Mountains. The sky had become decidedly overcast when they awoke the next morning, the air cooled from a light drizzle. At first the ground, barely touched by rain, gave forth a cloud of dust which rose behind the wagons. "This dust is getting into everything, including my throat," choked Jenny, tightening her lips.

The low rumbling of thunder increased, clouds covered the hot sun and soon rain came down in torrents. The night closed in black as pitch. The next day a gentle drizzle continued from sunup to sundown.

"At least there's no dust," commented Jenny.

The ground became slippery making it hard to keep wagons and animals on the road. Camping that night was a nightmare. When Richard finally managed to get the tent up, everyone huddled inside it, wet and cold.

The next day the sun came out again. The essence of wet earth and brush loaded the air with exquisite fragrance. They could smell the wild rosebuds as they passed the bushes, damp and intensely sweet.

Progress slowed through the gently rolling upland broken by broad river valleys and numerous hills and ridges. Jenny worked untiringly to amuse the girls. She helped them examine the rich, dark, shining foliage of the magnificent magnolia tree and the large, glossy leaves of the oak. They watched jeweled-winged hummingbirds dart among the flowers. They smelled, tasted and felt the out-of-doors. As they awakened their senses to all of nature, Jenny could see why poets, musicians and artists everywhere looked to God's handiwork for their inspiration.

"Look at that slender maple. Beside it are two tall pines with needles of dark green. They're holding their arms out to us!" she exclaimed. "And see the great massive oaks standing between the trees making a windbreak for them all."

Jenny never seemed to run out of stories to tell the girls and rhymes to teach them. She extravagantly talked Richard into stopping a bit early so they could all pick wild strawberries for a tasty treat and dogwood blossoms for a bouquet to brighten their evening meal.

Richard stopped the wagon and leaped down. He broke off a spray of blossoms and handed it to Jenny without speaking. Their eyes met in perfect understanding. She was profoundly moved, not by the act alone, but by what it stood for—the connotation of love, contentment and unity. Jenny knew it was a peace offering after his reluctance to let her take the girls and the resulting arguments. She blinked hard to keep her eyes dry. There may be persecution and sacrifice and other hardships to be endured for the sake of the truth, but they would weather it together.

––––––––––––

"Are we ready to get moving?" Richard asked for the second time. Everyone started climbing into the wagons except Sarah. She stood with her feet apart and planted firmly on the ground.

"And what is holding us up this morning?" he asked looking her straight in the eye.

"I'se not goin'," she announced.

"You're not going!" he repeated incredulously, as though he didn't believe his ears. "And just what do you plan to do?"

"I'se tired o' travelin'. I'se walkin' home."

Laura looked down at her twin, her eyes wide. Richard looked at Jenny with that helpless "What do we do now?" look. Jenny fluctuated somewhere between surprise and full-blown mirth as she tittered, then struggled to suppress laughter.

"Get yourself into this wagon, and don't let me hear anymo' of dat nonsense," commanded Mandy. "You decided to go, an' you don't change your mind now."

Sarah climbed into the wagon without another word of protest. Her mouth made a moody, pouting line as she moved to the back of the wagon, holding onto the hardwood sides to help lessen the jolts. Laura climbed back and put an arm around her sister. The hot Virginia sun shone down on their faces. Mandy stopped and tied sunbonnets on the girls, but Sarah found hers confining and uncomfortable. She kept pushing it back and soon her exposed skin was red and warm.

That night Mandy whipped up the white of an egg, and amidst Sarah's protests, spread the gooey stuff all over her face. As it dried she felt it pulling on her skin.

"I don' want this on me," she fussed.

"Don't," corrected Jenny.

"It will help pull the feber out of your skin," Mandy insisted.

"I wish I hadn' come," said Sarah, thoroughly tired of the long, monotonous days on the wagon. "I'se tired o' lots o' things," she wailed. "I'se tired o' Aunt Jenny tellin' me how t' talk. I want to go home and see Greene and Sully and play with the kittens."

Laura looked at her sister with concern. She, too, was tired and listlessly clung to Mandy. She silently fought off tears as long as she could, then her dark eyes overflowed and the moisture made rivulets down her dusty face.

After supper Mandy held the girls, one on each knee, while they all watched a crimson sunset. They listened to the buzzing insects and to the voices of croaking frogs and crickets breaking full upon the evening stillness with a steady rhythm. In a strong, clear, beautiful voice she sang sad, haunting songs which gradually lulled them to sleep. Richard lifted the girls, one by one, into the tent. They slept fitfully that night.

The morning breeze felt fresh and delicious, like a bracing drink of cool water. The early morning rays of sunshine gladdened the travelers' hearts. They drank in the soft air scented with the delicious odor of pine needles and the twins forgot about their homesickness of the night before.

The heavily forested Blue Ridge area rose abruptly along the western edge then became a broad upland of mountains, valleys and plateaus. The road went along winding paths in valleys made by rivers and streams and through gaps or passes between steep mountain peaks. Ascents became steeper and steeper, the road more and more winding. The wagons almost tipped over in some places and in others slid precariously. Going downhill seemed particularly frightening because the wagons were so hard to control. The drivers wound back and forth to keep the wagons from going so fast they overran the horses. The road was well marked out, but traveling was slow.

Jenny felt an intense responsibility for the safety of these two children she had insisted on taking from their home. Accidents, fevers and epidemics took such a high toll of the young. So many children were injured or killed by falling out of a wagon and getting run over by the wheel.

Sarah found it impossible to stay in one spot. Mandy couldn't keep Sarah still because her hands were busy with the reins, guiding the horses over the sometimes treacherous terrain. Jenny tucked Laura in the wagon beside Mandy and put Sarah between her and Richard. Now Sarah fussed to ride with Mandy. "If you promise to sit still on the seat beside her, I'll let you ride with Mandy next time we stop," Jenny promised.

Sarah couldn't stay still for long, and was soon climbing all over the wagon and Jenny would have to take her back. Sometimes Jenny would walk for a ways with the girls. They needed the exercise, and it gave them a change of pace. Sometimes they practiced memorizing and reciting Psalms. It was hard work to keep their interest. This trek with kids took more energy than dealing with a whole school full of unruly scholars. It seemed more fatiguing than anything Jenny had ever done. At least school kids went home and you had the evening hours to rest and recuperate.

"Boy, are my legs cramped and my muscles tired," she complained rubbing the outside of her thighs.

"So's mine, so's mine," said Mandy.

"Yes, it's a lonesome old life," thought Mandy, as she listened to the slow clip-clop of the horses pulling the wagons. She missed Sully so. She missed the companionship of her friends. She missed the work and routine which had filled her life for so many years. The monotony of the long drive was becoming almost unbearable.

Puddles of mud dried back into dust that stuck in your throat, tickled your nose and made your hair feel heavy on your head. Mandy's limbs, shoulders and back ached from the bumpy wagon and holding the reins to drive the team. By evening she wanted nothing more than to collapse onto her bed. It wasn't easy, this driving a wagon across the country and sleeping under it at night, though she had chosen to sleep there. She would feel terribly awkward sleeping in the tent with Richard and Jenny.

Richard and Jenny treated her well. As they worked side by side, Jenny treated her almost like one of the family. Mandy began to feel more at home with them than she had with any white people she had ever known. She felt them to be friends in a guarded sort of way. It was a new experience for her to be treated almost as an equal, after years of plantation life, where slaves knew their place and kept it. Sometimes she wasn't sure what she was supposed to do; occasionally this new touch of freedom made her intensely uncomfortable.

Mandy felt herself to be a very stay-at-home type of person. She had not been off the plantation for years except to visit close neighbors. Being with the twins, who had become as dear to her as if they were her own, helped console the ache that filled her heart. She felt almost jealous of Jenny, who was so good with the girls, and could give them the education Mandy was not capable of giving them. Mandy knew she could have at least taught them some of the basic skills if she hadn't been a slave, but she did not dare let anyone know she could read and write.

When the twins argued over who would get to ride with Jenny and Richard, Mandy turned her face away and pain swept through her. She thought of the many times she had held them in her arms and taken the place of the mother they had never known. She thought of how Eliza had warned her about becoming too attached to these girls that had been dumped into her lap. She remembered being encircled in her own mother's arms and the feelings of warmth and love she felt. At these times, scenes from those other days came vividly to her mind.

Chapter Six

On a day filled with flowers and sunshine, Laura sat beside Richard in the wagon. Sometimes this new experience was exciting, sometimes boring. She touched his arm and said, "Look Uncle Richard—Azaleas!" He drew in the reins and brought the team to a stop. Mandy pulled up beside him. "What wrong?" she asked.

"Just a rest break," he replied. The twins climbed out of the wagons and ran to the colorful flowers. Each came back carrying a blossom, rich in color and perfume. Sarah handed hers to Jenny and Laura gave hers to Mandy, which put smiles on both women's faces.

That evening when they camped by some willows, Richard reached up with his knife and snipped off a willow branch hanging low over his head. The blade slid easily through the tender limb. He cut a piece about three inches long and notched it near one end, then worked the bark loose and slid it off.

"What you doin', Uncle Richard?" Laura asked.

"Just wait a minute and you'll see," he countered. He put a groove from the notch to the short end of the twig then popped the bare twig into his mouth wetting it with saliva to make the bark slide back on easily.

Laura watched intently as he pulled a face at the taste of the sap and wondered what on earth he could be doing. He slid the bark on, then put the newly made whistle to his lips and blew a high shrill note. He handed it to Laura, who hesitantly put it to her lips.

"Blow it," he instructed.

She blew softly. Her grave little mouth curved into a smile at the noise it made.

"Can I do dat?" asked Sarah, reaching for the whistle.

Laura held the whistle out to her sister.

"No," said Richard, reaching to cut another twig. "Laura, you keep it. I'll make you each one."

The girls whistled until Mandy exclaimed in exasperation, "Stop dat fo' awhile. Put dos whistles in yo' pockets and leave dem der de rest of de day. Dat noise drivin' me t' distraction!"

As the girls snuggled in their bed that night, Laura turned to Sarah and confided, "I wish Uncle Richard was our daddy."

––––––––––––––

Through Jenny's eyes, the Patterson River loomed larger before them than it was in actuality. Richard reigned up on the bank and surveyed the area. The bridge had been washed out. He looked around for the best spot to cross. The water flowed high from recent rains, and the bank was undercut. The wagon Mandy drove pulled up behind them.

"Let's make camp for the night, and take some time to find a good crossing," Richard decided.

They unhitched the horses and Richard made a campfire. While the women fixed supper, he ambled southward towards a small bluff overlooking a spot that showed signs of once being used as a crossing. He sat on the rocks awhile and looked down at the river. They would have to camp for a day or two until the water level lowered and the swift boiling water calmed some, he decided.

He looked at the sky for a clue as to what kind of weather to expect. It was clear, clear as a new glass windowpane. Richard walked back to the wagon. The aroma of beans and bacon cooking in the large pot over the fire filled his nostrils and made his mouth water. He looked at Jenny and felt the air thick with her fear. He put his arms around her and whispered sweet words of comfort into her ear.

"We'll wait until the river goes down a bit. It might take a few days, but I can work on the wagon, and maybe I can bag some game for you and Mandy to dry. Our supply is getting a bit low."

She relaxed some in his embrace, but he was only putting off the ordeal of the crossing, and they both knew it had to be done.

For three days they tarried on the riverbank, but Richard's efforts at hunting were unsuccessful. On the fourth day, Richard hitched up the team and led the reluctant horses to the bank. They refused to plunge into the still raging waters. He climbed onto the back of old Doll, the dapple gray mare with a steady disposition, and urged her into the water.

The swift waters pulled against the wagon and it swayed from side to side. Jenny tried to hang onto both the wagon box and the twins beside her. "Hang on tight," she yelled. Water splashed into the wagon and was soon ankle deep, soaking their feet, their clothing and all their belongings. Daisy and Doll plunged and reared, and the water drowned out the sound of Mandy yelling at her team crossing behind them.

The two horses stumbled onto the west bank, barely able to stand up. They looked back to see how Mandy was managing, and to everyone's horror, one of her horses was down.

The animal had stepped into a hole and fallen. The twins began wringing their hands and screaming in terror. Jenny pulled herself together and tried not to let them see how terrified she felt.

Mandy was whipping and yelling at the animal, which finally struggled to its feet and plunged on across the river. When they were safely on the west bank, Richard unhitched the animals and rubbed them down with dry grass. The family lay on the grass beside the spent teams, too exhausted to move. Later that day they had to unload their wagons and dry everything out before repacking and continuing on their way.

One morning, Jenny opened her eyes to a pair of deer drinking from a pond of water just a few feet from their camp. She poked Richard awake and pointed at the animals. He slipped quietly out of bed, grabbed his gun and shot the young buck. He grabbed his knife to slit its throat and re-move the glands from its back legs which would give the meat a strong wild taste if left in the animal. It would provide welcome fresh meat. The doe ran, leaping, across the clear-ing and vanished into the trees.

In seconds the whole camp came awake. "You killed it!" Laura said accusingly.

"Land sakes, chile, we needs food, that's why," retorted Mandy. "You've eat venison before."

"I didn't know venison meant deer," Laura said defen-sively, "or I wouldn't have eaten it."

"Well, you be darn glad to have it this time," asserted Mandy, "and you'll get awful hungry if you get too uppity for your own good."

They cleaned, skinned and quartered the animal. That evening Mandy tended the fire and revolved the spits, while they roasted a hind quarter for the evening meal. The fresh meat provided a pleasing change from their normal fare. The delectable smell of cooking venison made them all terribly hungry. Even Laura couldn't resist the succulent treat. The travelers sat down to their dinner, thinking it was better than a banquet, as the flickering flames cast shadows among the oaks. They laid over the next two days and cut the venison into thin strips which they dried over the camp fire.

Richard fixed a wagon wheel which had been cracked by driving over an unexpected rock. The twins watched in fascination while he deftly removed the metal rim from around the wheel, fixed the wheel, then heated the metal and slipped it back onto the wood. He plunged it quickly into cold water to cool it enough to shrink the metal against the wheel and also keep it from burning the wood rim.

"Save all the bacon grease you can for greasing the wheels," he told Jenny. "I can't believe how fast I've been using the grease lately."

A few days later Richard shot a plump, young rabbit. "Poor little bunny," Laura lamented.

Mandy soaked it all night in oil, thyme, rosemary and garlic. The next morning she built up the fire and put it on to simmer before the sun kissed the horizon. By the time they were ready to eat, it tasted tender and delicious. Richard took a small bite. "Umm, I've never had rabbit that tasted so good!" He accented the statement with a huge second bite.

At Cumberland, Maryland, they reached the Cumberland Road and headed toward the Ohio River. The road had been built by the federal government. Authorized by Congress in 1806, this first section had been completed in 1818.

Not originally a toll road, it had recently been turned over to the state, who charged tolls to keep the road maintained.

Days stretched into weeks and the girls began adjusting to this new life. Fresh air and exercise helped make them strong, their skin started to tan and Jenny noticed their appetites improving. As they slowly covered the miles toward Missouri the girls began blossoming. Sometimes Richard would hold one, then the other on his lap and let them help drive the team. He had to confess he felt enchanted by these two petite beings. Jenny spent hours of time teaching them to read from the Bible and the Book of Mormon. Sarah and Laura could soon read quite well. "I'll bet they're ready for a third reader," Jenny bragged.

They also learned numerous facts about the flora and fauna of the area. The adults felt delighted with their progress. The most difficult part of the trip was the same monotonous routine day after day. They were up at five-thirty, had breakfast by six-thirty, then they packed the tent and tools and Richard hitched the horses to the wagons. They were ready to travel at seven. They stopped for dinner and to rest the horses at eleven-thirty, then resumed travel until evening when Richard found a place to camp. Everyone felt so tired they dropped into their makeshift accommodations each night and fell asleep almost instantly. Sometimes Richard muttered in his sleep. Each morning Jenny found it almost impossible to believe she had slept all night, yet could still feel so exhausted.

They urged the horses up a steep mountain, then stopped to drink in the fantastic view. As far as the eye could see, there lay mountains and valleys and forests and rivers—a breath-taking sight. They all looked out at the view ahead and sat there a few moments in silent wonder.

Richard stopped to talk to a leather-faced settler. "Thousands of people come through here every year," he told them, "most of them going west into Indiana and Illinois. How's it going for you folks?"

"I've been on the trail three weeks. In some places the road is good and in others it's so poor I can't make any time at all. In places the mud's been over my boot tops, but people keep telling me the road's fairly good."

The settler tipped back his head and laughed.

––––––––––

The Harris family finally reached the banks of the Monongahela about sixty miles south of Pittsburgh. At Pittsburgh the Monongahela and Allegheny Rivers joined to form the Ohio, a broad waterway to the West. Every year more and more grain, hogs and tobacco were floated down the Ohio and Mississippi to New Orleans and foreign markets. These rivers were the major highways of the West. Richard felt a wave of nostalgia as he assessed the freight wagons coming and going to the river.

"Just wait until you see Pittsburgh!" Richard told Jenny. "It's a great town with its docks and iron mills, its big houses, tall buildings and busy stores... It's quite a sight."

Jenny looked at the mighty river and shuddered. She felt she would rather die than get out on the water. There were canoes, arks, bateaux, flatboats and pirogues carrying barrels of salt, sugar, tobacco and other products. On the docks people crowded about watching the boats arrive and depart.

Reading the look on Jenny's face, Richard put an arm around her and said, "I know you hate the water, but it will save us a lot of time we can't afford to lose."

Richard arranged for passage on a large flatboat. It was a good twenty feet wide and a hundred feet long, with an overhead roof to protect both people and goods from bad weather or attacks from the shore. Amongst others, they loaded their wagons, horses and Rosie the cow, onto the boat and prepared to quit land travel for a while. Wide-eyed, Sarah and Laura were all over the place, fascinated by everything.

They were barely on board before Jenny, feeling the motion of the boat, became horribly sea sick. She lost her breakfast into the river and wanted nothing but to collapse on the bank and lie on dry land again.

"You'll get your sea legs before long, then you'll be okay," Richard said compassionately.

In his business, he had been down the Ohio many times, buying animal skins, cotton, tobacco and sugar and arranging to ship needed goods back to the new villages on the river plains.

Richard looked at Jenny's colorless face and hoped she would soon be able to hold something on her stomach. "One man described a flatboat as a log cabin, a fort, a floating barnyard and a country grocery," Richard noted, trying to cheer his wife.

Side by side were men, women, children, horses, pigs, chickens, cows and dogs. Piled on deck were kegs of powder, dishes, furniture, farm implements, tools, weapons and produce. Everyone except Jenny laughed and talked. The people were eager to start, but they had to wait on deck for half an hour before the boatmen began to shout to each other. The deck hands loosed the ropes that held the boat to the dock and they began their journey downriver.

Mandy finally grabbed a twin in each hand as they looked at everything with wide eyes. Jenny felt too queasy to look at much of anything, but she glanced at the boatman, who was now in charge of their safety and was barking orders. He appeared tall and strong, his face tanned to a dark brown. He wore a bright red shirt, a loose blue coat—called a jerkin—and coarse brown trousers. On his head sat a cap of skin and he wore leather moccasins on his feet. A leather belt, from which hung a hunting knife and a bag of tobacco, encircled his waist. He seemed to know exactly what to do and how to handle the deck hands and the boat.

Whenever they passed a village, people came down to the water's edge to see them pass. The boatman brought out a bugle and its notes rang out up and down the river. Villagers waved at them.

When they came to narrow, dangerous rapids, the boatman jumped into action, shouting commands to his men like a shrieking madman, as with great strength he guided the boat away from the sharp rocks. Jenny thought she would faint dead away before the danger was past and the boat again moved into the broad, calm river where clouds and color reflected in smooth, calm water. Sometimes the men sang as they worked, and their rich, sonorous voices rang skyward or broke full upon the evening stillness.

Pittsburg was indeed an impressive city. Its iron mills belched forth smoke onto the tall buildings and big houses. The dock was positively crowded with people and boats unloading and loading their cargo of passengers and freight. Jenny, Mandy and the girls resisted Richard's proposal to go ashore for a short time while their boat transacted its business. "We'll just stay put, right here, until we're on our way again," insisted Jenny, who knew it would be hard to keep track of the girls in all this confusion. Richard looked at Jenny and noted her cheeks carried a tinge of color, which had been absent for the first part of the river journey.

At Cairo, located near the southern end of Illinois, the Ohio River came into the Mississippi. There were only a few houses at the little settlement where the big rivers joined. Here they transferred to a steamboat and headed northward on the mile-wide Mississippi walled on both sides with solid timber.

The pilot-house of the steamboat housed several pilots who had come down to take a look at the river. This part, between Cairo and St. Louis, was known as the "upper river," and when low, it changed its channel regularly. Pilots whose boats had to lie in port a week often ran up the river on another ship inspecting it and keeping abreast of its changing conditions—a cheaper alternative than staying ashore and paying board.

A pilot had to know not only the names of all the towns, islands, and bends, but must know every snag and cottonwood along the banks of the river and every sandbar—even in the dark. The boat picked her way through snags and blind reefs, invisible wrecks which could tear the timbers of her hull apart and around islands. The smallest mistake could destroy a quarter of a million dollars' worth of steamboat and cargo and as many as a hundred and fifty lives.

Heading upstream nothing stopped them but fog. Downstream was different, with a stiff current pushing behind the boat. It was not customary to run downstream at night, especially during low water.

Visiting pilots were guests of the ship, and useful since they were always willing to assist at the wheel, go out in the yawl and help buoy the channel or help in any other way. Proud of their occupation, they talked incessantly about the river.

The captain disappeared into his stateroom. The captain was in charge and had the final say about everything on the boat. Jenny had heard that steamboat captains received a fabulous wage—sometimes as much as two dollars a day. She wondered what anyone would do with that much money.

At St. Louis, where the Missouri joins the Mississippi, the river was more than a mile wide. They quickly unloaded their possessions. Jenny felt delighted to put her feet on dry land once again.

"We'd better not tell anyone we're Mormons," Richard cautioned. "It might be dangerous."

The town abounded with rumors about the Saints. As they tried to sort out what was happening, they avoided people as much as possible. Richard was glad he had warned them not to say anything about the Church. It wasn't the time or place to profess their affiliation to the Mormons.

When they stopped for supplies, a thin man with straggly whiskers and cold eyes warned them, "You'd better watch out for the Mormons. They're a bunch of robbers and cold-blooded killers. You aren't safe traveling alone; you'd better team up with other wagons."

"We're not afraid of Mormons or anyone else," Richard said.

The stranger shook his head.

"Don't say you weren't warned," he said with a nasty edge to his voice. "They're a bunch of abolitionists," he added, eyeing Mandy, "and they're threatening to take over the whole state. We drove them out of Jackson County. The people of Clay County sympathized with the bastards for a while, but they soon realized their mistake and got rid of them."

"Where are they now?" asked Richard.

"They moved east, up into the Shoal Creek region—into country nobody else would want, and be damned if they haven't turned it into a blooming city. A settlement of four or five thousand people sprang up overnight. They called it Far West. The state legislature even gave them a new county, and named it Caldwell," he continued, eyes cold with hate and mumbling as he moved off.

"I don't like that man," said Sarah under her breath, glancing at her twin.

"I don't either," said Laura.

Richard sighed. All of a sudden he felt tired. The nation was tottering on the verge of war. In Missouri, no charge could be made that would arouse more intense emotion than that of being an abolitionist. He felt a sharp pang of concern lest they fall into the hands of angry mobsters before they could even find the Mormons. How would they be accepted by the Church members, bringing a slave woman with them, and what would the future of the Mormons be in Missouri? Was he taking his wife and his brother's children into a far more dangerous situation than he had realized? He had learned to love the twins dearly, but perhaps he had been unwise in giving in to Jenny's insistence that they take them.

Jenny turned intent eyes upon Richard, then looked uneasily toward Mandy. Richard looked into his wife's anxious face and said quietly, "We'll just have to deal with that when we get there."

He made that same side-of-the-mouth click of his tongue they all knew so well by now and lifted the reins. The horses responded. The wagons headed out of town, and the Harris family turned their faces toward Far West. They had to continue traveling if they were to find and join the Saints, but it didn't look good for their people in Missouri. Very soon they would see for themselves what the situation was in the new city the Mormons had built.

Though Richard had heard about the rapid influx of converts he felt unprepared for the city he saw rising above them as his eyes took in the landscape of what would be their new home.

"Look!" he said excitedly. "There it is!"

Jenny, lulled to drowsiness by the endless miles of travel, sat up straight and squinted. The city could be seen for miles in any direction.

"We're almost there!" she told the girls who were engrossed in conversation. Sarah and Laura gazed at the town, then exchanged looks.

"Wow!" said Sarah, "They do have houses here. Just look at them!"

"I guess we won't have to live in our wagon," said Laura.

Another wagon, loaded with lumber, pulled up beside them. "Hello," yelled a short, sturdy, balding man with a friendly smile. I'm Jim Hansen, and this is my wife, Miriam and daughter Mary. Are you coming to join us in Far West?"

A young girl, about the size of the twins looked out from between her parents. She looked thin and had long auburn hair which fell in tight curls. Sarah waved at her and she waved back. Laura smiled shyly, her nose wrinkling.

"I'm Richard Harris, and this is my wife, Jenny and the twins, Sarah and Laura. And Mandy," he added nodding in Mandy's direction. "My wife and I are from New York." Richard looked around him, "I can't believe the size of Far West and how quickly it has sprung up."

"Most people arriving here are surprised at the city," said Jim. "New converts join us daily. They come from nearly every state and many foreign countries: England, Germany, Denmark, Norway, Sweden, the isles of the sea… Converts come in wagons and on foot, but by the hoards they come."

Richard and Jim Hansen were soon in deep conversation about Far West, how it was laid out, land prices, and how the Harris family might get settled in their new surroundings.

"Our next door neighbor is disillusioned with both the Church and the settlement. If you have any cash money, which most people arriving don't have, you might talk to him. He's been considering selling, but is not yet ready to just abandon the place and leave without getting anything out of it. He has some corn and wheat planted, and logs hauled in for a house, but they're living in their wagon box."

"I'd like to talk to him," said Richard.

As they neared the city, they were joined by others. Up the road leading to Far West came a procession of men, women and children. There were men on horseback, people in various types of carriages or wagons and people walking. Their friendly banter and exchange of news made Richard and Jenny once again feel a sense of belonging. Other wagons filled not only with converts, but with lumber and building materials headed towards the settlement—a jovial, slow-moving throng of human beings. Most were hopeful and eager in spite of the persecution mounting against them.

When they stopped to rest the horses and eat lunch, the men uncoupled the sweating animals and staked them in the tall grass. Miriam, her youthful appearance heightened by her slender form, did not move from the wagon seat until Jim returned. As Jim lifted her from the wagon, Jenny saw she was missing her left foot. Miriam, anticipating her shock, explained that she had frosted her feet when the Mormons were being driven out of Independence and one foot had to be amputated, but she got around reasonably well.

Miriam looked at the twins and took in her breath. "Oh, Jenny, they're adorable," she said smiling. "You'll have to let them come over and play with my Mary. I know they'll be great friends, and we'd find it delightful to spend some time with all of you. I hope you'll be our neighbors."

"I can't wait to see the prophet Joseph Smith in person," Jenny confided to Miriam as they spread their food upon a blanket.

"What's a prophet?" Sarah asked loudly.

"A prophet is a person who communicates with God, and who tells people God's will," Richard explained as he and Jim joined the women and children.

"Joseph is not in Missouri now," said Jim. He's in Kirtland, Ohio.

"I thought the Saints were being instructed to gather in Missouri," said Richard. "Why is the prophet still in Kirtland?"

"We are, we are gathering in Missouri," said Jim. "Miriam and I have been here for a long time. Twelve miles west of Independence we laid the foundations of a settlement which was to be our 'Zion.' We all entered into a covenant that we would obey the laws of the land and the laws of God in this new home and we would teach others who came after us to do the same thing."

"I can't see why that would arouse persecution," said Richard thoughtfully.

"We purchased a great deal of land and Joseph designed a city. You should have seen it—so very different from the usual. It lay a mile square, divided into blocks of ten acres with streets eight rods wide. Center blocks were reserved for public buildings. Houses were set back on the lots leaving room for front lawns with flowers and shrubbery. In back of the homes we were to raise vegetables and fruit. Everyone was working hard and excited about building up Zion."

"What happened?" asked Jenny. "What caused all the persecution?"

"Our non-Mormon neighbors and the Saints did not get along very well," said Miriam, "and no wonder—we are so very different. We believe in a personal God; in miracles, visions and healings; that our priesthood is the true priesthood and that apostles and prophets are as necessary today as in Biblical times. These ideas are foreign to others and they hadn't yet had time to get to know us!" She paused a moment, then continued.

"The old settlers resented our religion and the way the area was building up," added Jim. "Our belief that there had been an apostasy from Christ's church didn't set well. They pictured us as the 'common enemies of mankind.'"

"Most of us were Yankees, and they resented that, too," said Miriam.

"Trouble arose over politics. The old settlers were afraid we would out-vote our neighbors and gain county offices with their salaries and power. Missouri is linked with the South as a pro-slave state. They don't want a bunch of abolitionists here," explained Jim.

"I've been concerned about that," said Richard.

"One early spring night, a mob broke the windows in our houses, burned our haystacks and shot into our homes. After that violence continued to increase," Miriam went on, shuddering as she remembered the experience. "A year later, a mob of five hundred men rode through the streets of Independence, waving a red flag and brandishing pistols, clubs, and whips. They swore they would rid Jackson County of the Mormons," Miriam's eyes misted and she pressed her lips together as she recalled the terrible experience.

"It's hardly fair to expect people to give up their homes and their Constitutional rights," said Richard.

"There wasn't anything we could do except agree to leave, but we knew we needed some time. We told them we would leave the following spring," said Jim, "but within days they were back to breaking into homes and threatening us. We appealed to the Governor, and he told us to take our case to the local courts. That was a joke," Jim laughed, his voice bitter. "The judge of the county court, two justices of the peace, and other county officials were leaders of the mob. Our appeals only incited more mob violence against us. An abused minority can expect no relief from a politician."

Richard glanced at Jenny, who listened with wide-eyed apprehension.

"By the end of October armed men rode through the streets day and night destroying our possessions, setting fire to homes, burning haystacks, trampling crops, stealing our stock and whipping and assaulting men and women," he added, his features set grimly.

"At gunpoint they drove every man, woman and child who claimed to be a Latter-day Saint out of the county. By then it was November and we were freezing, but that made no difference," added Miriam, anger and pain showing in her face as she folded her arms across her chest and shivered. Suddenly her eyes misted, as she fought hard to hold her tears. "That's when I froze my feet." She looked at them with kind of a hopeless anger, then lifted her hand to push her hair from her forehead.

"That's awful," exclaimed Jenny, hardly able to believe the dark and terrible things she was hearing. It sickened her soul to think one human being could be that vicious to another. "Couldn't you do anything to protect yourselves?" Jenny asked. She thought back to the way people had treated them in New York, but their friends and family there had been nowhere near as viscous as these people in Missouri.

"We found temporary refuge in Clay County where we lived under wretched conditions. We did all kinds of odd jobs for the settlers there, from chopping wood to teaching school," said Miriam. "I set up a school for several months that winter."

"How interesting," said Jenny. "I taught school in New York until we joined the Church and I lost all my pupils. We'll have to get together and talk about it." She remained quiet for a moment, then asked," But why isn't Joseph Smith here with his people?"

"The failure of the Church to establish Zion in Jackson County makes it necessary to keep a settlement at Kirtland so converts migrating from the East can be temporarily provided for there," explained Jim.

Jenny couldn't help staring at Miriam. She was young and pretty with long blond hair lying in soft curls against her thin face. She had a frail look about her. Jenny wondered how Miriam had ever survived the persecutions they were telling about. She hoped she wouldn't have to experience this kind of thing. They were arriving in Far West at a time when severe poverty and intense persecution was plaguing the Church members in both Ohio and Missouri.

CHAPTER SEVEN

Aaron Hale, who had been living with his parents, moved into Jenny and Richard's home in Buffalo, New York. He kept the place clean and in good repair—dusting the shelves, furniture and bric-a-brac, and watering the flowers while waiting patiently for Jenny's return, which he convinced himself would be inevitable. He was sure his sister would come to her senses and return home before long, and if she didn't, or couldn't escape from her husband and the Mormons, he vowed he would surely carry out his threat to kill Richard for what he had done to his sister. Meanwhile, her home could not be left empty. It would be an open invitation to the riff-raff of the city.

Aaron thought back to when he and Jenny were youngsters. They certainly had their spats then. Her temper was nearly the equal of his. He could never win a battle with Jenny. But she had matured as she grew and gained unbelievable control. She would never lose her determination, he thought with a rueful smile. It was a pity she hadn't been born a boy.

Aaron's parents refused to talk about Jenny and Richard. They had threatened to disinherit Jenny if she left with her husband, and when Aaron approached the subject, Mrs. Hale said, "Your sister, as far as we are concerned, is dead, and we do not want to hear anything about her."

Jenny had everything a woman could want here in Buffalo, Aaron thought for the hundredth time. Her home was comfortable; her school had been doing extremely well. Why would she want to leave? Just thinking about it made him hopping mad. The lilacs she had planted in the yard and up the lane bloomed in a profusion of flowers and their sweet scent filled the air, but Jenny did not return and could no longer enjoy them.

Aaron had worked with Richard in the shipping business. Now, he found to his surprise that everything there had been legally turned over to him. Perhaps he should feel thankful to his brother-in-law, but he felt this was just one more indication that Richard had schemed for some time before abducting his sister and that he did not plan to ever return.

Aaron had finally located the address of Richard's brother in Virginia. He immediately sent a letter to Tom Harris. A few weeks later he received a reply saying Richard and Jenny had been there, but had left for Missouri. Tom Harris apparently had no idea that Aaron's relationship with Richard was not ideal at this point or he would not have disclosed their plans so freely.

Aaron's contacts in the business painted a somber picture of the Mormons and Aaron grew more and more concerned about his sister's welfare. He decided he would leave as soon as his affairs could be put in order. He would try to find her and help her escape and return to civilization.

But Aaron's affairs would not be put into order. Real estate dropped suddenly, making it hardly worth the cost of taxes. The shipping business declined and he fought to keep it solvent. The bank failed and he lost what available cash he had saved. Everything seemed against him. The country reeled under depression. He decided he would have to wait until the following spring to go—travel would be too difficult during the winter months which were approaching rapidly.

Richard stepped back and looked at the cabin built of rough logs with two good-sized rooms, dirt floors, a heavy door at the front and one paneless window covered with oiled paper in each room. Several neighbors perched on the roof busily nailing on the roof boards.

Though converts were arriving by the hoards, all were made welcome and helped to get settled by those already in Far West. They called each other "brother" and "sister" which Richard was just beginning to get used to. He had been here three weeks now. The cabin was up and their household about to be established.

The former owner hadn't built a house, but he had planted over half of the land in wheat which was already tall and would soon be filled with kernels of grain. Most of the rest of the land was planted in corn. A garden, already producing fresh vegetables, would help provide much needed food for winter months. Richard had been lucky to come along just as Jim Hansen's neighbor had decided his convictions weren't strong enough to survive the Mormon way of life. Since Richard had cash money, the man had been willing to sell the piece of land for much less than its worth.

Their cabin was located on the outskirts of town, on the north side of the city where farms now dotted the countryside. It would be good to try his hand at growing things again, though it would be much different than on the plantation. It had been years since he had worked the soil. He looked across his ten acres of rolling prairie land and a wide grin spread across his face. He felt good that he had been able to secure a piece of land—even a few acres.

They were within walking distance of the stores and yet next to the country, which gave him that splendid feeling of having his own space. The place seemed ideal. Richard felt thankful Jim had told him about this spot before anyone knew the family planned to leave the area. Places were at a premium and it would have been quickly snatched up.

The swarm of faces and extended calloused palms hardily shaking their hands which Richard and Jenny encountered when they first arrived at Far West was less confusing now. As he became acquainted with neighbors and their families, they were beginning to register in his consciousness as individuals.

Richard studied the cabin thoughtfully. The biggest room would be a living room, kitchen, dining room and bedroom all in one. The half-attic would provide a sleeping room for the girls. The room in the back would serve as a bedroom for Mandy at nighttime, and as a school room for Jenny during the day when the tick, used as a bed, could be moved and benches set up.

Richard knew Jenny could hardly wait to unpack her trunks which contained precious school books and slates. The close neighbors also acted excited about her plans to open a school. She had talked with several of them and seemed sure she would have more than enough pupils. Money was almost nonexistent, but neighbors would be willing to trade milk, butter, eggs, flour and the essentials the Harris family would need, for their children's education.

Teachers were encouraged to teach morals, religion and manners as well as reading, writing and arithmetic. Jenny planned to hold Saturday classes for the girls in sewing and other domestic arts. It seemed a tall order, but Richard felt sure Jenny could measure up. She approached him now and put her hand in his. "Oh, Richard, it's wonderful! I can't believe you men have done so much today."

He hadn't seen Jenny so excited since the day Tom had agreed to let the girls come with them. He smiled down at her. The twins had charmed everyone—Sarah with her outgoing personality and Laura with her demure ways. Laura had come out of her shell so much he could hardly believe she was the shy, uncertain child he had first met at the plantation a few months earlier, though her smile still had a hint of shyness. Right now they were sitting on the ground near the lilac bush that Jenny had planted so carefully, playing tick-tack-toe in the dirt. Sarah gave Laura a threatening glare as her twin yelled "Tick-tack-toe," and drew a line across three Xs, but it didn't seem to bother Laura, who no longer felt unable to assert her rights.

Even Mandy had been accepted in good style by most of their neighbors. If they were surprised to see a southern Negro in their midst, they didn't say so or let on they were. Richard had heard a few southern families who had joined the Church and come to Far West had their slaves with them, ones who when offered their freedom, had begged to be able to stay with their masters, but they hadn't yet seen any of them.

Jenny brought a bucket of fresh water, and as the men came down from finishing the roof of the cabin, one by one they dipped the long handled tin dipper into the bucket of water and refreshed themselves. "Brother Harris, I believe you can handle the rest," Jim Hansen said with a smile. With a bit of chinking and some finishing work this will make a mighty respectable home."

At first Richard had thought Jim a homely man. He looked heavy enough to almost be considered fat, but Richard soon realized it was all muscle. His dark brown, intense eyes set in a round face bored right through you. His light brown hair with streaks of grey rimmed a balding head. As they became better acquainted, Richard saw Jim in a new light and knew he was exceptional. He could always sense just what was needed and seemed so willing to help his neighbors. His wife also seemed special. From Miriam, Jenny was learning a lot about the way of life here and Mary and Laura were already becoming fast friends. He realized his family was lucky to have the Hansens for neighbors.

––––––––––

Jenny quickly made friends with the women of Far West. The twins provided an instant conversation piece, though the ladies invariably asked, "Don't you have any children of your own?" They didn't mean to be unkind, just wanted to know, but for Jenny, pain always accompanied the question. It was fortunate she had her school materials and plans. The school would keep her busy and happy as well as helping provide necessities. She and Miriam Hansen poured over the books and supplies she had brought and discussed the school Jenny planned to open.

"We badly need more schools for the children here," Miriam said as she picked up the third reader. "I loved to teach before I got my feet frozen, but after that it was very difficult for me. If I can help you any, I'd be glad to. There is such a shortage of teachers, books and materials."

Jenny straightened up from the trunk and handed a stack of spellers to Miriam. Miriam set them beside a pile of New England Primers. She picked up one of the primers and it was evident as she leafed through its pages she enjoyed it like the company of an old friend.

"Did you know that eighty-seven percent of the contents of the New England Primer, which has been the textbook of American schools and inspired our fathers and grandfathers for a hundred and fifty years, comes from the Bible?" Miriam asked.

"That much of it? I'm impressed. How did you know that?"

"I read it recently." Miriam admitted, a smile twitching at her mouth.

"I wasn't able to bring nearly as many of my school materials as I wanted, but I sacrificed a lot of personal things in order to bring this trunk full of school supplies," Jenny sighed.

Miriam took a sip of hot chamomile tea from the cup on the table beside her. "That's admirable," she said. Suddenly she looked serious. "I can't think of anything more important than teaching our young ones. The parents are so busy just providing necessities that they don't have time to teach them at home. Few people have any cash money, but most have something they can trade for your services." She thought a moment then added, "A lot of the adults are interested in continuing their learning. Have you ever thought of having some evening classes for them?"

Just then the front door opened and Sarah and Laura, their long hair pulled back into neat braids, burst into the room. They looked impressive dressed in matching pinafores Mandy had sewed for them before they left the plantation.

"Aunt Jenny," they whooped in unison, "Can we go with Uncle Richard to the store?"

Richard stuck his head in the door. "Are you girls going with me?" he asked. Then seeing Miriam, he added "Good morning, Mam. I didn't know we had company."

"Can we? Can we?" the girls begged. Jenny nodded her head in agreement and they rushed out and quickly climbed over the wheel hub and onto the wagon seat.

———————

Jenny opened her eyes from a comfortable dream. Her gaze swept across the rough board roof to the log walls and down to the small window opposite her bed. Then she remembered—she no longer lived in New York in her attractive, pleasant home; she lived in Missouri in a crude log cabin. Her gaze rested on the table, chairs and cupboard Richard had made of split pine. In one corner sat the green metal trunk. She sighed and shut her eyes tightly, then vowed silently she would make this rough cabin worthy of the name "home."

The women had chinked the spaces between the logs well with straw-filled clay. Richard made a chimney of homemade bricks which widened from the roof to the large fireplace and Jenny flanked it with hanging pots and pans. They filled their bed ticks with dried grasses until harvest time when fresh, clean straw would be available. Jenny crocheted curtains to grace the two small windows. Richard covered the windows with shutters which they could close at night or in bad weather. The cabin gradually took on an air of homey comfort. Jenny and Mandy kept it immaculately clean. Miriam Hansen gathered rags and helped Jenny and Mandy braid rag rugs to cover the well-packed dirt floor in the front room. The girls helped tear the rags. The women spread dried grasses under the rug before laying it, to provide some cushioning. They made small area rugs and placed by the door and in front of the bed where they knelt for prayers. When they finished, Jenny wiped away a tear with her apron, then looked at Mandy and said, "It's so grand to have a home again!"

"Yes," agreed Mandy, "movin' 'round takes the starch right out o' me."

Mandy, at the stove, helped Jenny cook the evening meal. The kettle of water, filled with corn, boiled merrily and the aroma of baking biscuits filled the cabin. Sarah and Laura spread the rich, creamy colored Belgium linen tablecloth Jenny had brought from her home in New York and carefully set the table. Belgium linen was said to be the best in the world, with the color imparted by the chemical content of the waters of the river Lys in which the flax was retted, or soaked to separate the fibers. Jenny insisted on a properly set table and good table manners.

Jenny lifted the yellow corn from the steaming kettle. A few minutes later the family sat down to a platter of scrambled eggs, corn, warm biscuits, strawberry jam, and a pitcher of fresh milk to drink with cookies. After Richard blessed the food, Jenny looked around the table from one to the other of her family, encompassing them all in her love. She smiled across the table at Mandy and the twins. "We're so lucky to have all of you as part of our family," she said, her eyes misting.

In the evening, after supper, while the women cleared the table and washed the dishes, Richard put a big log on the fire and pulled up his favorite chair so he could capture the light from the dancing flames. He picked up the Book of Mormon from the table where it sat beside the old family Bible.

When their evening tasks were finished, they gathered daily around the fireplace and Richard read aloud to them. Jenny used this time to knit or crochet doilies and other articles to beautify their home. Her hands were doing some useful work every minute of her so-called leisure hours. Restless hands never laid idle in her lap.

Richard's smooth, deep voice could be heard clearly above the crackling of the fire. The twins watched the small red and yellow flames lick a new log until it burst into a bright blaze. By the time the log burned down, they were almost asleep, curled up like kittens between Mandy and Jenny. Richard shut the book and set it on the table. He went to the fireplace and poked at the coals, getting them placed just right before banking the fire so it would keep until morning. Every day closed as it began, kneeling in family prayer.

The coverlet on Jenny and Richard's bed was another of Jenny's rare treasures. She had put almost a year of her life into making it. Before Jenny was married, under the direction of her mother, they had planned the pattern of eight pointed snowflakes and the pine tree border. They dug roots and collected plants and barks to make dyes. She spun and dyed the yarn, then the hum of the spinning wheel was followed by weaving long hours on the hand loom.

Jenny became an artist, breathing the sublime air of that sphere where beautiful things are created. Her weariness always fell from her when she seated herself at the loom. She signed the coverlet by weaving her name, the date and New York into the corner. She felt exhilaration when the treasured work of art was finished. She had created it with her own hands.

Now its beauty of color and design showed to great advantage in the frontier cabin with plain walls and simple, sturdy home-made furniture of split pine rubbed to a soft finish with bee's wax.

The twins had rarely been so excited; they had hardly been able to eat their breakfast. Richard had promised to take them to the store to shop.

"My money! Where did I put my money?" exclaimed Sarah.

Jenny picked up Sarah's handkerchief from the wash stand and handed it to her. In the corner was tied the shiny dime Sarah had earned, penny by penny, from endless berry picking, making jam and helping weed the Hansen's garden while Mary was away visiting her grandmother.

"Thanks, Aunt Jenny," she said hurriedly. Laura was already out the door with her few coins. She had also been sewing and working for the neighbors, scrubbing the rough floor boards of Mrs. Miller's kitchen every Saturday morning.

"I'm coming, don't leave me," Sarah shouted as she lifted the latch of the door.

As she clambered into the buggy and sat beside Laura, Richard gave the reins a flick and the horses started off on a trot. While Jenny's birthday was only a week away, she had no idea the girls had planned this shopping trip to buy something for her. They told their aunt they were going out for a treat, all by themselves. They had asked Richard to take them to the store several days before. He played along with the charade, telling Jenny he was going over to the feed store and to check on some harness parts, and would leave the girls at Burton's store so they could buy their treat.

"Have you decided what to buy?" Richard asked.

"Not yet," they chorused.

"Are you going to put your money together and buy one big present or each get something separate?" he asked. The question started a controversy.

"What about some perfume?" asked Sarah. "If we put our money together we might have enough for a small bottle."

Sarah recalled when she and Laura, on one of their explorations into the locked room at home–that spot they had been forbidden by their father to explore–had found the little bottle in their mother's top drawer. The fragrance smelled heavenly, but Mandy had been furious when she caught a whiff of perfume, and insisted they both have a bath and a hard scrubbing with lye soap to eradicate the telltale scent before their father returned.

"I thought maybe Jenny'd like a thimble," said Laura, always the practical one, "or some new needles." She thought a moment, "I think a thimble would be best. She's always pricking her fingers when she sews."

"A plain, old thimble!" exclaimed Sarah. "I want to get her something special."

"A thimble is special, and it's something she needs," retorted Laura, pulling a sour face at her sister.

"Now, now, girls," said Richard. "Maybe you'd better just shop separately." Then hoping to change the subject, he said, "Isn't it a nice day for a buggy ride?"

They drew up in front of Burton's store, where Richard jumped out and tied the horses to the hitching post, then helped the girls from the high seat. They bounded up the steps and through the heavy wooden door.

"Mornin'," Mr. Burton's voice said from behind a pile of newly arrived freight. He stepped into sight.

"Morning Mr. Burton," said Sarah and Laura. He went to a glass jar on the counter and extracted a piece of hard candy for each of the girls.

Sarah already stood by the showcase eyeing the treasures it contained. "What can I show you?" asked Mrs. Burton as she came into the store from the part of the building where the Burtons lived.

"I have ten cents, I earned it myself," Sarah noted.

"That's nice," nodded Mrs. Burton approvingly.

Sarah glanced around the store and thought it had never looked so intriguing, perhaps because she had her own money to spend. The room contained everything from Barlow knives marked two-bits to barn lanterns, tallow candles, cloth, needles, pans, harmonicas and a few trinkets.

Laura at the other end of the store, looked at a rag doll with button eyes and yellow colored yarn for hair. The price tag said ten cents. Laura liked dolls—she looked at it for a long, longing moment.

"The girls are looking for a birthday present for Jenny," Richard explained. "I'm going over to the feed store and I'll be back to get them in a few minutes." He headed for the door, but turned and reminded the girls, "Don't touch anything. If you see something you want to look at, let Mr. or Mrs. Burton show it to you."

The twins moved about gazing at the numerous items for sale. Sarah looked longingly at a soft, brown pair of gloves made of doe skin. She didn't even ask the price because she knew it would be too high.

"I would like to see your perfume," she told Mrs. Burton. The fragrance filled her nostrils with wonder, but the prices were all more than she and Laura had, even if they pooled their money. On the verge of tears, she moved on to other things. A beautiful white lace handkerchief might be nice.

Laura gazed with sparkling eyes at a shiny silver thimble. "How much is it?" she asked, holding her breath for fear it would be too much. She counted her money again and found she could buy it and have a few cents left over. "How much is a needle?" she asked, and nearly jumped up and down with excitement to find she had just enough for both. Then her eyes fell on a beautiful little blue needle case. It looked as blue as the evening sky and she knew Jenny would love it, but Laura would have to pick between the needles and thimble or the case.

Sarah looked at a little red bag with a drawstring. How she would love to have it, she thought. She stooped down to see it from the underneath side of the glass in the showcase. It wasn't large and wouldn't hold much but it was so attractive. She wondered if she would have money enough to buy it and still get a present for Jenny.

She wandered over beside Laura. "Have you decided what to get?" she asked.

"I don't know whether to get the thimble and needle or the needle case," said Laura, pointing out the beautiful little case to her sister. "She needs the thimble and needle, but the needle case is so pretty. I know she'd love it."

Sarah examined the case. At last she said, "Why don't you get the thimble and needle and I'll get the case."

"Wonderful!" said Laura, jumping up and down with excitement as she threw her arms around her sister. "That'll be perfect."

Sarah gave the little red drawstring purse one longing last look, then untied her money from the corner of her handkerchief and handed it to Mrs. Burton.

The girls had just finished paying for their purchases when Richard returned. Mrs. Burton wrapped the gifts with a small piece of tissue and tied the package with a length of red twine. The girls thought they had never seen a present look so attractive. They happily went out the door, talking a mile a minute. They could hardly wait until Jenny's birthday.

Jenny opened her doors for school on a Monday morning. Miriam was right; the people of Far West were anxious to see their children get an education. Sam Hill—a lanky kid with long arms and legs attached to hands and feet too big for the rest of him—arrived first, trying his best to look grown up. Jenny liked his young, serious smile.

His dark brown hair had been slicked down carefully. His light brown eyes intense and his young face sincere, he told her, "My pa says I need to get some learnin' and he's right. I want to learn all about everything."

Jenny smiled in spite of herself. He looked so young, so enthusiastic about life.

Mary and Miriam Hansen were next to arrive. Jim brought them over in the buggy so Miriam could help Melissa that first day. Dressed in her best pinafore, with large, blue eyes shining with excitement, Mary regarded Jenny soberly.

"Good morning, Mrs. Harris," she chirped.

Four children from the Rawlins family arrived with the older ones shepherding the younger. They had shaggy hair; big, wistful eyes and thin faces. Their clothing looked drab and nondescript, but clean. A tall, bewildered-looking boy approached her, a shabby hat still clutched in his thin hands. "Good morning, Mam," he said. "My name is Thomas, and my brother and sisters are Joe, Martha, and Ellen. My parents would like us to go to school."

Daniel Hyde was also tall and thin for a ten-year-old, and arrived barefooted. A few washed-out freckles spotted his nose. He informed Jenny he had already finished the third reader. Bill Coombs was a big, awkward kid with hair the color of ripe wheat in the sun. Jenny soon noted he looked out for Daniel, who acted shy and quiet.

Isaac and Minnie Miller's mother delivered them to Jenny's doorstep. They had just turned seven and Mrs. Miller had dressed them in Sunday-go-to-meeting clothing. She cautioned them not to get dirty. Jenny felt excited to have another set of twins in her school, even though they acted very differently than Sarah and Laura.

Alice and Adeline Wilson, ages eleven and twelve, accompanied their brothers, John and George, nine and ten. Their homespun clothing had patches everywhere, but the children looked clean and well groomed. Alice and Adeline, exceedingly plain girls, wore their straw-colored hair loose and uncurled. Jenny looked at them and felt a curious tingling sensation in her heart. It seemed evident their family had little in the way of material possessions.

Rose, Elizabeth, and Lucy Clark, nine, eleven and twelve respectively, wore heavily starched pinafores and their hair hung in long ringlets. Lucy, the talkative one, chatted almost to the point of annoyance. With visible distaste, they looked at the Wilson children and moved across the room. Alice and Adeline Wilson looked at each other knowingly and Alice shrugged her shoulders in an attempt at lightness. Jenny had the feeling being shunned was not a new experience for the Wilsons.

Ambrose and Ezra Palmer, seven and eight years old, arrived last. Both sallow skinned, small and quiet, their long-lashed eyes filled with longing. They spoke in hushed whispers and Jenny could barely discern their names. They stared up at her fearfully, looking as utterly wretched as only frightened children can.

Jenny's glance roved about the room. Tears blurred her eyes as she felt the great need of the children. There were so many it would be awhile before she could keep them all straight. She could see she had a group with widely varying circumstances and abilities. It would be a challenge. One thing most of them had in common was the same eager, anticipating look. They smiled at her—impressed because she was to be their teacher. She ran her hand self-consciously over her skirt, straightening it. She felt almost as nervous as the children. When they were seated on the rough wooden benches Richard had made for the schoolroom, Jenny signaling for silence, said, "Let's all stand and say the Lord's Prayer."

———————————

Jenny and the girls found plenty of ripe wild currants, raspberries and green summer grapes to pick on Saturday afternoons. The women made jams, jellies and preserves. They would taste delicious on warm biscuits during the long winter months, which would be coming soon.

By late September, the wheat stood tall and heavy and had ripened ready for harvesting. Jim Hansen declared he had never seen a better looking stand. Neighbor men worked through the long, burning days to help Richard cradle and bind the grain into sheaves. These they hauled into a large pile between the barn and the house.

Now, at sunrise on Saturday morning, several men and a group of young people joined with the Harris family to help them thresh their grain. Mary Hansen, Bill Combs, Brother Palmer, Brother Miller and Daniel Hyde arrived almost in unison. The Rawlins and the Wilson children were all there. Everything sparkled from the sun shining on the morning dew.

Sam Hill came with his father, John. Jenny had to smile as she saw them standing there in exactly the same position, with feet far apart and one shoulder thrown back in a peculiar slant. The sunlight striking their hair showed it to be exactly the same color and it curled the same soft way over their well tanned foreheads. John rubbed his chin and Sam copied the motion. Jenny had noticed Sarah seemed to be quite interested in Sam.

"We have a good breeze this morning," said Jim Hansen wetting his finger in his mouth, then holding it up to determine the exact direction of the wind. "I hope it holds."

The men laid out an immense canvas on the ground and fastened it down firmly with pegs at the corners. The sun came out, warming the air. Richard stepped forward into a pale shaft of sunlight and smiled. "We're ready for the bundles," he informed the waiting crew of young people.

Sarah and Laura joined the others in carrying a circle of sheaves onto the canvas. "You put the heads toward the center," brother Miller told the twins, who had not helped thresh before. Sarah dropped her bundle, then slowly brushed the dust off her hands and the front of her dress. She pulled a disgusted face, then started off for another bundle. She's a prissy little thing, thought Jenny. Laura seemed to enjoy being a tom boy and had not yet become overly conscious of her appearance.

Richard nodded to Brother Palmer, who sometimes played the harmonica for dancing. Brother Palmer tapped one foot as he called out rhythmically, "Now get in there and tramp, tramp, tramp the bundles." The young people began tramping the grain, knocking the heads from the straw. Sarah and Laura hesitated a moment, then followed suit.

When Brother Palmer seemed winded, Brother Miller whistled and clapped his hands to a rhythm as the young folks marched round and round, sometimes singing to the whistled melody as again and again they tramped circle after circle of bundles. Richard called a rest and they sat on the shady side of the cabin laughing and talking. Mandy and Jenny came out with cold pitchers of apple cider to refresh the band of workers.

After a short rest, Richard and the other men winnowed the grain with the help of two pans and the breeze. Jenny watched Richard pouring the grain from one pan held high in the air to another held lower, as the breeze blew away the chaff. She could see the hard strength of his hands and wrists, and marveled at his vigor. When the wheat was fairly clean, he poured it into the waiting sacks.

The group repeated the process over and over again and the pile of grain sacks grew almost as high as the cabin. When Jenny called dinner, over half of the bundles had been threshed. The youngsters lathered their faces and hands with the homemade lye soap and rinsed in the wash tub of water set outside the door for that purpose. Sarah turned up her nose and complained, "I can't believe threshing is such a dusty, dirty business."

Mandy and Jenny brought out plates of home-cured pork, dried corn, squash and potatoes. Fresh biscuits from the bake oven, spread with yellow butter and currant jelly would make the meal especially tasty. After washing up, Sarah, Laura and Mary Hansen helped Mandy pour mugs of cold, creamy milk. The hearty smell of the food seized everyone's attention, and conversation turned toward the feast at hand.

The men lined up and waited their turn to scrub the dust from their hands and faces in the little tin wash basin which stood on the wash stand near the door. Two of Jenny's pupils, Martha and Ellen Rawlins, had been enlisted to stand beside the table with long willow boughs to keep the flies away while the hungry threshers ate.

The men's laughter grew merry as they sat at the table in the clean, log-cabin kitchen and discussed the crop. It looked like they would have plenty of wheat to furnish bread for the Harris family for the winter and a little left over to sell or share with those who had none.

The young folks sat around a cloth spread on the grass in the shade of the cabin, and laughed and joked as they ate. Sam and Sarah stretched out by the back corner of the cabin, just far enough away to be out of earshot, and talked with animation. Jenny noticed Laura and Mary Hansen looked rather envious of Sam's attention, but soon they, too, began talking and laughing with some of the other girls and boys. Jenny looked around at her family and neighbors and felt amazed that anyone had enough energy left to talk.

When the men had finished the last trace of ham, vegetables, home baked bread, jelly, and freshly baked apple pie, they filed outside for a twenty minute rest to let their dinner settle before beginning the afternoon session. Mandy stood for a moment with hands on her broad hips and surveyed the scene, then began gathering up the dirty dishes.

Everyone resumed work until late afternoon when the bundles had all been tramped, the grain winnowed and the sacks hauled into a rough shack Richard had built to store corn and grain. John Hill called to his son, Sam, who again stood talking to Sarah, "Let's go, Sam, so we can get our chores done before too late."

"See you this evening," Richard called as the neighbors left in small groups to go home and do their own chores..

When the blaze of color faded from the western sky, they all returned for a bonfire party. The boys gathered willows and brush for the fire. "Pile it here it on the opposite side of the house from the clean straw so the straw won't catch fire," Richard instructed the boys.

"Here, girls, get a broom and sweep this canvas," he called to Sarah and Laura. The girls swept the threshing canvass, then Richard and several other men moved it to the side of the cabin by the bonfire and stretched it tightly over the ground. The sun, near setting, threw long, uncertain shadows over everything. The men had brought their wives and the couples danced on the canvas until almost midnight to the music of four harmonicas and Brian Palmer's fiddle. Everyone joined in the fun, the girls in new calico dresses and the boys in clean shirts.

Jenny and Richard held their arms high to allow the other dancers to pass through as they did the Virginia Reel, and Richard looked deep into her eyes. The moon took on a sudden brilliance. How she loved to dance. Fiddle music set her blood to leaping and put color in her cheeks. As he held her in his arms, Jenny's heart thrilled at the strong bond which welded her and Richard together.

The flames from the roaring fire threw light onto a long table with log legs which Richard and Jim had quickly constructed for the occasion. There side pork and cornpone gave forth savory odors and fresh butter glistened like gold. Jugs of milk and cider waited to quench the thirst of the dancers.

Jenny looked around at her family and friends. All the young people seemed to be having an amazing amount of fun. She noted that Sarah smiled at Sam from the corners of her eyes as her feet beat time to the music. Laura and Mary Hansen were talking to the Wilson children.

Mandy sat beside the bonfire with some of the older people and watched the huge flames sending sparks toward the stars. To some this was the best feature of the day. Mandy seemed to enjoy just being with everyone and watching the festivities. She usually caught the edges of the conversation as she served the people who had become their friends, and knew the whole picture of what was going on more quickly than anyone else.

The flickering red light of the fire burned close to the embers and coals became dim as the Sabbath day approached. Richard closed the dance with a prayer of thanksgiving for the bounteous harvest. The air, crisp with a slight tinge of sharpness, signaled that autumn waited just around the corner and would soon appear. Everyone started down the moonlit paths towards their various homes, some of the young people singing as they walked.

Jenny and Richard felt exhausted, but pleased. Even in the darkness, Jenny could feel the smile on Richard's face. Every moment of back-breaking work had been worth it. Jenny was not sorry she and Richard had joined the Church and come to Missouri, so different from their home in New York.

Richard and Jenny could hear the girls chattering away in the loft, but their voices became slower and quieter until they ceased altogether. Richard reached over and let his fingers trace the outline of her mouth. Jenny smiled as he pulled her into his arms and began kissing her soft lips. She snuggled against his strong, firm body. All these years since their marriage and they were still romantically in love. Richard could still thrill her with his embrace. Their love making had not cooled like that of some couples, but always held the same passion it had from the beginning.

Jenny felt happy the Mormon creed recognized the necessity of recreation and the social needs of the people were not overlooked. While their days were fully devoted to working, they often held parties or dances in the evenings. Frequently, after dinner, housewives would invite the neighbors in for a piece of old-fashioned jelly cake, mince or squash pie, doughnuts or cider and the evening would be spent telling stories, singing and dancing.

Young folks made popcorn balls and enjoyed taffy-pulls. On moonlit evenings they gathered and played kick-the-can, tag, hide-and-seek or other games. Their lives included working, playing, sleeping and a certain amount of time set aside for worship and prayer.

CHAPTER EIGHT

Monday morning Jenny held no school—the straw had to be taken care of. Jenny and Mandy took the quilts and grass-filled bed ticks outside. They washed the quilts then emptied all of the old straw from each tick to ready it for washing and drying on the line in the hot sun.

Meanwhile Richard carried the braided rag carpets outside, and set each one on the grass. The girls swept them all clean. The women helped sweep and gather the faded, dirty, well-trodden dry grass and weeds from the cabin floors into an old sheet and dumped it in the pile with the filling from the ticks. Jenny and Mandy cleaned the walls and floors and furniture, then left the cabin to air and dry while they all sat outside and ate slices of hot salt-rising bread and drank mugs of cold milk.

When the ticks felt dry, the women and girls stuffed them with fresh, clean straw and Mandy began sewing them shut. Richard brought the wheelbarrow to the straw pile and with the pitchfork, began filling it with the sweet-smelling straw, while the twins helped pile in arm loads full. When it was heaping full, Richard rolled it to the house, and they spread the sweet-smelling straw evenly onto the dirt floor.

Sarah and Laura danced on the carpets and played in the tents made by quilts and blankets hung over the clothesline for drying. Everything that could not be washed was beaten until it was dust-free and fresh smelling. Richard helped spread the new large rag carpets the women had recently finished braiding and sewing together over the fresh straw. The furniture made little, puffy imprints in the padded carpets and the whole house smelled sweet and clean. The ticks were carried in to make foundations for the beds. Jenny looked forward to the time they could have chickens and their ticks could be filled with feathers like her beds had been in New York—goose, duck and chicken feathers.

It had been a long day and was time to do the evening chores when they finished. That evening Richard burned the stuffing that came from under the carpets and inside the ticks and they ate supper outside beside the bonfire. Bonfire smoke was as much a part of fall as the fragrance of blossoms and the croaking of the frogs in the meadow grass were of spring. Again they washed up outdoors before the girls undressed and put on their nightgowns.

The twins laughed at the crunching sound as their bare feet sunk into the fresh padding of the carpet. They squealed with delight as they climbed onto the high tick mattress and sunk into the soft crunchy straw. They pulled the clean patchwork quilt over them and giggled as they turned from one side to the other. Richard and Jenny looked at each other and smiled. "I'm so glad the girls became part of our family," Jenny volunteered. She didn't have to look at Richard to tell what he was thinking. Having the twins had enriched both of their lives.

On Tuesday morning the school children delighted in the sweet smell of the school room and the thick padding of the carpets, as they would for many days before the newness wore off. Jenny had laid by a supply of clean straw to use in teaching the girls how to make brooms and hats the Saturday after the threshing party. Richard stored the balance of the straw in the barn to use for bedding down animals in the winter and for covering garden vegetables, which he would store in pits to keep them from freezing.

That evening, Jenny sorted the family's clothing. "This," she would say as she picked up a worn pinafore, "isn't fit for anything but dusting and cleaning cloths. These," holding up one well-worn pair of Richard's homespun pants, "will make a nice stripe in a carpet."

The material of an apron where the edges were not worn, would make quilt blocks. Now, with teaching the girls to sew and do domestic tasks, she needed plenty of material to work with. Jenny liked to keep carpet rags and quilt pieces worked up so they did not become a burden.

Autumn was always a busy time. The women made sweet and dill pickles, mincemeat, plum puddings and Christmas cakes. They gathered hops and laid them by for making yeast and root beer. They gathered herbs such as yarrow, catnip and peppermint for making medicines.

Corn, a valuable crop, provided food for both people and animals. The settlers used husks and stalks for ordinary fuel as well as for fuel to smoke fish, hams and bacon. Jenny and the girls dried many pounds of sweet corn, peas and other vegetables to put away for winter. "Spread them carefully on the racks so every piece can dry," Jenny instructed the girls after cutting up a large pan of carrots and blanching them in boiling water. Squash hung from the rafters of the kitchen to dry. Richard saved some seeds from each vegetable for planting crops in the spring.

Jim asked Richard to help him kill their pigs that fall. Jenny and the girls went over to help Miriam take care of the meat and render the lard. Jim was bringing another squealing pig from the pen. "They aren't going to kill that poor pig, are they?" Laura protested.

"Don't be a baby," Sarah chided. "They killed the pigs on the plantation, and we watched them. Don't act like you never saw a pig killed before."

Jenny reached out and brushed back a strand of hair that had fallen across Laura's face. "We have to have meat for the winter, darling," she said quietly, now you and Sarah ask Mary if she has some carpet rags you can tear into strips.

Mary produced the rags quickly. "Here girls, if you'll tear these into strips just this wide," she said measuring with her finger, "it will help me a lot." She seated them where they couldn't see the activities outside.

Heavy black smoke rose against the sun as Richard threw another pine log under the tubs of boiling water they were using to scald the hair from the skin of the hogs while butchering. Jenny paused to look out Hansen's window as the laughter of their husbands and their pleasant voices drifted in. Jenny loved to hear Richard's voice and watch his precise movements as he went about his outdoor tasks. He always knew exactly what he intended to do, and did it. Though this was the work of slaves on the plantation where Richard had been raised, he seemed to know the procedure well. Richard had told Jenny he spent a lot of time with the slaves on the plantation during his growing up years, and his skill at menial tasks reinforced what he said.

The men stuck each pig in the neck with a knife. When the blood had drained from the animal, leaving it lifeless, it was quickly dipped into the boiling water, which loosened the hair on the hide. A slit was cut between the tendon and bone of each back leg and a thick branch of wood put between the legs to hold them apart and provide something from which to hang the pig. The men hung the animal and scraped off the hair before slitting it open to remove the entrails.

They used almost everything on the animal. Jenny and Miriam scraped the meat, fat and brains from the pig heads for making the rich rolls of headcheese, a delicacy which they would slice and serve with meals or put on sandwiches. They boiled the heart, fried the liver and salted the bacon and hams by soaking them in a liquid brine.

Then Jenny and Miriam washed the intestines and stuffed them with sausage, used the stomach tissue for tripe, saved the hocks for cooking with beans and pickled the feet. They filled large kettles on the stove with fat and heated it until the grease was cooked off.

The women had washed the buckets from the pantry shelf sparkling clean, ready to receive the slightly smoky grease they were rendering from the hog fat, which would make lard for winter baking and frying. The lard, after being used, would be recycled for soap making and lighting. Grease of any kind was put into a dish, with a wick, and used when candles were not available. They called this type of light a "bitch."

Jenny poured the sizzling grease into the buckets then piled the rinds from the fat, now called "chitlings," carefully into a huge bowl. It seemed Hansens had raised an unending supply of pigs this year, and the task of butchering and caring for the meat would never end. Jim washed out the bladder of the pig he was working on and blew it full of air, then tied the opening into a knot. The girls were soon having a great time playing ball with the pig bladder. Jim strode into the room and rubbed his cold, red hands together before the fire. "We use everything on the pig but the squeal," he bragged.

Jenny looked at the Hansen place and thought it simply radiated Miriam's touch, from the roses climbing up narrow sections of white lattice at each corner of the house to the crocheted curtains on the windows. She had made an orange, yellow and brown braided rug to cover the floor. Jim had made her a small open bookcase of native maple to hold her precious volumes.

The kitchen window looked large and sported a window seat—a place where Miriam could sit watching an azure sky and drink in the beauty of nature. Few others in Far West had glass windows. Pegs by the door held hats, a shawl and a pair of gloves. The total effect seemed colorful and homey.

When the butchering had been completed, the Hansens sent Richard and Jenny home with meat, chitlings and lard. "That's too much to give us for a little help with killing the hogs," Richard objected. "I couldn't have done it without your help," Jim insisted. "We have plenty left for the winter, and you know you will need meat and lard for your family."

Occasionally someone killed a beef and brought Jenny a piece of fresh meat for their school tuition. The women prized beef suet for making mincemeat and plum puddings. They made six or eight puddings at a time which they hung in their cellars until some festive occasion, then steamed them for a special treat. The Clark children brought two plum puddings and Jenny was delighted with the rare delicacy which she put away to save for Christmas dinner. They also brought a small amount of beef suet, which Jenny used to make mincemeat for pies. When the children brought mutton tallow, she and Mandy made candles or salve for chapped hands.

———————

Neighbors all helped one another here in Far West. The men helped build barns and cabins, harvest the crops and butcher the animals. The women combined their efforts in making rag rugs to cover the dirt floors of their homes and in manufacturing of cloth–shearing the sheep, spinning and weaving on hand looms. These processes were lengthy and time consuming.

An endless round of Saturday afternoon quilting bees, spinning bees, carpet-rag bees and husking bees were held as people prepared for winter. Jenny became acquainted with many of the parents of her students as they swapped patterns, shared their knowledge and helped one another.

The women were often warned by their leaders about the evils of gossip, but curiosity occasionally ruled. These get-togethers provided an excellent time to broadcast the latest events, such as engagements, marriages and births. They devoured each bit of news greedily, especially any news from back home.

They didn't mean to be malicious, and when the conversation took a critical turn, Jenny noticed Widow Wilson had a way of turning it around. Her tall, gaunt form leaned over the quilt as her bony fingers put small stitches into it. Her hands were gnarled and roughened from toil-worn drudgery, but she possessed an innate dignity. "Have you heard about the Bennett family?" she asked.

"No. What about them?" asked Miriam.

"They just moved in next door to us, and they have the cutest boys. My girls are all in a dither about having them for new neighbors."

"Those Bennetts are a strange lot," said Mrs. Clark as she snipped off a thread with her teeth.

"What do you mean?" asked Widow Wilson.

"There's something unusual about them. They don't act like normal boys, they're so quiet and considerate of each other."

Jenny looked at young Mrs. Clark, who probably didn't know which side to milk a cow from, and wondered how she could be so critical. It made her blood boil.

"They're a nice family, and a great addition to the town," insisted Widow Wilson. Mrs. Clark's eyes turned a little icy and she shrugged her shoulders.

"Did you know that Nancy Burns had a baby boy last night?" asked plump, jolly Mrs. Miller.

"No, I can't believe it!" said Mrs. Palmer. "It seems like it was just last week that she was starting out her pregnancy. Did everything go well?"

"Yes, she and the baby are both doing fine."

I'll have to take over some fresh biscuits and butter, thought Jenny to herself.

"The Brown girl is engaged to that nice Cluff boy," announced Miriam. "I think they make a lovely couple."

"When will the wedding be?" asked Mrs. Wilson.

"Sometime next month," said Miriam. "By the way, has anyone seen Clara recently. David's death was surely hard on her. It's rough to lose a husband; we should all go see her."

"I saw her last week and goodness, how she has aged," noted Mrs. Clark.

"Yes, I noticed," said Mrs. Miller. "She is my age. Am I as gray and wrinkled as Clara?"

"You would be if you'd been through what she has," said Widow Wilson quietly.

The various "bees" played a major part in the social life of the community. Sometimes the participants enjoyed refreshments of molasses candy, parched corn, raisins and other dried fruit or almonds. Once in a while supper was served. Whatever they ate, the spirit of cooperation and fun usually attended their activities and most of the women tried hard to keep it that way. Many of these ladies had left homes of culture and refinement and were always reaching out for enrichment and striving to improve their skills.

Laura loved to be outside when the sun rose. She breathed deeply as a soft breeze caressed her cheek. The undisturbed morning dew felt damp against her skin. Her bare feet left prints in the moist soil. She bent to examine a sparkling spider web which clung to a yellow rose bush.

The old pig in the pen behind the house began grunting, expecting her breakfast. She hung over the fence and scratched the sow's back with a stick. The pig, which relished being scratched down her neck and across her back, rubbed up against the fence and stretched. Laura sighed as she thought about Richard killing Mary's pigs for bacon, ham and roast pork for the winter. "Poor things," she said softly, "I'm glad you are needed to have little pigs for us." She had heard Richard say when he bought the sow, he planned to keep her at least until she had a litter.

The horses made a little whinny to welcome Laura, and she found a lump of sugar in her pocket to give each of them. She patted Daisy and Doll on their thick necks. She threw her arms around Rosie's neck and hugged her, and was rewarded with a low "moo."

She walked far out along the edge of the corn field. The corn had been harvested, and the stalks would soon be cut. The leaves, drenched with dew, were shiny even though they were turning yellow. She loved early morning walks; things were so special when the air held a tinge of leftover night.

Laura tucked a note into the crack in the post marking the northwest corner of Richard and Jenny's property then dropped onto her knees to examine a wild daisy growing at the base of the post. It had begun to dry out, but still struggled to survive. She sat there for a moment while her thoughts stirred round and round. Her soft, young forehead creased with tiny, thoughtful lines.

Laura's thoughts turned to the dolls the girls had fashioned from hollyhocks in Mary's yard the day before. She loved dolls of any kind. In Virginia she had beautiful ones, now she was grateful for even corn cob or hollyhock dolls. Her life had changed greatly, but she loved being with Jenny and Richard. She missed Greene and Sully. Her eyes misted as she thought of her friends. And her father, what had become of him, she wondered. He always appeared so sad and cross, while Richard seemed happy and full of fun.

Soon her legs felt cramped and she got up and peeked around the post. During the summer the post had dried and a crack almost a quarter of an inch wide ran from the top half way down the length of the pole. Laura and Mary Hansen had become bosom friends and when school was going were inseparable. This post was now their secret hiding place, and the girls had lots of secrets. Both Laura and Mary learned to read and write quickly and now writing notes to each other had become an intriguing pastime.

No one was out yet. She picked a dandelion, slipped the large end of the stem into her mouth and curled her tongue around it. She pulled it out and in, out and in, until the end began to curl into two even little circles. She ran the curls clear up to the golden flower then picked another and began again. She anchored the curled flowers into the post beside the note.

Mary, like Laura, was small for her age. She was not particularly beautiful. Laura was fascinated that Mary's auburn hair almost matched the color of Jenny's and her face and arms were covered with small brown dots. Jenny called them sun spots, but others called them freckles.

Laura walked back toward the house. "Laura!" Mandy scolded with both relief and irritation in her voice as Laura entered the dirt packed area they called a yard, "how many times have you been told not to sneak out of the house so early in the morning. It isn't safe."

The Prophet Joseph Smith came to Far West in October of 1837. Everyone in the Harris family felt so excited.

"I can't wait to see Joseph Smith in person!" Jenny exclaimed. "We've waited so long."

"That's what we said when we first came to Missouri," said Richard. "Yes, we've waited a long time," he added as he tried to fasten the top button of his shirt collar.

"You're gaining weight," laughed Jenny as she noticed his difficulty.

"Get your dress on and let's get going before we're late," he said, avoiding the subject.

They joined the crowd of people gathering for the services. 'The Stand,' where services were held, consisted of a platform on which the Church leaders sat at outdoor meetings. The audience sat on benches of split logs or on the grass.

The wind whizzed through the dry stems of last year's grass and seemed determined to bite its teeth into Jenny's very bones. Her fingers pulled her Paisley shawl, which draped over her crinoline skirt, closely about her shoulders.

She realized with a start how soon winter's winds would be upon them.

Jenny felt thankful she had brought two shawls from New York—a thin, cotton, light colored one for summer and this dark, heavier one made of wool and silk for cooler days. The continuous weave of the Paisley made it soft and pliable. Her mother had insisted that no bride's trousseau was complete without at least two shawls.

Richard and Jenny's little family worked their way to the front of the congregation and stood in breathless awe as the Latter-day Saints' prophet appeared. There wasn't any mistaking his identity. A feeling of presence and size accompanied him. Tall and broad shouldered, with his dark hair and his black cutaway coat, he towered above the others around him and Jenny could not distinctly see anyone else.

There, in the actual flesh, stood the man they had heard about so many times! Then he looked at her and Jenny had the feeling those intent, deep blue eyes could penetrate her being and read her very thoughts. She felt an electrifying thrill as warmth and peace enveloped her from head to toe. As she listened to the words of instruction and counsel which fell from his inspired lips, she knew the Gospel message Joseph had restored to the earth was true. In her heart she knew they were listening to a Prophet of God. She felt thankful she and Richard had embraced this restored Gospel.

It seemed a spiritual feast to her just to gaze at his face. It radiated a simple honesty, without pride, though hundreds of eyes were fastened upon him. She could feel deep love flowing from him toward the congregation and from the people toward him. Jenny knew that love for any man cannot be dictated but must flow spontaneously from hearts which have been deeply moved by heart to heart communication. There was no doubt these people had experienced that feeling. She

hoped her family would have a chance to get better acquainted with their prophet.

After the service Richard grabbed Jenny by the hand.
"Let's go talk to him," he said excitedly. They made their way
through the crowd to shake hands with Joseph. He was busy
shaking hands with all the people—men, women, and children. His face broke into a broad smile, his deep blue eyes
twinkled, as they introduced themselves.

"I hear you have a school, Mrs. Harris, and that you're
doing a wonderful job of teaching our young folks." He held
his hand out and shook each of theirs with a firm clasp. When
he took Jenny's hand she felt new life and vitality penetrate
her innermost soul. "Education is so important to our people," he added with an intensity that came from the depths of
his being. "Education never had a stronger advocate than the
Prophet Joseph Smith. He had instructed his people 'to seek
diligently...out of the best books, words of wisdom; to seek
learning, even by study and also by faith.'"

Turning to Richard he stated, "A few of us are getting together at the home of Brother and Sister Phelps this evening.
Why don't you and your wife join us?"

Richard and Jenny felt so excited they could hardly wait
for evening to come. It seemed a day had never been so long.
They finally arrived at the Phelps' place breathless with
anticipation.

The guests listened eagerly to Joseph's every word as the
men discussed important issues of the day. "The numbers of
the Saints are increasing rapidly in Missouri," said Joseph.

"I understand the early settlers of Missouri are mainly
from the mountain regions of the Southern States, and many
were induced by politicians to move into this area before
1820, so it would be admitted as a slave state," said Richard.

"How can we expect these people to respond to thousands of Mormons entering the state who are not in favor of slavery?"

"We have no intention of upsetting the slavery status of Missouri, but the older residents of the state are becoming alarmed as our numbers increase," said Joseph.

"I'm not surprised," Richard said thoughtfully. "Missouri was admitted as a slave state by a narrow margin, and whether or not we preach freedom for slaves, the people here know the Mormons will not vote for slavery at the polls."

"I realize that slavery is a major problem," Joseph said, shaking his head. "Missouri is a slave state, and our stand on slavery is not popular with the old settlers." He sighed and paused a moment before continuing. "Though we've been careful to say nothing about it, Missouri's status is threatened by an influx of Northerners. No charge can be made that arouses more intense hatred and violence from the old settlers than that of being an abolitionist, and our beliefs about slavery make us open to suspicion."

"The sentiment about the Mormons was evident as we came through Independence," said Richard. "I heard the Saints had been driven out of that area."

"Yes," said Joseph, "Our foes declared us 'common enemies of mankind' and it was said we ought to be destroyed. They charged us with being idle, lazy and vicious, and with being the very dregs of society. Have you seen any laziness here?"

"I've never seen such industriousness," said Richard. "The people are truly a busy and religious group."

"It depends on what the word, 'religion' means," said Joseph. "If a man conscientiously holds to a certain standard above his own self-interest, for which he would sacrifice the things that other men desire, that man is a religious man.

Many in our midst would fit that description, but some are constantly looking out for only their own interests."

His smile vanished and Richard saw deep pain fill his usually sparkling eyes. "Our men have been tarred and feathered, our women defiled and our property destroyed. Twelve hundred Saints were driven out of Jackson County and two hundred and three homes destroyed. The courts were powerless to protect us."

"I didn't realize it was on that large of a scale," said Richard.

Joseph's eyes darkened with emotion. "The shore of the Missouri lay lined on both sides of the ferry with men, women and children. Goods, wagons, boxes of provisions were constantly being taken across, but the rain descended in torrents, and our people suffered greatly. Some were in tents but many had no shelter from the elements, trying to keep warmed by their fires. Husbands, wives and children were often separated and hunting for one another. The scene was indescribable."

Joseph paused, "Over two hundred volunteers marched from Ohio to the aid of their brethren, but with the Governor—who had previously seemed sympathetic to our plight—turning against us, we had to disband the camp and will have to wait for a season to establish Zion. Now we must direct our energies toward building up new communities here north of the Missouri.

"The citizens of Clay County showed us great kindness, but soon asked us to leave." His voice choked, "If only the Saints would repent and live as we've been instructed to, these things would not have to happen. Those who have fallen away from the Gospel have brought many of the problems upon us. It's heartbreaking to see the persecution and know the sorrows of our people."

Richard knew Joseph worked with unremitting labor to help the Saints and that he set his people a personal example of self-sacrifice.

"I haven't seen many slaves here," Richard observed.

"Oh, there are a few who did not want to leave their masters, and have chosen to stay with them," said Joseph, "but there are only a few." He looked momentarily troubled. "We are just beginning to send missionaries to the Southern States, and it is inevitable that some slaves will be brought with their masters to join the Saints. I would urge anyone who has slaves to let them go free. It isn't right that one person be held in bondage to another." Then he added quickly, "But if they want to remain with you, they should not be turned away."

"I agree," said Richard, "but since Mandy belongs to my brother, I have no right to interfere."

"I understand your position," Joseph agreed, "and we will make her welcome here. She must be treated with the same respect as any other human being. We are all children of God."

———

Tom picked up his newspaper and saw more headlines about St. Louis. The area was a hotbed of instability. Last year, papers across the country had all carried the story of Elijah P. Lovejoy. He had started a religious journal in St. Louis writing scathing editorials attacking slavery and urging emancipation of the slaves. A mob invaded his print shop and destroyed the printing press. Lovejoy fled across the Mississippi into Illinois where he set up offices in Alton and ordered a new press. Alton was a free town, but doing business with, and dependent upon slave holding states for profit. In November the new press had arrived and he moved it into a warehouse guarded by friends. The second night a mob set the warehouse afire and shot and killed Lovejoy.

Calm, clear logic disappeared when mobs took over, Tom thought. He had heard that now mobs were persecuting the Mormons in Missouri. He wondered how Mandy and the twins and Richard and Jenny were doing. They had been gone for several months now.

Tom had heard more and more derogatory reports about the Mormons. He received occasional letters from Jenny and Richard, and they never mentioned any disillusionment with their new religion. He couldn't imagine his brother being allied with anything as bad as the Mormons were reported to be, but he couldn't help wondering if he had made the right decision when he decided to let the girls go with Richard and Jenny.

It had been good for him, though he missed them more than he had ever thought possible. He had lost much of his earlier bitterness about life, and was even able to think about Christina occasionally without feeling anger about losing her. Just last week he had gone to the Mitchell plantation and met a little blond woman who had come to Virginia for a visit—a sister of William—and she had quite taken his fancy. She had been sitting playing the piano that day he and William had entered the house.

"Have you met my sister, Ruth?" William asked.

Their eyes met and as her expressive, deep brown ones stared into his, he didn't want to let them go. Her mass of blond hair was combed back, braided and wound into a large bob at the base of her head showing off the fine whiteness of her skin. It seemed an unusual combination, her dark brown eyes with blond hair and fair skin. Her features were finely and delicately formed. Little wrinkles at the corners of her mouth showed that she smiled often, but her chin and mouth gave the impression of strength and determination.

"Did I hear you playing a Chopin waltz?" he asked. "Would you mind playing it again? Chopin is my favorite."

"Mine, too," she murmured.

When she finished playing they smiled at each other and made small talk. Then he found himself telling her about losing Christina. He realized with a start it was the first time he had spoken his wife's name since her death without a painful pause. He had promised to come to dinner on Tuesday and now as he stood looking at the western horizon lit up with reds and golds, he found himself looking forward to the evening.

CHAPTER NINE

Autumn in Far West drifted into winter. The fireplace put up a losing fight against cold sifting in around the door and window frames. The Harris family made quilts to hang over the windows and the doors to keep out the cold. As the area continued to grow rapidly, new neighbors settled close to the Harris home.

Jenny sat knitting in the oak rocker she had bought to rock her own babies in—babies which had never come. The chair was comfortable and fitted Jenny's form. She had made a new cover for the plump cushion on the seat and for the back-rest which eased the straightness of the back. She kept the wood waxed and polished to a high shine.

Cold skies clouded up with a flurry of snowflakes. She heard children playing in the first sprinkling of snow, and mothers calling to them. She closed her eyes and prayed softly, "Oh, Heavenly Father, please let me be a real mother. I know I have the twins, and I thank thee for this opportunity, but Richard would be so happy if I could give him a child of his own."

Every moment was still being taken up with routine tasks, but Jenny enjoyed her work. She was proud of her house, its snug warmth, its comfort. The two-room cabin was always filled with odors—food cooking, the smell of wash-suds, fresh milk and new cheese, ripened fruit demanding attention.

One November evening the odor of sweet spices from the kettle of apple butter simmering on the fireplace filled the air. Jenny set out a kettle of cream and the churn. She sang as she kept time to the swish, swish of the churn dasher, whose revolutions slowly thickened the cream until it broke into globs of golden butter. It seemed a monotonous task, but they would have fresh butter for the next morning's breakfast, and she would send some over to Widow Wilson, who never had any luxuries.

They had cleaned the house and finished the dishes quickly after an early supper so the twins could visit the Hansens, where they had been invited to sleep over. Mandy was off assisting another sister in childbirth. Jenny looked forward to a quiet evening with just herself and Richard at home.

Jenny could hear the strokes of the ax, sharp in the twilight, then Richard's footsteps on the path. She would know the sound of them anywhere. Richard came in with an armful of wood, kissed her quickly on the cheek and departed again. Even chore clothes did not hide his handsome form. The wind howled faintly. When she again became aware of Richard's footsteps on the walk, her mind also registered the faint jangling of harness buckles.

"Oh, no," she sighed, "not tonight."

But Richard, unaware of her objection to the task at hand, lugged the heavy hames and tugs into the house, his entry accompanied by a little snow storm swirling around his feet. He deposited the formidable pile on Jenny's immaculate kitchen floor next to the table.

"It's harness oiling and fixing time. I guess I'd as well get it done while the twins are gone and it's quiet around here."

He set the harness oil on the corner of the table and went back out the door. Jenny dusted her hands on her apron and rescued the family Bible, Book of Mormon, and the doily she had crocheted from the center of the table. Returning shortly with a piece of flat hardwood, Richard set it on the corner of the table and pulled up a wooden chair beside the heap of leather strips and buckles. He checked each rivet and if the fastenings were not secure, used the block of wood as an anvil to hammer each one tight. Buckling, unbuckling and hammering, the work progressed.

Jenny finished the churning then poured off the buttermilk, added cold water, and began to work the remaining buttermilk out of the soft lump of butter. She worked the butter and changed the water repeatedly until the water came out clear, then added a little salt. She molded the butter into a round ball, put it in a bowl and covered it with a clean cloth and set the bowl in the cool corner cupboard which served as a pantry.

Jenny seated herself on the other side of the table from Richard and marveled at the precision of each hammer stroke. Richard, always pleased by Jenny's presence, smiled across the table at her as she leaned toward him.

"Happy?" he asked.

"Couldn't be happier," she replied.

"I know this isn't much of a home compared with what you're used to," he said, "but I'll build you a better one as soon as I can."

He wished he could find a way to tell her how grateful he was for her love, how important it was to him to feel the bond between them growing day by day. His eyes were saying, I love you, and I appreciate you being my wife. I appreciate the cooking, the cleaning, the many hours you spend working to make life happier for all of us. In spite of her tiredness, straggly hair, a little extra weight, and a nose more than a little shiny, Jenny radiated that star-drenched happiness and aura of beauty a woman feels when she knows she is truly loved.

She looked at Richard and thought him about the most handsome man in Far West. His eyes danced when he spoke and his mouth seemed to always sport a smile. She believed herself the luckiest woman in the world that he had fallen in love with her.

The yellowish filter of sun coming in the cabin window became dim and Jenny lit the candles. She beamed and the freckles across her nose shone in the candlelight. The wind made whistling noises down the chimney.

"Sounds like the Almanac is right," said Richard. "we're due for a stormy spell."

When he had completed the repairing and oiling of the harness, Richard shoved his chair away from the table, came around it, and took her chin in his hand to tilt her face upward for his kiss.

"I guess you'll be glad to see this pile of harnesses out of the kitchen and back to the barn," he said, then looked around with a sigh, "I've made a mess of your clean kitchen. I'm sorry." He smiled a tired smile. "I guess I could do this in the barn, but like I've always said, the kitchen is the heart of the house, and I enjoy being in here with you." He sniffed the air and added, "Besides, your kitchen is always filled with such heavenly aromas! The earth's loveliest fragrance has to be the smell of baking bread."

Jenny looked at her kitchen; it was a mess, but the magic of the evening outweighed the inconvenience. She felt the quiet peace of one that has something more precious than gold, and knew why she had never regretted leaving her home and family to come west with this man whose love made her world worthwhile. She would not hesitate to go to the ends of the earth with him. Their little home was full of love—so full it seemed the walls would burst—but not so full as Jenny's heart. She bowed her head in thankfulness to God for a perfect day.

That winter seemed long and hard. The wind shrieked and blew the snow into great drifts. The children's clothing dripped puddles of water onto the braided rug Jenny, Mandy and the mothers of the students had made for the school-room. The population of the Church in Missouri continued to grow. The city of Far West came right up to Richard and Jenny's doorstep, but Richard still had his ten acres of wheat and corn fields.

Christmas Eve day came and with it tiny snowflakes which fluttered to the ground like goose down. Mandy helped Jenny clean and stuff chickens. "Laura dear, bring me a threaded needle to sew up this fowl." Jenny called to the girl who was in the other room.

They rolled out mince pies and made two extra for the Wilsons. Practically immersed in Christmas, Jenny sang "The Mistletoe Bough," an old English ballad while she made "curly gingerbread" by a recipe brought from England by her grandmother. The pudding the Clark children had brought that fall bubbled over the fire, permeating the air with its fragrance as it steamed.

The girls hung their stockings over one of the chairs. The last thing before being tucked into bed, they sat before the fireplace and Jenny read the story of the birth of the Christ child. Jenny and Richard wanted the children to know Christmas is not because of Santa Claus, but because the birth of the baby Jesus is celebrated on that day. When the girls were in bed and quiet, apparently asleep, Jenny dropped some candy and cookies she and Mandy had made and a new pair of mittens she had knitted into each stocking.

———————

Richard stopped milking Rosie in the late winter, and for a time, their only milk came when brought by one of the school children. Then one day in early spring, Richard took Laura and Sarah out to see the newborn calf—a heifer. Richard felt elated.

"Don't get too close," he warned the girls. Rosie, who had always been docile, was fiercely protective of her new young. After the calf nursed, Richard milked Rosie and fed the first nine milkings to the pigs before the family again enjoyed fresh milk for household use.

As the last tiny edges of snow melted, and spring 1838 touched the earth, patches of black began to appear. The mud looked deep, fertile and sticky. Melody poured from the swollen throat of a meadow lark. Richard restlessly kept examining the ground to see if it was drying out enough to farm.

The mid-spring mornings were cool and crisp. "I didn't know you were such a dedicated farmer," said Jenny, as she saw love for his land shining from Richard's brown eyes.

"I guess it's in my blood," admitted Richard. "I love spring; it's like a miracle to see the world awakening and to feel myself part of it when the warm earth stirs and begins to live and breathe again. I love the clear blue sky and being able to see, smell and taste nature," he noted as he chewed on the stem of a dry weed. "I like the look of newly turned earth, the furrows ready to receive the seed, the first green showing above it ..."

"Yes," agreed Jenny, "it's wonderful when after the cold and dark of winter, earth again turns to sunshine and a splendor of leaves and blossoms. The birds sing, the flowers bloom, the lilac blossoms burst from their buds. There is the feeling once more that all is right in God's world."

Jenny reached up on tip-toes and gave Richard a kiss on the cheek. "We're all weary of winter and will be ready to go to the fields when spring planting time comes." Jenny gazed across their ten acres and the Hansen place across the field and drew tranquility from the scene. "The world is so beautiful and peaceful. Why can't our lives be that way?" she wondered aloud.

Jenny felt a wave of nostalgia when she looked at the one struggling lilac bush she had brought to Missouri. A thousand pictures filled her mind. She pictured herself home in New York walking among the lilacs in the spring, half delirious from their smell and rain-wet leaves and her own marvelous dreams.

The seeds, struggling to break through the soil, reminded her of the effort it took for her own life adjustments. To Jenny, flowers had personality and identity. Like the flowers, she must take root in this new environment, leaving her former life behind. The work ahead could not be done in this frame of mind. She could not live in the past, she told herself.

The warm sunshine and spring breeze helped to again lift Jenny's spirits and renew everyone's energy. Richard came in after morning chores and took Jenny into his arms and waltzed her around the room, then snatched her off her feet, holding her well off the floor.

"Put me down," she begged as he looked at her with love shining behind his teasing eyes. "What's gotten into you?"

He set her on her feet and kissed her firmly. "The fields are dry enough to begin working them," he declared proudly.

That day Jenny announced that school would close until the crops were in. The children were all needed in the fields.

"We will start spring planting tomorrow," Richard said that evening as they sat at the supper table.

The twins squealed with delight.

He turned to his wife. "Well, Jenny, we have a field to plant, but thanks to your generosity, barely enough seed grain to put in a crop and still have bread until it matures."

Their wheat crop had seemed so ample in the fall; it was hard to believe it was nearly gone. Jenny knew Richard did not begrudge the grain she had given away. He had given plenty himself—to the Widow Wilson, to a family with sick children and no wheat to make bread, to an old man still living in his wagon box. They had the satisfaction of knowing they had done what they could to aid their neighbors when there was a need.

The next morning Jenny awoke as faint light entered the window. As soon as breakfast was over, the whole family hurried to the fields to work. Jenny couldn't believe how quickly her arms and back began to ache from this type of labor.

Richard stopped, leaned on his shovel and looked over at Jenny. "How you doin', sweetheart?" he asked.

She brushed her arm against her forehead and smiled, then looked at the shovel in her right hand and wrinkled up her nose. "I'm not used to being a farmer," she said. "My hands are already getting blisters. I don't know how you handle doing this kind of work all the time!"

Richard had to admit it wasn't the quickest way of breaking the sod, but machinery was scarce and shovels were all they had. They were lucky to have good metal shovels. He glanced over to where Mandy was helping the girls. She measured out the seed corn and demonstrated to the twins how to place the small kernels of seed in just the right places. Richard knew Mandy's joints were stiff with rheumatism and hated to have her doing so much bending over, but they all had to do their part. Mandy never complained, but always remained agreeable and willing to do whatever was needed.

He turned and looked out across the field to the west and saw someone approaching. "I wonder who that is," he said with a slight frown. Then he recognized the short, stout, familiar figure. "Oh, it's Brother Hansen." He put one foot on the shovel and pushed it into the rich, brown dirt so it would stand upright, shook the dust from his hat, dusted his face with his handkerchief, and walked toward his neighbor.

"How's it coming?" Jim asked. "I see you've put the whole family to work," he added noting the cooperative operation. "I won't say it's coming fast," Richard replied as he brushed the perspiration which was making gray lines down his dusty face from his brow, "but it's coming."

Jim smiled, "I just finished putting the last of my corn in. I'll bring the plow over tomorrow morning for you to use. It will help you break the sod on this piece a lot faster."

"That would get these last few acres turned in quick order," Richard agreed, relief showing on his face.

Jenny walked closer and sighed, "That would be wonderful, Brother Hansen," she beamed.

"Let's take a break and have dinner," Richard said. He didn't have to say it twice. Everyone dropped what they were doing and started toward the house. "Won't you join us, Jim?"

"I just ate, but I'll walk over that way with you."

Richard and Jim were bringing up the rear, engrossed in talk of farming as they strolled toward the cabin. Jenny had to laugh as she filled the wash basin with water. The faces of the twins were dirt-colored masks through which their eyes and teeth flashed startlingly.

"You look like little black children," Jenny said as she brushed Sarah and Laura's long hair back out of their eyes with her hand. They washed and dried, then sloshed the basin of dirty water into a bucket beside the wash stand. When Jim left, Richard came in and began rolling up his sleeves, then took a handful of soap and used it vigorously. Jenny mechanically handed him the towel. Her mind was busy thinking how thankful she felt Brother Hansen would loan them a plow to turn the soil of their land instead of having to do it by hand.

"Mmm," Richard said as Jenny removed the lid from the bake oven, "I think I smell scalloped potatoes! Whatever did I do to deserve this?"

"There's fruit cobbler, too," Jenny laughed. She extended her plump, blistered hands expressively. "Look at me; I'm no lady of leisure. These hands were meant to mix bread, hold a rolling pin, flute the edges of a pie, wash a tub full of clothes." Then she added ruefully, "but I'm not sure they were made to turn the soil. They seem a little soft for that."

Richard's warm, brown eyes caressed her. He put his lips to her hand and kissed the blisters, and they both began to laugh. With an arm around her shoulders he walked her to the table. "You deserve a rest," he said as he pulled out her chair and seated her in spite of her protests that she must serve dinner.

"Laura and Sarah, it's your turn to help serve dinner."

"Will you drive Daisy and Doll on the plow?" Jenny asked. Daisy and Doll were always dependable.

"I thought I'd try the young ones and see if I can't get them used to farm work."

"Be careful," Jenny cautioned. "I know you will be—you always are," she added as an afterthought.

Jenny arose the next morning thankful that the women-folk could stay in the house and work. She could hear the consistent squeak of stretching leather, the click of single-trees, and the steady tramp of the horses as they pulled the plow. At dinner time, she took Richard out a sandwich and milk. He stopped the horses and waited while she stumbled across the plowed furrows.

"How's the young team working out?" Jenny asked.

"They're a little skittish, but not near what Daisy and Doll were when they were first worked," he replied. "They work together well."

Richard came in after dark for supper, tired and dirty, his clothes soil stained and sweaty. He took off his dust-covered jacket and hat and rolled up his sleeves to wash. He felt tired, but the plowing was going well. Jenny bowed her head and thanked God for good neighbors.

Light entered the window and Aaron Hale opened his eyes. He sat up quickly and rubbed his head. He had been dreaming of a wedding—his own. He had been standing be-fore a strong, imposing man, dressed in a cut-away broad-cloth suit, and the girl beside him was the prettiest woman he had ever laid eyes upon. In fact, she was radiantly beauti-ful—perfect in every detail, from her slim body to her fine featured oval face framed by a halo of golden hair which fell in soft, downy waves upon her breast. Her cheeks, pink with excitement, mirrored the rosy clouds of morning and her eyes the blue of the sky. Aaron laughed at himself. His "dream girl" was a real beauty. Matrimony was the farthest thing from his mind at this time. What's more, he was sure there wasn't a woman living that was as perfect as the one in his dream.

The day had finally come when he would be leaving to find Richard and Jenny. Aaron had practiced quick draws and target shooting all winter. Now, he was not only in a position where he could leave, but he felt ready to get revenge on the man who had ruined his sister's life. His stomach knotted as he mulled it all over again, starting with the unpleasant scenes with his parents when Jenny and Richard had taken up with the Mormons—his father shouting, his mother squeezing the arm of her chair, as she lowered her head and silent tears ran down her cheeks.

He tried to picture Jenny in his mind the way she looked the last time he saw her. She would be fixed that way in his memory—long red hair piled high on her head, green eyes sparkling… Fun-loving Jenny, who could have had the world under her little pink thumb; imagine her throwing it all away for a husband with some perfectly mad idea about religion!

Aaron, himself, had liked Richard at first, until Richard met up with the Mormons. He remembered, as though it were yesterday, his disappointment, then fury when he had found their home deserted. There had been a few weeks when he and his parents had kept reassuring one another that Jenny would soon return, then the final realization that she would, or could, not do so.

His mother had tried to discourage him from going after Jenny. "Haven't you read the news?" she asked. "The Missourians and the Mormons are killing and destroying each other. Will you insist on going and running into danger and death? Isn't it hard enough that I have lost my only daughter, but am I now to lose my only son?"

"Don't worry, Mother," he assured her, "I don't intend to get myself killed. I will rescue Jenny from the Mormons and bring her home. I'm sure she was abducted, or she would never have left in the first place."

Mrs. Hale shook her head and looked away. "Jenny chose her own course," she said quietly. He could see his mother's eyes were moist.

Aaron dressed carefully. He knocked the mud off his boots before putting them on. Then he buckled on his gun belt, took his hat from the peg by the door, and carrying his small bag which contained one change of clothing and a few toiletries, stepped out into the dawn of a beautiful spring morning.

Deep quiet enveloped the yard. A dry, untrimmed rose vine still clung to the wall by the bedroom window, but the grass along the path looked green and vibrant. The lilac bushes were heavy with buds. Jenny had loved flowers, remembered Aaron for the hundredth time, especially the lilacs.

Aaron walked down the street enjoying the morning breeze blowing on his face from off Lake Erie. He entered a waterfront cafe and ordered breakfast. A short, dumpish looking waitress brought him a bowl of mush, and a plate overflowing with ham, eggs, and fried potatoes. He habitually ate at the waterfront cafes where he could hear the latest word about the Mormons from passing travelers. He paid for his meal and continued down the street to the stage station, where he boarded the stage for Pittsburgh.

Aaron arrived at Pittsburgh and checked into a riverside inn. The next morning, he ate quickly and stood alongside the pier where the wooden steamboat, with its huge paddle wheel on the stern, steamed up the Ohio and docked for loading.

Captain Dugan was a brusk sort of person with a stocky form, bushy brows, a swarthy complexion, keen brown eyes and a cigar hanging from the side of his mouth. Aaron had known and done business with him for a long time. The captain remained unquestionably in charge of everything he set his hand to.

"Welcome aboard," he bellowed as he clasped Aaron's hand firmly. "What brings the pleasure of your company to us this time?"

"Merely an errand," said Aaron. The thought ran through his mind that you didn't tell a casual friend you planned to kill your brother-in-law.

Richard and Jenny became acquainted during the winter with the young woman named Eliza R. Snow, who had written some of the Church hymns. Jenny had heard a great deal about her from Emma, who had nothing but praise for Miss Snow's fantastic abilities.

Eliza, born of New England parentage, had a quiet and refined manner. She stood slightly above medium height with her slim figure, clothed in a full-skirted, silk dress, looking for all the world like a fine Dresden china doll. Her high forehead wrinkled as she talked about the great need for education among the Mormons. Jenny thought Eliza's most striking feature, her deep, penetrating eyes, filled with poetic fire when she talked about things dear to her heart.

Eliza came to visit Jenny and they were deep into a discussion of schools and teaching methods when the girls dashed in. "These are our twins," Jenny told Eliza.

"Girls, this is Eliza R. Snow. She has taught Joseph Smith's children and is a writer and a poet." The girls bobbed a curtsy and smiled at the stranger. Sarah showed immediate interest, watching Miss Snow in a curiously intent manner.

"What do you write?" Sarah asked.

"I've written stories, poems, and songs," said Eliza.

"Wow!" said Sarah, "I'd like to be a writer. I've been writing some poems."

"I think they're really quite good for her age," said Jenny. "We've been studying and writing poetry, and she really took to it. Sarah, why don't you get one of your poems and read to Miss Snow."

Sarah scurried off, but soon returned and read to Eliza:

> My sister, Laura, is my twin
> We are not much alike
> But sometimes when we lay and talk
> Quite late into the night
> I find we really feel the same
> About a lot of things
> We both enjoy sunsets at night
> And butterfly's bright wings.

"That's really nice," said Eliza. "You have a knack for writing poetry. You must do it often."

The Harris family and Eliza soon became fast friends. She was now living with her parents and brother in Adam-ondi-Ahman, but when she came to Far West she often dropped in for a few minutes. Her appearance was always a special treat, especially for Sarah, who wrote poems with renewed vigor to show to Miss Snow.

"I really believe she has a lot of talent," Eliza told Jenny. "You must encourage her all you can."

"Eliza is a brilliant and talented woman," Jenny told Richard that night. "She is a student of literature and a poet, and has written the words for several of the songs in the first Church hymnbook."

Richard lowered the book he was reading and gave her his attention.

"Can you believe that at the young age of twenty-two she wrote a requiem for the newspaper for John Adams and Thomas Jefferson. Her first-prize story was published in Godey's Lady's Magazine."

Richard lifted his eyebrows and Jenny could tell he was duly impressed.

CHAPTER TEN

Working with the young people helped fill that curious hunger Jenny felt, that incessant need to make her life count for something. Jenny's Saturday morning classes with the girls became a great success. She remembered her own home, her mother's face and her tireless hands sewing Jenny a new dress for the Fourth of July celebration, the attractive table she set for the evening meal, the knitting and crocheting she did. Jenny tried to impart to these young women all of the homemaking skills she had learned in her own home. There was very little cash money in Far West, but she would teach them how to make a house a home by the work of their own hands.

Their first lessons were in mending. "Mending, is an important part of homemaking and should be done with exactness and skill" Jenny told the girls.

She showed them how to cut patches on the straight of the material, sewing them on so the lengthwise and crosswise threads in the patch exactly matched the lengthwise and crosswise threads in the article being patched.

"A hemmed patch," she instructed, "is a sturdy mend. It is commonly used on a hole or a frayed cut or tear. Before beginning this patch cut out the smallest possible square or rectangle that will remove the uneven edges of the damaged area. Cut along crosswise and lengthwise threads, then clip diagonally at each corner, about one-fourth inch, and turn the edges under. Slide a matching piece of cloth under this square or rectangular hole. Make sure any design matches perfectly."

Jenny paused and looked at the girls who seemed to be listening with rapt attention, then continued. "The patch should be about one inch larger all around than the hole. Baste it in place and hem the turned under edges of the hole against the patch with fine invisible stitches. If the patch is light weight, turn under the edges of the patch and hem them. If heavy, overcast the edges closely. This patch will barely be noticeable on the right side and is good for clothing that is tubbed. It will withstand the rubbing on the washboard."

"Wow!" said Lucy, who at thirteen was thin, long-legged and taffy-haired. "I didn't realize patching was such a big job!"

Jenny smiled tolerantly at the young girl. "This is only the beginning," she said. "We will learn how to make a lapped patch where sturdiness is more important than appearance and to mend woolens and knitted articles next week. The following week, we'll patch linens and household articles."

Lucy let out a long sigh. Jenny looked at her and thought how much she had changed from a year ago; how with a little education she seemed to have taken on a more positive character, but she was still the talkative one.

Jenny taught the girls to embroider in many different stitches, and each girl made a sampler—a moral platitude embroidered upon a square piece of cloth, using the various stitches they had learned. In one corner they embroidered their name and the date.

She taught them how to help shear the sheep, then wash the sheep's wool, card it and spin it into thread. They gathered berries, bark, roots and other natural materials for dyeing the yarn before it was woven.

"Weaving is like living our lives," Jenny told the girls. "Whatever we put into our lives shows in the pattern we end up with, as we weave on time's loom."

"What an interesting thought," said Mary.

A series of parallel threads called the warp were set out on a loom, to the desired width of the fabric.

"Every girl must learn how to thread the loom," insisted Jenny. "When weaving, the warp may break and you'll need to know how to thread it again. The warp must be done evenly so the tension will be the same on all the threads."

The warp made the background, and so the threads had to be of sturdy material such as wool, linen or cotton. The weft threads were thrown under and over the warp threads with unvarying regularity as the homespun material was fashioned. Jenny used cotton warp overshot with wool when cotton was available. The girls learned to make various shades and even plaid materials from which to sew dresses and suits. They wove linsey with a flax warp and wool weft for dresses and for sheets and blankets. Jenny sent them each home with some flax to spin into yarn and bring back the next week.

"Some day," she told the girls, "you will want to make a coverlet for your trousseau. They examined the one on her bed carefully and she showed them her name and the date in the corner. "It takes many, many hours, and by the time you have finished you have devoted almost a year to this work of art."

"I could never do that," said Lucy, as her girlish face wrinkled up at Jenny imploringly.

"You could if you set your mind to it," said Jenny

Jenny remembered her mother telling her, "Creative work is part of a balanced life. Learning to appreciate and love the beauty in little things we do enlarges our horizons, and we learn to see the beauty in all life."

Within the four walls of the crude log cabins of Far West there was often little time to think of adornment or art, but the artistic longing women felt, made them anxious to make something to beautify their homes. Often that artistic bent was expressed in quilts.

Jenny taught the young girls to piece together scraps of material of various kinds and colors into patchwork quilt tops, then to make a quilt back and put a bat of wool between them. They learned to sew the quilt together with tiny, even stitches they called "quilting."

Jenny demonstrated how to make some of the old favorite patterns: the Star of Bethlehem, Churn Dash, Water Mill, and Eight Hands Around. It took up to forty blocks to make a quilt, and often as many as twenty pieces to create a block. The small cabin seemed literally crowded with old clothing which had been ripped apart to use.

Applique for quilt-making was popular, and Jenny showed the girls how to apply the designs and stitch these "laid-on" quilts, which were considered by some to be more elegant than the humble pieced quilts. But elegance was not what the little settlement of Mormons needed most at this time. Economy was a necessity and patchwork was created of scraps of material not otherwise used. There was such need for warm covers for beds and hangings for doors and windows to help keep out the cold of winter.

They hooked rugs from old socks and knitted materials and braided rag rugs from strips of cloth. Jenny gave the girls careful instructions, just as her mother had given her at that age: "The proper width to tear the rags depends upon the weight of the material. Thin rags must be torn about two inches wide, twisted and rolled up to the size of your little finger. This method will enclose the seams so no raw edges are left."

The cabin filled with busy girls, tearing, cutting and sewing rags. Rags which were sewed were wound into balls. While they worked the girls chattered like little brown sparrows.

"This will take forever," moaned Lucy. "We'll never get enough rags sewed to make a rug."

"It takes about four pounds of sewed rags for each twenty-seven by fifty-four inch rug," Jenny told them. "I'm sure we'll have enough to make a small rug for each girl's home if we keep working at it. We can use up materials that might otherwise be wasted, and make useful articles."

Jenny instructed the girls in the little practical tips which help make a home stay nice. "When making a new carpet, always save the ravelings for use in darning the carpet on some future day. The colors will match better than any yarn you are likely to have."

Jenny taught the girls to make clothing for small children from larger garments. They learned to measure, tuck and cut cloth into dresses to fit themselves and each other. Jenny reminded the girls, "widths and lengths of the figure are the basic measurements used in patterns. Acceptable work is based on accurate measurements."

Sarah shook her long hair back impatiently as she struggled with the task at hand. Laura bent over her work with her long braids flipped over her shoulder. Laura showed a real knack for dressmaking, and was soon being asked to sew for others in Far West. Mrs. Miller asked Laura to sew new outfits for Isaac and Minnie. When Jenny examined the neat handiwork of her niece, she felt extremely proud of her work.

––––––––––––––

Aaron Hale had spent most of the time on the boat in the captain's quarters catching up on all the news of the trade. The captain on a steamer had supreme power. He stood no watch, came and went when he pleased, his orders were obeyed without question and he was accountable to no one. As his guest, Aaron had the run of the boat.

Spitting forth fire and smoke, the boat covered the nine hundred sixty-seven miles to Cairo, Illinois, in record breaking time. They were soon down the Ohio and starting up the mighty Mississippi. The closer they came to Missouri the more restless Aaron became.

On deck one moonlit evening when he could not sleep, Aaron looked out at the big river and the stars twinkling above. Several lights were also twinkling. From upstream, a lumber raft with a lantern in its middle crept toward them. He heard a man yell, "Heave her head to starboard!" The raft floated past and went out of sight around the shoulder of an island on the Missouri side of the river. They continued up the river, creating waves which lapped against the shore. They passed other rafts drifting down the great river, with wigwams in their center—some as many as four or five—to shelter the men from the blazing sun, wind and rain. One made its presence known by a fire burning on a thick bed of dirt piled on its deck.

Towns on the black hillsides showed up only as a cluster of dimly lighted windows. They maneuvered around towheads, or sandbars, with cottonwoods as thick as flies on horse manure.

They passed a boat caught on a huge rock which had splintered its hull. The cyprus woods in the background helped give an eerie appearance to the scene. Aaron shuddered at the sight.

The captain emerged from his drawing room in the forward end of the texas—a structure on the hurricane deck of a steamer containing the cabin of the officers and the pilot house.

"I'd rather see the new moon over my left shoulder than a sight like that," the captain sighed. "That's about as bad as one's luck can get." He rubbed his hand across his brow. "She sure killed herself on that rock."

As they bore down on the steamer, Aaron could see the dark shadow of her upper deck above water. It was a sad sight and the two men watched silently as they passed the paddle box, the stern and then she disappeared into the darkness. Aaron and Captain Dugan stayed on the deck a long time, talking in subdued tones.

Toward midnight, thunder and lightning rent the sky. The wind screamed as the lightning lit up the river and showed whitecaps for half a mile in each direction. Soon it began to pour, and a solid sheet of water fell from the skies.

"No use staying out in this kind of weather," Aaron said, as he bid the captain goodnight and started toward his berth. The storm didn't last long. By morning the sun was shining.

The days went by quickly as Aaron socialized with the captain and the pilots. They smoked and talked and ate and talked. Captain Dugan ran a no-nonsense boat, without entertainment for the passengers, becoming so popular on the Mississippi.

"This is not a showboat, it is a freight and passenger steamer," he declared. "My job is to get people and freight

from place to place quickly and safely, not to entertain travelers," he added as he tapped the big bell three times, giving
the signal to land.

Their speed slackened and they stopped about three
miles above a small town where they spent a couple of hours
taking on freight.

They would be docking at Independence the next morning. From what Aaron had heard, the Mormons had moved
northeast of there into the wilderness. Deep furrows appeared in his brow as he thought of his sister. He would soon
find out what had happened to her, and if she were still alive,
bring her back to New York to her family. He stood a long
time on the deck before retiring to his compartment.

Aaron was one of the last off the boat. As he looked toward shore, at those who had just reached the landing, he
couldn't believe his eyes. There, in the flesh—unless he was
dreaming—was the girl he had dreamed about. She looked as
perfect as she had in his dream. Aaron stood stock still, his
mouth open. He blinked his eyes.

"Are you going to stay with us for the return trip?" asked
Captain Dugan who had somehow appeared at his side.

"Who is that woman?" Aaron asked, ignoring his question
as he pointed unashamedly at the her.

"Which woman?" the captain asked, craning his neck in
the direction Aaron was pointing. But the woman had disappeared into the crowd.

Aaron rushed about the waterfront, searching, asking,
but finding no clue to the woman's whereabouts. He rented
a room at an inn and for three days searched the area unsuccessfully. He found himself hardly able to eat or sleep, his
purpose for being in Missouri almost forgotten. The third
night, gazing at a crystal moon high in the sky, he decided

he must continue on. He would forget this nonsense and in the morning he would purchase a horse and follow the Mormons. Perhaps he had been dreaming again, he told himself.

Early the next morning he found a sturdy bay gelding the owner proclaimed to be the fastest horse in town. After paying a good price for the animal, he mounted and started out of town in a northeasterly direction. As he gazed back at the small settlement, looking quite rustic in the early morning light, a rabbit jumped out of the brush right in front of the horse. The horse shied, took several jumps sideways, then began to rear. Aaron was a tolerably good horseman, but taken off guard, was no match for his new mount. The ground came quickly up to meet him.

Aaron felt consciousness returning to his aching body. A faint odor of baking bread filled his nostrils. Was he in heaven? No, he decided, the pain throbbing through his body wasn't compatible with what he'd heard about heaven. He must still be alive. Was he dreaming? If so, it was a nightmare.

He could feel the softness of a bed beneath him and a pillow under his head. Someone was taking care of him. He opened his eyes, then closed them quickly as pain shot through his head. He didn't want to open them again, but felt compelled to. He waited until the pain passed, then cautiously opened one eye at a time. As they focused, he could see the smooth rubbed wood of a pine table at the end of the bed. He had to find out where he was.

Thinking brought back the pain. He forced himself to lay quietly until it subsided, then eased his head to one side. His "dream girl" was sitting in a rocking chair beside the bed, knitting. This girl was turning up in the most inopportune places!

"Well, you're finally waking up!" she said in a voice sweet and melodious to his ears. "I was beginning to think you never would."

He blinked, stared, and blinked again. He tried to lift his hand to rub his eyes, but hadn't the strength. "Where am I?" he finally managed to get out as he tried desperately to shake the fog from his brain.

"You're in Far West, Missouri," the girl answered. "You had a close call between the head injury and the broken leg. For a while we didn't think you were going to make it."

"Far West?" The name rang a familiar bell in his consciousness but he wondered why. "How did I get here?"

"We picked you up just out of Independence and brought you here in our wagon. Apparently your horse threw you. In the damp earth, we could make out where the horse had shied. And the ground bore marks of your landing. We saw a bay gelding running riderless toward town just before we found you, injured and unconscious. Tell me your name. Where did you come from?"

It was coming back to him now. Aaron clenched his hand as if still gripping the reins of the gelding. A throbbing pain again cursed through his head. He remembered the Mormons and starting out to find his sister. The memories of the Mormons combined with his present helplessness filled him with anger.

"You aren't one of those...those Mormons?" he asked, his face uneasy. He marshalled all of his strength and tried to sit up. It wasn't a smart move. His head pounded almost unbearably as he let it fall back onto the pillow. The effort left him exhausted. He became aware of another pain, this one in his leg. He groaned.

She lifted her chin as her gaze met his, then gave a little laugh. "Yes," she said, "we're all some of those…those Mormons. And you?" A low whistle filled the air as the kettle on the fireplace began to boil.

"Well, I'm certainly not a Mormon, he said wearily, but my sister is."

July 4, 1837, dawned with robins chirping outside and a light breeze gently pushing the curtains back and forth. Jenny lay for a few minutes watching the trickle of light coming through the lace curtains over the new glass pane Richard had put in the window. She knew, in spite of the morning breeze that this day would be another Missouri scorcher. It was an exciting day. It would be celebrated by laying the cornerstone for the temple the Saints planned to build in Far West.

While Mandy went to milk the cow, Jenny poured water into the basin on the washstand. First she bathed her face and hands, then dressed and combed her hair before the little mirror above the basin. She pulled the auburn strands neatly, straight back from her forehead, with a big bun at the nape of her neck. When she finished fixing her hair, she started breakfast. She soon had ham sizzling in the frying pan and biscuits in the bake oven. Richard loved her biscuits with fresh butter and honey. Today she had a special treat—fresh strawberry preserves. She spread a clean linen cloth on the table.

The girls began stirring. Mandy came in with a bucket of milk from Rosie and started to strain it.

"Get dressed in your best dresses, girls. It will soon be time to go," she yelled up to the twins.

The family gathered and said their usual morning prayers. Richard gave thanks for the freedom they enjoyed on this anniversary of the country's independence. The girls were bubbling over with excitement.

Jenny turned to Mandy, who had started the day with a frown which still hung on her face. Mandy's dark eyes lacked the usual sparkle.

"It's so nice to have a Fourth of July celebration. It was always such a gala affair back home," Jenny said happily.

Mandy shifted from one foot to the other. "I'se never cottoned much to what yo' call Independence Day Marsa Harris. It always been a sad day fo' me. It just remind me dat I's not free—jus' like rubbin' salt into de' wound."

Jenny looked at Mandy with a new burst of understanding. "Oh, Mandy," she said apologetically. "I never even thought of how you might feel about the Fourth of July. I'm so sorry."

"The Fourth of July is yo's, not mine," Mandy reaffirmed. "It jus' show de distance 'tween us."

"You know if it were up to me, you'd had your freedom long ago. I don't think of you as a slave, I think of you as a friend—an indispensable friend that helps me so much. I don't know what I'd do without you."

They sat down to breakfast and just as they finished the dishes, they heard the sound of the wagon arriving out front. Laura reached for her shawl that Jenny had laid out to take along in case the weather turned cool.

"Do I have to take this ol' shawl along?" Sarah asked, looking disdainfully at her wrap.

"Just bring it in case you happen to need it," Jenny insisted. "You don't have to wear it, but a well-dressed lady always carries a shawl." Sarah grabbed the shawl and went out the door grumbling. Laura gave Jenny a knowing grin as she followed her sister. Jenny gave Mandy a quick hug, then exited and pulled the door closed behind her.

Richard helped the girls into the wagon so they wouldn't mess up their dresses. He reached out a hand to Jenny and helped her up beside him in the driver's seat. He had taken off the common, plain sides of the wagon and fixed on boards which were handsomely painted. He had placed flat hoops in mortises and spread and tied a painted cloth over the whole. He felt quite proud of his wagon's new look.

The spot for the temple lay one hundred ten feet in length and eighty feet wide. It was a happy day for the Saints of Far West as they laid the cornerstone. Perhaps they could build their Zion here. After all the persecutions they had suffered, maybe they would find peace and happiness in northeastern Missouri. As they celebrated this day of freedom, they thanked God for the respite from mobs they now enjoyed.

The Independence Day ceremony was followed by band music and a parade. Little did the people know the conditions of peace and progress which they celebrated were to be short-lived.

Heat waves shimmered across the landscape and people's feet kicked up a cloud of dust. It felt hot, hot enough to make you dizzy, Jenny thought as she watched the girls talking to their friends. A young woman, barely eighteen at most, came up to Jenny. As she approached heads turned in her direction. She was a strikingly beautiful girl.

"Are you Jenny Harris?" she asked softly.

"I am," Jenny answered.

"My name is Anna, Anna Morris," she said. "I have good news for you. Your brother, Aaron, is at our house. He has been injured by a fall from a horse, but is starting to recuperate."

"Aaron! Aaron! What on earth is he doing in Far West?"

"He hasn't told me that," said the girl, "but I thought you would be anxious to know he is here."

One county had proved too small to hold the Mormons. Twelve hundred had been driven out of Jackson County, but now fifteen thousand members located in northwestern Missouri. Joseph had engineered the laying out of new towns to accommodate the great influx of people. These included Adam-ondi-Ahman, Gallitin and Millport in Daviess County, De Witt in Carroll County, and Haun's Mill in Caldwell County. Joseph advised the people to live within the cities with their farms on the outside. He discouraged small clusters of homes away from the central locations.

Young men with little formal schooling became missionaries and went forth to other countries and to isles of the sea. Converts came from many countries, bringing traditions of their former homes to Missouri. No matter what customs they had known before, faithful Mormons were all interested in working for the same objectives. Non-Mormons looked upon them as a strange people. First they tilled the soil that life might be sustained. They built homes that their families might be sheltered. They worked together to build their Zion. They believed that "the glory of God is intelligence," as did John in Biblical times, "Ye shall know the truth, and the truth shall make you free."

Joseph Smith reinstated the ancient law of tithing—a principle pronounced in Biblical days and recorded in Malachi. It had been the law of God to his people in Abraham's day and in the times of the prophets who had followed him. Now God's people would again be tithed; all members would pay one-tenth of their income annually. The men of the settlement would be asked to spend every tenth day working on the temple, tithing their time as well as their increase. That way everyone would share in the burden of building the temple. It seemed a fair way to do it.

Jenny, Richard and the girls stood beside Aaron's bed. He opened his eyes, and shut them again quickly.

"It's me, Aaron, your sister," Jenny ventured.

"I don't have a sister," said Aaron, his voice harsh and strained, his eyes dropping.

The air of the room hung tense, expectant about them.

"Yes, you do, Aaron Hale," Jenny cried, a note of hysteria in her voice. She felt angry in spite of his evident condition. "Look at me," she commanded, her eyes narrowing.

With a sharp intake of breath and a quick glance upward, Aaron looked at her, grudgingly at first, then his eyes opening wide with wonder. She didn't look unhappy or mistreated, in fact her eyes sparkled with a shine he hadn't seen there in years.

Her composure regained, she looked squarely and a little hard into his dark eyes behind their bushy eyebrows, then tossed her red locks defiantly.

"What on earth are you doing here?" The tone of her voice insisted on an answer.

"I'm not here by choice, but by grim necessity," he said, looking around the small cabin.

"Don't be ridiculous," Jenny said. "What are you doing in Missouri?"

Aaron, a trifle abashed, did not answer.

Richard stepped forward with his hand extended. "It's good to see you again, Aaron," he said, "whatever your business might be."

Aaron frowned up at him, ignoring the outstretched hand; his eyes gave a hard unwelcome. Then slowly he began to laugh, as though he had just heard a joke. The laughter trickled out of his open mouth in a slow, thin stream—softly at first, then a roaring guffaw. It hurt his head and brought tears to his eyes.

"I came here to kill you, you sonofabitch, and to rescue Jenny from the Mormons. That's why I'm here. We thought she had to be plain crazy to leave the comfort and security of her home and go out into a wilderness full of savages and wild animals. Either that, or she was abducted by her husband, and I decided on the latter."

Anna gave a little gasp and everyone's mouths flew open, then an electric silence followed.

"Well, I don't need rescuing," Jenny finally said with a firm voice. "But it looks, Aaron Hale, like you're the one who's been rescued."

Aaron leaned back against the pillows, as if he needed some support to steady him and shut his eyes.

"To love is much more fun than to hate," piped up Sarah.

"This is Sarah and Laura, our twins," Jenny said presenting the girls.

"Where did you get twins," he asked. "Was I unconscious that long?"

They're Richard's brother, Tom's, girls," Jenny explained. We're keeping them for a while for him."

"Oh," said Aaron, "I know who Tom is, I wrote to him. But I didn't know you had his girls."

"What I don't understand," he said thoughtfully, "is how people could give up everything they have and choose hardship and danger for some crackpot religion."

"Because God is marching right by our side," Anna quickly answered, "and this isn't a crackpot religion. You don't know us or you wouldn't be talking that way."

Aaron looked at her thoughtfully, contriteness in his eyes. "After what's happened to me, I'm not sure but what you're right," he sighed. He laughed again, a depth of unresolved pain beneath his outward humor. He felt a numbness, perhaps something to do with shock.

In spite of herself, a tiny grin tugged at Jenny's mouth. "Sometimes blessings come in the blackest of disguises," she said. Then turning to Mr. Morris, who had just come into the room, she asked, "Do you think he could be moved?"

"I don't think it would be a good idea for a while," Mr. Morris responded. "His leg is in pretty bad shape. I set the break and Anna has been treating it with herbs and poultices, but the infection is still strong. His leg probably should have been amputated, but if anyone can save it, Anna can," he said with confidence. "She learned healing from her late mother."

Jenny looked at the two and felt their evident concern. The room looked neat and clean and the young girl seemed to be quite competent. "We'll come to see him often," she conceded.

Resentment crept back into Aaron's tone. "You can come to see me, as long as you don't try to make a Mormon out of me," he said, then closed his lips tightly and fell grudgingly silent.

CHAPTER ELEVEN

Election day fell on August 6, 1838. William P. Peniston, a candidate for the state legislature, told the old
settlers that if the Mormons were allowed to vote, other settlers of the area would soon lose their rights.

"I don't think you should try to vote this time," Jenny
told Richard as she shooed the chickens from the doorstep.
"It looks like there might be trouble."

Richard looked as though he couldn't believe his ears.
"Do you think I'm going to sit here and let some idiot scare
me away from exercising my Constitutional right to vote?"
he asked, his voice incredulous. "What kind of a coward do
you think I am?"

Jenny shook her head. Richard certainly could not be
called a coward; that created the problem. If trouble erupted, he would be in the thick of it. She felt Richard becoming
more and more angry at the injustices the Mormons were
expected to endure. She could feel his building wrath and
scorn for the acts of their enemies. While he had a great
deal of admiration for Joseph Smith and believed he was di-
vinely called to be a prophet, he couldn't help but wonder
how much persecution his people would be expected to endure. Would they be expected to suffer insults and injustices

forever? Whenever he heard of mob injustice, he felt his hackles rise. Hate was beginning to spread inside him like a poison. He and Jenny never discussed it, but his anger began to seep silently into every crevice of their relationship.

Jenny stood motionless in the yard and watched Richard mount his horse. He rode over beside her, his eyes meeting hers with forced unconcern. He leaned down and planted a kiss on her forehead. "Don't worry, honey, I'll be back before nightfall," he assured her, then waved to the girls and turned his horse toward the county seat at Gallatin.

Jenny continued to stand motionless, hugging herself as if to hold herself together, and watched him ride off until the sky and the rider became one. She swallowed, trying to dislodge the lump in her throat, but it didn't move. "Please God," she prayed silently, "keep him safe."

The girls stood there beside her with their bare toes in the warm, gray August dust. A hawk sailed through the clear sky, casting its shadow along the edge of the yard. Jenny shooed at the chickens with her apron.

"Sarah, Laura, chase that hawk away before it gets some of our chickens," she called. The girls started throwing rocks at the predator when it again circled the yard. Jenny couldn't help but notice Laura's accurate aim.

Jenny watered the lilac bush, finally taking hold and showing a spurt of growth. She went inside and closed the door, then in the kitchen paced up and down along the side of the rag rug, pulling up sharply in front of the table. Her eyes fell upon the two books lying there—the family Bible and Book of Mormon which Richard usually read aloud from in the evenings.

"What de matter?" Mandy asked, noticing her restlessness. "It's nothing," she snapped, her tone more harsh than she expected. She picked up the mush kettle, then set it back down. She picked up the dust rag and dusted this and that. She walked into the school room and straightened the benches. It would soon be time for the children to be here.

All the joy of the last few months felt lost in the agonizing present. School was a godsend for Jenny that day. While working with the children she had little time to think of anything else. Ezra was striving so with his reading, and she wondered if Isaac would ever learn to spell. She made a mental note that she and Mandy needed to knit some new hats and gloves for the four Wilson children before winter. Widow Wilson was having a real struggle to provide for her family.

When school let out, she asked the Wilson children to stay a minute, and sent them home with a pail of milk Daniel Hyde had brought her that morning and a small sack of grain. They would not need the milk tonight before they milked Rosie, and she didn't feel like dealing with making butter or cheese right now. She wondered if she would soon be a widow like Mrs. Wilson, but forced the unwanted thought from her mind, and set about cooking Richard's favorite dinner. The walls of the kitchen seemed to close in about her, suffocating her. Richard was still not home at supper time. By now the whole family was worried and they ate in tense silence.

When the table was cleared and dishes finished, Jenny put on an old sweater. Mandy took the milk pail from its peg beside the door and headed toward the barn to start the evening chores. Jenny looked at the long faces of the twins. Sarah's delicate face looked unusually pale in its frame of dark brown hair.

"Put on your wraps and go out and see if there are any more eggs," she told them. "When you've finished that bring in some wood."

The evening shadows were beginning to lengthen across the lawn. The chickens wandered about looking for night bugs. While Mandy milked Rosie and the girls gathered the eggs, Jenny scattered a handful of the precious grain in the straw and the chickens assembled in wild disorder to scratch for the few kernels. She fed the pigs some corn and watered the horses. After Mandy finished milking, she took the bucket of milk and poured half of it into the trough for the pigs. "Give Rosie a handful of grain to keep her milk production up," Jenny told Mandy. It was good the new wheat crop was almost ready to harvest. Jenny felt they could spare a few kernels for the animals, though they had to be careful or their supply would not last through the winter.

A gust of wind stopped her in her tracks, whipping her long skirts about her ankles. "There's a storm brewing," she said mechanically to herself and yelled for the girls to come inside. Back in the house, Mandy strained the milk, put a towel over the clean bucket and set it to cool. Jenny picked up an English prayer book, one of the treasures she had brought to Missouri. It had belonged to her grandmother. She looked outside and noted the evening's fast-diminishing light and the approaching storm, then, feeling every one of her twenty-seven years, sat in the rocker, her body, mind and soul all aching from weariness. Mandy glanced at her anxiously, then both lapsed into an awkward silence.

This had always been Jenny's favorite time of day—this in-between time just before candle lighting. That hour between dusk and dark when everyone in the family returned home from wherever they might be earlier in the day; when the sun's rays kissed the world goodnight and she felt the deep contentment which comes at the end of a work-filled day. Now she felt the air heavy with gloom and disaster. She rose and began poking the fire, then sat down again and tried to look calm, but her hands were pleating and unpleating a corner of her apron.

A burst of rain, carried by wind, swept around the south corner of the house and banged the window shutter loose. Jenny thought about how much she depended upon Richard. With him she felt strong and capable. Without him she would be unable to endure the endless days, the interminable nights, the excruciating loneliness of life, and the persecutions they might be called upon to endure. Their marriage was one of love and unity. She ran her hands through her hair, then her elbows dropped to the rocker arms.

"Richard, please come back, I need you so," she whispered softly, then opened the prayer book and began to read.

Dark enveloped the area by the time she heard hoof beats. Jenny ran to the door, with Mandy and the girls right behind her, as Richard rode up. His face and shirt were covered with blood. Jenny took one look at him and let out a little scream.

"I'm okay," Richard assured her as he dismounted.

"What happened?" they all gasped.

"Peniston's men were there in force to keep us from voting, a jolly good fight ensued and a few heads were cracked— nothing serious," said Richard.

Mandy took the horse to the barn and Jenny took Richard into the house. "Get a basin of water and a wash rag," she told Sarah. Jenny had noticed Sarah didn't become squeamish at the sight of blood during recess at school, if one of the kids got a nosebleed or minor injury, like most of the girls.

The dried blood looked even worse in the candlelight, but Jenny found a cut on Richard's forehead which seemed to be responsible for his bloody appearance. "I'm hungry. How I could go for a bowl of fresh baked bread and milk!" he said.

Jenny laughed, "Just like a man, always thinking of food."

After Jenny cleaned and bandaged Richard's head, she sent the twins to bed and gave him his supper. That night, as she snuggled closely against Richard's warm body, she welcomed the patter of the rain which seemed to be cleaning and restoring the world.

———————

The episode in Gallitin would have been only a minor incident, but for the consequences which followed. When the Mormon men gained the upper hand, Peniston's men withdrew to take up arms. An exaggerated report of the conflict quickly reached Far West, and another group of men went to investigate. They found no problem and started back to Far West. On their way they called on Justice of the Peace Adam Black, and obtained a paper from him to the effect he was peaceably disposed toward the Mormons and would not take up with any mob.

Enemies of the Mormons, including Justice Black, later signed an affidavit saying that five hundred armed Mormons had gone into Gallitin to do harm to the non-Mormons there. This falsehood acted as a match to a pile of straw. Distorted reports circulated daily. The majority of the settlers knew little of the Mormons and had no way of knowing about these new settlers except from rumors, the press and ministers preaching against them. Misunderstandings and renewed persecutions resulted, but among those well acquainted with the Saints, stood many whose friendship and acts of kindness continued throughout the persecution.

Avowed anti-Mormon of Jackson County days, Lilburn W. Boggs, had become governor. Reports sent to him stated that the Mormons were in insurrection, that they refused to submit to the law, and that they were preparing to make war on the old settlers.

———————

As cold winter winds whistled through Far West, Jenny began to feel a vague discontent and realized it must be homesickness for her old home, for her father and mother, and for her brother, Aaron. She couldn't bear to think of how they must feel. Though she was grown and a wife herself, and mothering two twin girls, she longed to feel her own mother's love–to be able to talk to her once again. Leaving under stress without the usual tearful goodbye, left her missing the assurance that she was really loved by her family. She didn't even dare write home or try to contact them. She loved and resented her mother in almost equal portions. It wasn't right that she should be required to choose between her religion and her family. It was as if she didn't have a family. She felt like an orphan.

———————

Joseph returned to Kirtland in December. Occasional word brought to Far West showed him kept constantly in the courts there on one trumped up charge after another. A little over a month later, in January 1838, Joseph Smith, Brigham Young, and Sidney Rigdon, with their families, again joined the Saints in Missouri. Jenny was taken by surprise one evening when she answered a knock at the door to find Joseph standing there.

"Brother Joseph! Come in, come in," she exclaimed.

He ducked coming through the door so as not to hit his head on the door frame, and entered their cabin. Richard, just fixing the fire in preparation for their daily scripture reading, stood and brushed his hands off on his britches before holding out a hand to the prophet.

"This is a pleasant surprise," he said. "What brings you here?"

"We were forced to flee from Kirtland to save our lives from an angry mob," Joseph told them.

"Is Emma here with you?" Richard asked.

"Yes," said Joseph, "we stopped among friends, sixty miles to the west, until our families could join us."

"It must have been a difficult trip this time of year," Richard said, thinking of the challenge of their trek to Missouri during summer months when conditions were almost ideal.

"The weather seemed extremely cold, and we were often obliged to seclude ourselves in our wagons to elude the grasp of our pursuers, who chased us more than two hundred miles from Kirtland."

"They chased you that far!" exclaimed Richard.

"Yes," said Joseph, "and they were armed with pistols and guns and were seeking our lives."

"How did you ever escape from them?"

"They frequently crossed our track, and twice were in the houses where we stopped, once we tarried all night in the same house with them, with only a partition between us. We heard their oaths and threats concerning us if they could catch us."

"Weren't you frightened half to death?" Jenny asked. Joseph smiled at her, "The Lord protected us. Late one evening they came into our room and examined us, but decided we were not the men they were looking for. At other times we passed them in the streets, but they did not recognize us."

"That's amazing," said Jenny. "Do you plan to make your home in Far West now?"

Joseph nodded.

"It will be wonderful to have you and your family here in Far West with us," Jenny said.

"Won't you join us in our scripture study this evening?" Richard asked.

"I'd love to join you," said Joseph, whose warmth, informality, and personal charm had captivated the family from the first time they had met.

After the twins and Mandy retired, Joseph talked with Richard and Jenny for a long time.

Jenny felt happy Emma would be in Far West. It wasn't good for couples to be separated. She was quickly taken with the tall dark-haired and dark-eyed Emma, whom she found striking. They became fast friends. Emma, both versatile and cultured, had a definite air of femininity about her. Jenny marveled at her faith and reliance on God. There was no bitterness evident, only sorrow, when she told Jenny of their first-owned home in Harmony, Pennsylvania, where their son was born and died and the infant buried in the McKune cemetery between the home of her parents, the Hales, and the Smith home. Emma, too, had come so near to death's door.

Here, also, they had been threatened by mobs, only held in check by the influence of the Hale family. From Harmony they had moved to Kirtland then to Hiram, Ohio. By the time they moved to Missouri, she had three small children— twins and a son, Joseph.

"Sometimes I wonder," said Jenny, "is it really worth the while–the sacrifices, the struggles, the giving up of comforts, pleasantries and niceties of living such as we knew before? Back in New York there is still the ease and loveliness we grew up with..."

"Oh, I know," said Emma. "It's easy to wonder, but I feel this is what we are supposed to be doing. Our job is to learn to love and serve one another."

Emma was certainly serving others. Her home was always filled with people in need of help–the poor, the sick, the temporarily homeless. She always went about her tasks with great diligence and zeal, despite occasional physical weakness, pregnancy, arduous toil, poverty and frequent moves from one home to another. She served as an inspiration to Jenny and many of the other Mormon women while she worked to help make the Saints comfortable in Missouri.

"We don't ask for an easy life," Emma said, "We ask, instead for strength to live through a hard one if it comes."

Jenny loved to hear Emma sing. Emma had an unusually fine voice and sang as she went about her work. Often in the meetings, she would accompany the assemblies of the Saints during congregational singing with an improvised obligato, her high, clear soprano soaring, true and beautiful, above the harmonies of the crowd below.

Emma had been directed to make a selection of hymns for use of the Church. These sacred hymns were arranged and revised for printing by W. W. Phelps and published under the title A Selection of Sacred Hymns by Emma Smith.

"The hymns we sing, speak what we are and what we believe," she told Jenny as she showed her the book. "It's a great responsibility. Sorrow, faith, hope and courage, trust and obedience, joy and thanksgiving all speak from the heart in our songs."

Emma gave a great sigh. "I was asked to do this once before. The first issue of The Evening and Morning Star in Independence carried some hymns from those I collected. Others followed until twenty-six had been printed, but in July 1833, our printing press and much material was destroyed," she said sadly.

Some evenings when weather permitted, sharing Emma's love for music, a small group of friends would gather on the porch of Joseph and Emma's home, and sing the songs of Zion. The Harris women and girls loved these special evenings and the break they afforded from grim reality.

Jenny thrilled to the words of "The Spirit of God Like a Fire is Burning." Mandy's voice rose strong in this hymn which she took a particular liking to. Emma showed them this popular hymn in the first Church hymnbook which she had compiled, and told them it had been sung at the Kirtland Temple dedication. She turned the book pages to the song "Great is the Lord."

"The words to this hymn were written by Eliza R. Snow, a talented young woman who lived in our home and taught our children," she told Jenny, then softly began to sing the words.

Emma was pregnant again, but nothing seemed to slow her down. Things were hard for the wives of Church leaders and others who had to be away so much, thought Jenny. She was so thankful to have Richard by her side.

The girls cleared the supper table, washed and dried the dishes and flung the dish water out the door. A loud knock sent Sarah and Laura running back to the door. Jenny looked at the two girls standing in the doorway, and marveled at how they were growing. Almost faster than a weed patch, she thought. Their slender bodies would soon blossom from long-legged girlhood into young womanhood. They were so sweet. At going on ten, they were at that half-woman, half-little girl stage.

"Aunt Jenny, can we play out?" Sarah asked.

Jenny walked over to the doorway. Several of the neighboring kids were waiting for her answer. Alice and Adeline Wilson, Mary Hansen, David Hyde and Bill Coombs stood behind Sam Hill at the door. It was about an hour before dark, but she worried about the girls whenever they were out of sight.

With conditions as they were, no one was safe. Bad things were happening to the Saints in Missouri. Mobs were harassing the outlying farms and several homes had been set on fire, women raped, and murder was not uncommon. People in outlying areas had been instructed to move into Far West. The Harris residence was within the confines of the town, but she still worried.

Sarah and Laura looked at her questioningly. "For a while," Jenny replied, "but you'll have to be in before dark."

They were out the door in a flash and joined the group that was filling the air with laughter and shouting. "Let's play hide and go seek," Sarah yelled. "I'm 'it'."

"Don't anyone go too far away," Jenny cautioned before going back inside. "It's almost dark."

Sarah leaned against the southwest corner of the house, shut her eyes, and started to count, "One, two, three..."

The kids scattered in every direction. There wasn't really a lot of places to hide. Laura and Mary ran behind the house, David and Bill disappeared into the corn patch and the dry stocks rose above their heads. Sam tried to make himself slim enough not to be seen behind the corner post of the pig pen.

"Ollie, Ollie, Ollie, here I come," shouted Sarah. She slipped down the north side of the house toward the corn field where she could see the grubby faces of John and George Wilson peering out from the corn. But Sam, seeing his chance to beat her to home, suddenly made a run for the corner of the house. Sarah heard his pounding feet and turned to dash back, trying to tag him. They arrived at almost the same instant and she slapped him on the back just as he slammed against the house.

"Home free," yelled Sam.

"Out," yelled Sarah defiantly.

"No way," shouted Sam. "I was in before you touched me."

"No you weren't," insisted Sarah.

While they argued, Laura and Mary slipped around the house and suddenly ran for it. "Home free," they shouted in unison. When Sarah didn't seem to care all of the others ran in.

"I touched you first," Sarah yelled again as she started to cry. "It's not fair," she wailed. "Sam was out, and now because of him everybody got in free." She stamped her foot, and said, "I'm not going to play. You don't play fair."

"Baby!" Sam taunted. This brought forth a group of similar insults and taunts from some and protests from others. They all began to yell at each other. Jenny appeared in the doorway.

"Come on, Sarah," Laura said, "I'll be it for you this time."

"Okay," Sarah agreed reluctantly, "but it isn't fair, Sam was out."

Laura turned her back, folded her arms against the cabin, leaned her head on her arms and with eyes shut began to count. Jenny went back inside. She liked to let the children settle things themselves, rather than interfere whenever possible.

Sarah headed into the corn field. She slipped deeper into the corn stocks nursing her imagined wounds. "They'll be sorry when they can't find me," she said softly to herself. She could barely hear the rhythm of Laura's steady counting and that faded away as she slipped farther into the field until she could only hear faint echoes of laughter and shouting.

She heard the thunder of hooves in the distance, and realized with a start that she had come to the roadway along the far edge of their land. She peeked through the corn at the edge of the field and saw a cloud of dust. A group of horsemen had just gone by. A terrible feeling of panic almost overcame her. It would be dark—pitch black—before she could get back to the house. It would be quicker to walk down the road.

CHAPTER TWELVE

All at once a lone horseman galloped up. Sarah didn't hear him until it was too late to hide.

"Well, well, what have we here!" he taunted, looking at her in a way which made Sarah's flesh crawl. "It must be my lucky day."

Sarah screamed so loudly it made her throat hurt and started to run, but his whip snapped against her back, and she cried out in pain. She fell to her knees, then began to crawl backwards into the cornfield.

"Stay right where you are," he ordered, and Sarah knew she could only comply—her body couldn't seem to move. Besides, he sat there with his whip cocked and a grim look on his face which conveyed his intention if she didn't obey his order. She felt gripped with terror at what was about to happen, whatever it might be. He was off the horse in an instant and grabbed her roughly. He threw her onto her back on the ground, then he was on top of her with a hand firmly covering her mouth. Her nose told her there was liquor on the breath of the attacker. She bit his hand and tried to scream. "You make one sound, and I'll kill you, you little Mormon bitch," he said leering at her. Sarah could tell he meant what he said.

Sarah was terrified. Her insides began to quiver. Her heart came up in her throat, but she dared not cry out, even though his hands were now busy prodding her all over, then he began ripping her dress off. She lay there flooded with pain, fear, and hatred. She couldn't believe this unspeakable thing was happening to her. She knew it would do no good to again try to scream. She was too far from the cabin for her screams to be heard above the laughter and shouts of the other children playing.

Richard stroked his knife deftly against the whetstone until it had a sharp, shining edge. Then he picked up the rifle and ran a greased rag through its barrel. The log in the fireplace crackled and bright flames licked its sides as it gave itself to providing heat for the cabin. He sighted through the barrel of the rifle, into the firelight.

Richard felt both fear and anger within him. He had quickly summoned neighbors and searched for Sarah's attacker, but to no avail. Sarah was a pretty girl, and just at that pre-adolescent age when this would be a fatal blow to her future. No man would want to marry her now.

He would like to kill the beast that did this to her, but the fiend had gotten clean away. He momentarily imagined himself shooting the man in the head, then stomping his brains out. He dismissed the thought in disgust. Was he becoming as bloodthirsty as the mobbers? He felt weak and helpless.

Jenny had always felt a thrill of admiration for Richards good looks—even the tired distinction of his face after a long day. But now his eyes were ringed with black fatigue and there seemed weariness in every line of his body. She saw something else there that frightened her. She had heard him talk of his temper as a young man, but she hadn't experienced that side of his personality. To Jenny, Richard had always been a tall symbol of security, keeping his head in any crisis. But lately, even before Sarah's misfortune, he seemed possessed by a fierce anger so intense it was almost frightening.

Jenny walked over and put a hand on his shoulder. He leaned forward and looked at her with hard, brown eyes. "It isn't right, it just isn't right. Our people have nowhere to go. They don't know where to run, where to hide, what to do to keep the mobs from destroying them and the ones they love. And our government, which should be protecting us, is encouraging our enemies." He shook his head. "It just isn't right," he repeated with savage hostility. The harshness in his voice was such an abrupt change from his usual warm tone it frightened Jenny.

"Come to bed," Jenny encouraged. "Mandy is sitting with Sarah for the first half of the night."

He loaded the gun and set it carefully beside the bed. "Life is like a dog with an uncertain temper," he said bitterly. "You never know what moment it may turn and bite you."

With a sigh, Richard followed Jenny into their bed, but sleep did not come for either of them. Jenny lay and wept beside her leaden spouse, while Richard told himself he must get a grip on his feelings. Unable to comfort one another, each staggered beneath the price young Sarah had paid in their quest for religious freedom and wondered what more would be demanded of their family in the future.

Morning came after an eternity of waiting. Richard went to care for the animals. He watched the old sow and her young pigs, now almost grown. "Those mobbers are no better than animals," he shouted as he doubled his fist and hit the fence post, almost unaware of the pain it caused and the small trickle of blood across his knuckles.

The Missourian mob was completely out of control and Richard was tired of his people being their unwitting quarry. Sarah hadn't been the only victim that night. Three houses on the northern outskirts of Far West had been set afire; sheep, cattle and horses had been driven off; several women had been raped and an elderly couple from Denmark, named Larsen, who tried to defend their property died of the injuries they received. The muscles of his throat convulsed. He felt guilty that his brother's daughter had not been safe in his care. He wished Jenny had not insisted on taking the twins with them. If she hadn't insisted on bringing them, this would never have happened. He had known it wasn't a good idea at the time.

Jenny walked out behind the house, hoping to comfort Richard or receive some comfort herself, but now, in a bitter mood after a wakeful night, he lashed out at her. "I told you we shouldn't take the twins, but you weren't happy until we had them. Now look what has happened!"

His words, hot and sharp, cut like a knife. Tears started running down Jenny's cheeks. Richard felt immediately sorry for the outburst, but the damage had been done. He squared his jaw and turned away. It gave him a sick feeling deep inside–humiliation, defiance and part shame that he had failed Sarah, Jenny, his brother...

His thoughts popped back to when he was a boy. He had tried so hard to make his father proud of him, but it was always Tom who received his parent's praise–dependable Tom who always did what was expected and kept his temper under control, something it had taken Richard years to do. Now the anger, hurt and pain came flooding back. He kicked open the door to the barn, breaking the latch. He kicked the door again. He was angry at the mobber for the harm he had done to Sarah, angry at God for letting such a terrible thing happen to an innocent girl, angry at himself for not being there to protect her.

All he could do was look on helplessly. Not only the ugly contusions and abrasions, but the terror he saw in the child's sensitive face, the pain in her eyes, brought a catch to his throat. He wondered why he had ever brought the women he loved to this raw, thinly settled frontier where they must suffer shameless abuse at the hands of their enemies.

Sarah closed her eyes and tried to slip back into the merciful oblivion of sleep, but it was no use. She struggled desperately to think of other things but the more she tried, the more what had happened to her intruded into her consciousness and she lay there shivering. Just when she thought she might be on the edge of gaining it, sleep would slip from her grasp once more and she would have to face shattering reality. She prayed she would find this a nightmare which would go away when she awoke, but the throbbing pain between her thighs told her it would not.

She could not shut out the cruel face hanging in her mind, sharpened by dark of night or closing of her eyelids. Closing her eyes did not shut out her thoughts. Sometimes she saw him in the form of a pig, other times as a bear or a snake, but always with that cruel and leering expression. She hated the man, whoever he was. Her eyes grew hot with rage and tears and she began to shake uncontrollably.

The sun shone through a crack in the chinking between the logs. Laura had been bundled off to Mary's house the night before.

Mandy entered the room bringing a blanket, warmed by the fireplace. She wrapped it around Sarah and held her in her arms for a while just as she had held her as a small child, but nothing could stop the shaking of Sarah's bones as she started to cry, softly at first, then almost hysterically.

"You'll be okay, Missy," Mandy crooned. "Just rest and don't think about it."

Mandy's voice quivered as she remembered holding her own daughter when she had been ravaged by a white man. Sarah could not look at Mandy as she spoke. Mandy knew she couldn't make this thing that had happened not be. After a while it would heal like a burn or a cut, but it would leave a scar.

Sarah felt wicked and dirty; she felt an uncleanliness that could not be washed away; she felt she would never come clean again. For the hundredth time she relived the horror of it all. She felt bewildered, terrified by what had happened and by its meaning; she was engulfed in shame. She wondered what terrible thing she was guilty of that God had turned his back on her. Was he punishing her for not listening to her aunt?

She wished she had screamed her lungs out, and bit and hit her attacker and that he had killed her. From bits and pieces of conversation she heard the word "rape." The word had such terrible overtones.

She feigned sleep, and Mandy laid her down and went downstairs. She clutched the warm blanket tightly about her. Soon she could hear Mrs. Hansen in the kitchen talking to her mother. Their voices rose and fell while Sarah lay in her bed staring into her nightmare.

Sarah heard Miriam laugh and wondered how anyone could laugh at a time like this. Then their voices fell and Sarah knew they were talking about her. Her heart began beating hard and her face flushed with embarrassment, even though alone in the loft. If only she hadn't disobeyed and run so far into the corn field that night. She thought of Sam. She really did like him. He was her secret boyfriend and had asked her to marry him when they grew up. No one will ever want to marry me now, she thought, her mind going over the terrible words she had heard Richard say. The hot tears again ran down her cheeks.

Sarah knew she was considered pretty. Sam said that she was the prettiest girl in the school and she was the most popular. But the other kids would laugh at her because of this. How could she ever go to school on Monday, she thought with trepidation. The small, two-room cabin provided little privacy—no place to hide from the stares and giggles of the other kids.

Just last week Brother Hansen had told Richard and Jenny, "Every time I see that girl, she's a shade prettier."

She wondered now if this was what he had in mind. You couldn't trust men or boys. They were dumb; they thought they were better than girls. It was all Sam's fault this had happened. If he hadn't insisted on being "home safe," none of this would have happened, she thought to herself, then knew at once she couldn't blame Sam. She saw the man's face again in her mind, terrible and frightening. Rape—she had heard the word several times, and wondered what it meant. Now she knew, but wished she had never learned the meaning.

Somehow Sarah made it through the day and the following night. Morning came and the family began getting ready for church.

"I'm not going," Sarah announced loudly.

"It's okay," said Jenny, "Mandy will stay here with you."

Sarah could not bear the thought of going to church ever again. She could not stand the thought of rows and rows of prying eyes peering at her, some showing pity and others just curiosity, or of those who would shake her hand and put on false smiles pretending nothing had happened. She was sure the whole congregation knew.

Sarah had learned the hard way that there were hazards all around her, that not all men were kind and loving like her Uncle Richard. The attack had painfully altered her tender childhood trust and she would never return to a state of innocence. She had been the unwitting prey of one of the worst cruelties of man to a young girl.

Everyone returned from church. While Richard picked Laura up from the Hansen's, Jenny whipped the potatoes to a white froth, cut large slices of bread—though her hands made the bread knife tremble—and filled the cups with milk.

Sarah usually giggled too much, but now her face looked wild and terrified, and she couldn't even meet the eyes of anyone in the family. No one could bear to look at her. Laura seemed totally confused as to what was happening. In spite of the tantalizing food, dinner became an ordeal.

Jenny and Mandy tried to fill the air with forced chatter, but it was broken by ominous silences. Sarah sat at the table and toyed with her fork, moving her food from place to place, but eating little. She spent most of the time looking down at her hands. The usual light-hearted banter of mealtime was absent and the electric silence seemed to permeate the house, the air prickling with it.

Jenny stared at the wall, wondering what her own mother would have done in a situation like this. She missed her mother so much, she thought, and a lump formed in her throat. She knew Richard was trying not to blame her for what had happened, but he was right—she was the one who had insisted on taking the girls.

"Let's take the wagon and go over to see Brother Joseph and Emma this afternoon," Richard suggested. "I need to talk to the prophet."

The twins loved to go over to see the prophet and his family.

"I don't want to go anywhere," Sarah insisted.

"I'll stay home with Sarah," Jenny said quickly.

Richard could understand why Sarah felt unable to face going to church. It was difficult for him, too. During lunch he proposed the wagon ride, hoping to ease the tension, but he found himself taking Laura and Mandy for a ride while Jenny attended to Sarah.

As the wagon pulled up in front of Joseph's cabin, the prophet came out to meet them. He patted the sorrel mare on the withers, then held out a hand to help Mandy out of the wagon.

"Hello," he said soberly. "I hear there was trouble out at your place Friday night, Richard. I was just getting ready to come over."

He turned to Mandy and Laura. "Emma is in the kitchen finishing up the dishes. Go on in, she'll be delighted to see you."

He paused until they were inside then turned back to Richard. "I'm sorry," he said quietly, and Richard could see the pain in his eyes. "I don't know how much indignation our people will be called to bear before we find a place where we can live in peace." He got a faraway look in his eyes, "It's far from over," he added.

Richard felt a fresh burst of anger as a feeling of utter helplessness surged over him. "How can these men even be called human? They're animals, beasts, that's all they are!"

Joseph looked at him gravely, with eyes that were almost hidden under a heavy frown. Then he laid a hand on Richard's shoulder. "Eliza is on her way over to talk to Sarah. She's a highly intelligent woman and so good with children. Perhaps she can help the child."

Richard felt somewhat relieved in the pit of his stomach. Sarah had loved and looked up to Eliza from the moment she had met her. Maybe she could help her at this time.

"How are the Larsen children taking this?" Richard asked.

"I spent most of the day yesterday with them, helping make arrangements for the funeral tomorrow and the burial," Joseph said, suddenly looking terribly tired. "It's a real blow to all of them."

Jenny and Sarah heard the far-away tinkle of tug chains and thought the family was returning. When the soft knock came on the door, Sarah ran into the back room, slamming the door behind her. Jenny gave a small gasp of surprise when she saw Eliza standing there, then threw her arms around her friend and began to sob. Eliza comforted her until she could talk.

"What have we done to deserve this?" Jenny asked with a cynical laugh. "We've hoped, we've prayed, we've worked, we've tried to be good neighbors…"

Deep lines in Jenny's face and eyes filled with great weariness and made her look as though the last few hours had turned her into an old woman. The weight of brooding words, both expressed and unspoken, crowded her aching heart. This was a hard experience.

Eliza reached down into a crack in the frame of the open doorway and picked up a large butterfly, with its wings frayed and singed. She set it upon her open hand and they both gazed at its beauty, ravished and broken. "You haven't done anything wrong," said Eliza. "I suspect that before this is over we will all be tested to the limits of our endurance."

Sarah heard Jenny talking to someone, but when the door opened her hands lifted protectively against her chest. Sarah just knew this woman she looked up to so much was thinking of how she looked when she finally dragged herself out of the corn patch that night, hysterical with fright and pain, trying to hide her nakedness in the few rags that were left of her dress. But Eliza talked softly and quietly about her misfortune. She didn't try to skirt around it or pretend like nothing had happened.

"It wasn't your fault," she said. "You have to quit blaming yourself. I know you feel terrified and angry, but you have to let God and those around you help you heal."

"There isn't a God," Sarah almost shouted. "If there was, he wouldn't have let this happen." Then she added, "and he wouldn't have let my mother die. My dad said so."

Jenny's reprimand stopped at her lips as Eliza held up a hand to silence her words. Eliza's eyes were steady and clear and her voice firm and measured. "I know you feel that way, Sarah, and who could blame you, but some day you'll feel differently," she said kindly. "It's hard to face the world just now, and especially school tomorrow. I thought you might like to come and spend a few days with me studying poetry writing and sharing some of the poems and songs I have written."

The family hadn't seen much of Eliza since she and her family were living in Adam-ondi-Ahman, but when they came into town, and she dropped in it became a rare treat. Sarah adored Eliza, who always listened to her latest poem and encouraged her efforts.

There was nothing Sarah would like better. For a moment she almost forgot her sorrow, then her face turned serious again. But Eliza didn't give her a chance to relapse into the awful world of reality.

"Hurry and get ready," Eliza said.

"Oh, can I, Aunt Jenny?" Sarah asked.

"You know I'll take good care of her," Eliza said softly.

"I think it's a wonderful idea," Jenny agreed.

Sarah climbed slowly and painfully up to the loft to get her things.

"She'll be okay," Eliza assured Jenny. "She just needs some time and a lot of love. Nature is always ready to give us a new beginning. She eventually covers bad experiences with a cloak of forgetfulness so that we can start afresh."

"I hope so," sighed Jenny

Jenny helped Sarah get ready and half lifted her into the buggy. She knew the wounds of the child's flesh would heal but the wound in the girl's heart would be long in healing, and her own heart ached for her. Sarah was facing a bitter tomorrow and the days after that; life would never be quite the same for her. Jenny watched them drive away before the strength left her. She sank down onto a chair beside the table. "Why? Why?" she repeated over and over. The listening silence gave back no answer.

Burying her head in her arms, she wept almost hysterically. Like the butterfly, it seemed that something within her, too, had died. Was it hope? It had seemed little enough, at first—a privilege to give up home, friends, and even family for the sake of the Gospel when the sentiment of their community had been bitterly antagonistic. They would have a new home in a thriving new community among others who shared their beliefs. Richard, too, had given up much, and had seemed to have no regrets for his sacrifices. They had never dreamed it would come to this!

Jenny sat there a long time. When she finally raised her head she had new light in her eyes. She would carry on—for the sake of her family, she had to. She rose, went to the wash basin and splashed cold water onto her face, then tucked a wisp of graying hair into place with a long hairpin.

Jenny filled the kettle with water and set it over the fireplace blaze. She took a wooden spoon and stirred the stew she and Mandy had prepared for their supper, then added a bit of water with a gourd dipper. When her ear caught the sound of wagon wheels approaching, it lifted her spirits, just as it always did when her family returned home after being away.

———————————

One of the worst experiences of Sarah's life was followed by one of the loveliest times she would ever experience. Eliza kept her so busy she hardly had time to think. She wrote outlandish poems and they laughed at the ridiculous verses until she ached.

"The thrill of creating brings happiness, whether that creation is a bit of handiwork or a poem," Eliza mused. "Poetry is simply the most beautiful and effective way of saying something. We want to be one of those poets who reaches for the stars and even if she can't quite touch them, leaves stardust wherever she touches."

"That's a beautiful thought," said Sarah.

"You're going to grow up to be a great poet," said Eliza.

"Thank you," said Sarah softly.

"Joy comes with every new thing learned and shared with others, so you must avail yourself of every opportunity to improve your talents."

Eliza encouraged her to talk with her about what had happened, and told her over and over again that no matter how badly she hurt now, things would get better.

"Though problems and pains make you feel that things are so wrong believing in God doesn't even make sense, He has great things in store for your future. He didn't say life would be easy, only that it would be worth it."

Sarah turned to the window, "And how do you know, Miss Snow, what is in the future...more pain, perhaps?"

"Yes, more grief and pain," she said softly, but you'll never know how much joy. If you fail to move ahead, you'll stay here always, in one spot, in the place of your anguish. I've seen people do that. Life must not be barren of hope and happiness."

"How can I be happy after what has happened to me?" Sarah asked.

"True happiness comes from a sense of inner purity, a joy or oneness with God. You still have that inner purity—no one can take that away from you without your consent."

Sarah shrugged her shoulders and Eliza wondered if anything she said penetrated Sarah's deep pain and sorrow.

Eliza moved about Sarah's life urging her to reach beyond the present sorrow, when she wanted to hide her head and heart in solitude. She started rolling the dough for biscuits and asked for Sarah's help with the task. She sand-scoured the floor and furniture to breadboard whiteness, and Sarah knelt and worked beside her. Tears rolled freely down her pale cheeks like rain on a windowpane, cleansing her soul.

Disappointment, disillusionment, and wracking pain all blurred into oblivion as she and Eliza worked at one task and then another. They took care of the flowers, the chickens and the vegetable garden. They crocheted lovely lace edgings on handkerchiefs. At times Sarah almost forgot what had happened to her, but when she thought about it, she fairly blazed with indignation over what had been put upon her. She poured out her anger in verse and felt a small measure of relief, but when night and the darkness came, with it came the nightmares. She tried everything she could think of to stay awake, but no matter what she did, her exhausted body eventually fell asleep, and sleep gripped her in terror. She awoke after only a short time, breathing in gasps, feeling the pain and terror all over again. She stayed awake for hours, her eyes searching the darkness for a would-be attacker. Sometimes she would sleep peacefully for a short time, but more often she relived the horror of that night in the cornfield over and over again, night after night. Both night and day, she could feel the closeness of the man who had violated her—when not in her dreams, hiding in dark corners of her mind. She shrank from his presence but could not shake it.

She awoke tired, with eyes sunk in their sockets, but even at this time of pain and sorrow, Sarah enjoyed the company of Eliza and Mother and Father Snow. Mother Snow, a gentle lady, was named Rosella, but everyone called her Mother Snow. Her face was etched with lines, many of them the imprint of courageously borne pain. Her head was full of such interesting stories and she was always ready to share them with Sarah. Eliza's brother, Lorenzo, was unobtrusive, but kind to everyone. He looked so handsome in his black broadcloths for Sunday.

Mother Snow quickly became fond of this slight half-adult, half-child with long dark braids and deep, sad eyes.

Sarah talked to the older woman in an unaffected, mature way, with quiet reserve in her manner.

Eliza seemed always busy and happy. She shared her books with Sarah, as they read together when chores were done.

"The printing press was one of the most important and far-reaching inventions we have," Eliza told Sarah. "It has revolutionized the world."

"Why is it that important?" asked Sarah.

"Books help to pattern our lives. They bring intellectual growth and spiritual development. They contain the wealth of the past, and can beautify the soul. They preserve the finest thoughts and ideas of the greatest men and women throughout the ages."

"I don't read a lot," admitted Sarah.

"You should," said her friend. "Books bring courage, comfort and peace in hours of turmoil and trial. They can also bring sheer enjoyment and wholesome delight. There is little time spent that pays as rich of dividends as that spent with books," added Eliza, as she gave the biscuits she was stirring a stout beat. "My books are a great comfort to me, as is writing poetry."

"I've never thought of books in that way."

"One of my favorite things to read when everything seems wrong is the Twenty-Third Psalm. Just listen to the poetry of it and the comfort it gives in time of trouble," she said, opening the Bible, but reciting from memory:

> The Lord is my shepherd; I shall not want. He maketh me to lie down in green pastures; he leadeth me beside the still waters. He restoreth my soul; he leadeth me in the paths of righteousness for his name's sake. Yea, though I walk through the

valley of the shadow of death, I will fear no evil; for thou art with me; thy rod and thy staff they comfort me. Thou preparest a table for me in the presence of mine enemies; my cup runneth over. Surely goodness and mercy shall follow me all the days of my life; and I will dwell in the house of the Lord forever.

"That's beautiful," said Sarah. "So poetic. I never really listened to it before."

That night Eliza lay beside her and held her in her warm, comforting arms. They talked softly until Sarah was so tired she fell asleep in mid-sentence. Twice she awoke in the night screaming, and several times sat up with a start. Eliza was always there to comfort her.

CHAPTER THIRTEEN

Laura didn't know what to make of the things that had happened. She had the shock of seeing her sister brought home, bruised and bleeding. Jenny had hustled her off to Mary Hansen's home for the next twenty-four hours. She and Mary asked numerous questions, but they were not answered. Everyone seemed secretive and embarrassed.

"The poor girl was taken advantage of," Mary's mother said in answer to their inquiries. "Now run along and play."

Laura thought it was evident Sarah had been taken advantage of—she was bruised and bleeding. But there seemed to be more to what had happened than any of the grown-ups were willing to talk about. She did hear the word "rape" several times.

At morning recess Monday, Joe Rawlins gave a graphic description of rape. Neither Laura or Mary felt willing to believe him, but when Sarah returned home, she confirmed to her sister that his description was accurate by her blushing cheeks and refusal to talk. Laura felt shock beyond belief.

When Sarah started back to classes, Laura thought the other kids treated her sister shamefully. When they chose up sides for ante-I-over, Sarah, who normally would be picked first for almost any activity, was not picked. When she was the only one left, Laura exploded.

"Just what's wrong with my sister?"

"Well," said Lucy who was the captain of one team. "My mother says I can't play with Sarah. She says she has lost her innocence."

"Just what does that mean?" demanded Laura.

"I don't know," said Lucy, turning the toe of her shoe in the dust.

"Well, I'm not playing," said Laura.

"Neither am I," said Sam and they followed Sarah around the corner of the house.

There were tears in Sarah's eyes, and Laura threw her arms around her sister. "Please don't cry," she said. "What happened wasn't your fault, and I hate anyone who thinks it was."

"She's right," said Sam. "I still like you."

Sarah burst into tears and ran into the cabin. Meanwhile Lucy and the other girls had decided to play jump rope. Laura could hear their chant, "Three-cornered square, black as a bear, tell me this riddle or I'll pull your hair." Of course the answer to the riddle was the clumsy, heavy, and slow flatiron the women used to iron their clothing and linens.

Sarah refused to come to school the rest of the day. She climbed into the loft and stayed until the other children left. When she returned the next day, some of the boys whispered remarks to Sarah which made her blush and sometimes caused her to cry.

"I'll bet that mobber had fun with you," said Joe Rawlins. "Or you had fun with the mobber," Thomas Rawlins added.

Sarah turned quickly to hide the sudden tears in her eyes and her trembling mouth. Sam felt filled with rage and red blotches of anger appeared on his face as he doubled up his fist and socked Thomas on the right side of the jaw. Jenny came out and told them they could both stay in from recess for a week. None of the children would tell what the fight was about, but Sam, whatever the cost, was always ready to defend Sarah.

Laura couldn't believe what was happening. Why would the kids tease and shame and hurt her sister, who had already been hurt enough. She hated them all.

Dinner that evening seemed a somber affair as the family fell to eating silently. Laura looked at the members of her family and smothered a sob with a sigh. Richard had anger smoldering in his eyes while Jenny had a determined look and tried to remain optimistic. Mandy had not been her cheerful self since the attack. She kept busy, treading heavy-footed around the house and talked in an equally heavy voice. Sarah felt nervous and unhappy and seemed impossible to talk to. Laura bit her lip. Her heart ached with an actual, physical pain, almost beyond the limit of endurance. When they finished eating, Laura attacked the dinner dishes, her lovely little mouth grim and her eyes rebellious.

Nights for Sarah continued to be pure torture. She lay on her back in her bed, so she could see in all directions and no one could creep upon her from her blind side. She kept her eyes wide open and searched the darkness for a would be assailant. Her whole body froze when she heard the slightest noise. She saw his face in the dark, and tried to fight him off. She tried to scream, but her voice felt imprisoned in her throat with no way to get out. Her lips remained frozen and unable to move. Her chest constricted so she could hardly breathe and her limbs felt paralyzed. Sometimes the nightmares seemed so realistic she didn't know if she were asleep or awake.

"No," she whispered, "please don't hurt me." She tried to run, but her legs would not move. His face kept coming towards her, that wicked smirk on his countenance. Panic rose up inside her as she anticipated what he would do to her and the terrible pain he would cause her. Her stomach tightened into knots of fear.

Sarah's heart pounded, her chest became tighter than the cinch on a horse who failed to inflate his belly while being saddled, and just as impossible to escape from. She tried to hide from her attacker, but he always caught her. She put forth one last effort and a scream of terror rent the night air. Jenny appeared almost instantly. Her strong arms went around Sarah, pulling her close. Jenny felt Sarah stiffen in her arms. She told her everything would be all right, but Sarah didn't feel all right. Everything was all wrong! Even as she spoke the words of comfort, Jenny knew neither she nor Sarah believed them.

Sarah felt exhausted and her nightgown had become soaked with sweat. She felt warmth between her thighs and knew she had wet the bed again. Now she felt additional shame as well as terror. Sarah wished she could just die and get away from what her life had become. She had no idea what time it might be. She wondered how time could creep by so slowly as she lay night after night in the dark, waiting for sleep which when it came, only brought terror and the terrible pain radiating upward into her stomach and downward into her legs.

Sarah began to sob and her whole body shook for what seemed like hours. Jenny and Eliza had told her all this wasn't her fault, but even if they were right, that didn't seem to make it hurt any less. It's only a dream, she told herself, but she could feel the coldness of his eyes, the strength of his grip, and her dreams came so often they had become a second reality. She found herself shuttering.

————————

These weeks were torment itself for Jenny also. Like one suddenly struck dizzy and unable to function properly, she went about her work. She continued to feel responsible for the girls being there and now this horrible thing had happened because of her insistence. It would have been hard enough to bear without Richard throwing it up at her when she tried to talk to him. She couldn't have felt worse if he had slapped her. Her face had burned with resentment and shame as she ran back into the house. Richard's jaw set at a stubborn angle, unusual for him and he turned away with a shrug. It was a nightmare from which she struggled to awaken, but found only ugly reality. She ran her hands through her hair and her fingers caught.

All the principles she lived by were suddenly suspect. Doubts, discontent and turmoil chilled Jenny. Were her convictions strong enough to survive all this grief and terror they were expected to live through, all this hopelessness and fear within herself? She tried to think. She tried to pray, but she could not get the words out. Pangs of anxiety gripped her and huge knots had taken up permanent residence in her chest and stomach.

Jenny's life had always centered about Richard, but now he had withdrawn from her until she felt their emotional paths never touched as they went mechanically about their daily tasks. It seemed Richard was no longer a husband, but a stranger—one to whose thoughts and feelings she was not privileged. She felt an immense loneliness and loss, as if she stood alone in the world. A great bitterness walled up inside her.

School became the only thing that preserved her sanity. Time passed during the school hours; at all other times it maliciously slowed to a crawl. At first, while Sarah was at Eliza's, most of the children pretended nothing had happened. Only Sam asked about Sarah—where she was and if she were okay. When Sarah returned to school there seemed to be a lot of dissention and trouble among the students which had never been there before. Sarah was getting left out of everything and the children said such terrible things to her—things Jenny didn't believe they could think up themselves. They must be hearing these awful things, unchristian as they were, at home. It just wasn't fair. Jenny wondered if it would help to cut out recess.

Mentally Jenny went over the bitter situation. Richard seemed so miserable and irritable. He didn't even mention it or thank her when Jenny made scones for supper. They were his special favorite and he usually at least commented on how good they were. Several times he had risen from the table having hardly touched his meal. An icy barrier of reserve was rising between them.

She and Richard had always discussed things openly, but now they seemed unable to communicate. The deep, potent anger which filled him, kept her from reaching him physically, mentally or spiritually. Jenny almost found it hard to remember how he used to laugh. He sat at the table, his head low between his shoulders and his angry eyes sunk deep in their sockets—though they still had a certain steadiness within them. The face was the same—the same clean-cut lines, the same mouth and eyes—but different somehow. Perhaps the set of his jaw made the difference. The lines at the corners of his mouth had deepened. He looked older and exceedingly tired.

Even Mandy fell strangely quiet. The two women cleared and washed the dishes from each meal in silence, put them carefully in their places and then tidied up the kitchen without saying a word. Shock had turned to anger and then to denial. Jenny wanted to have a heart-to-heart talk with Sarah about her terrible experience, but found it impossible. No one wanted to acknowledge this awful thing had happened; it lay too close to their hearts—too intimate. Jenny longed for the peace and happiness they had felt a few weeks before.

Mobs vowed to drive the Mormons from the state and violence increased daily. A central theme of Latter-day Saint philosophy was that the spirit of man is eternal and progresses through the experiences it undergoes. Jenny wondered how these ghastly experiences could bring growth to anyone's spirit.

As the winter wind howled like a fiend, she looked out at the field of stubble where the golden grain had once waved. The quiet gurgle of the stream froze into silence. She felt all of nature matched her somber mood.

Sarah often curled up into a ball in her bed or in a chair and refused to participate in what the family was doing. She had never been one to sit around and read the scriptures, but now Jenny noted there was often an open Bible or Book of Mormon in her lap. Laura, who usually read constantly, had not opened the scriptures since that horrible day.

One Saturday morning when Laura was at Mary's, Sarah refused to come for breakfast. Jenny had heard her sobbing softly in the night and tried to shut out the sound, not wanting to awaken Richard by slipping out of bed and going to her as she usually did. If only Sarah could be rid of these dreams which drifted out of the darkness, dreams which caused her to relive the horror of that night which ruined all of their lives, nightmares which she couldn't escape. The poor girl felt afraid to go to sleep until the light came and could finally drive the dreams away. There was a heart-tearing quality to the girl's weeping.

Jenny dried her hands on her apron. She went out and asked Richard if she could use his horse, which stood saddled and waiting at the hitching rail. "I'll only be gone to Miriam's for a few minutes," she explained. Jenny had thought of something which she hoped would help—it was worth a try. She made a quick trip to Miriam's, then returned to the house and climbed quietly to the loft where the girls slept.

Jenny stood at the foot of the twins' bed and looked at Sarah, who for once seemed to be sleeping peacefully. She clasped her hands, pressed them tightly against her lips and prayed, "Dear God.." She couldn't continue.

Sarah looked so small and slight she hardly made a swell in the bed covers. Poor little girls! What would become of them? Sarah's experience had touched both of the girls. Bitterness welled up in Laura's soul and ripened into a new cynicism which went deeper because it was unexpressed. She went around with her mouth pulled into a tight little knot.

Sarah turned over and glanced questioningly at Jenny.

"Good morning, Sarah," Jenny said, trying to sound cheerful. "Wouldn't you like to come down and help me finish that patchwork quilt for the Widow Wilson?"

"No, thank you, Aunt Jenny. I'd rather stay here." Her voice sounded mechanically polite.

Sarah lay on her bed, hair stringy and nails unkempt, puzzled lines in her young brow—so unlike the intelligent, well-groomed girl she had always been. She seemed both bone-weary and brain weary. Sarah was becoming more and more withdrawn, and Jenny worried about how to help her deal with her trauma. She wished Eliza were closer so she could talk with her more often. Eliza had helped Sarah so much at first.

Jenny reached into her apron pocket and pulled out a tiny yellow ball of fluff which gave a plaintive "Me-ew."

Sarah's eyes widened. "Oh," she squealed, "It's a kitten!" She sat up and reached out for it. Jenny set the tiny animal in Sarah's hands.

"What a darling little kitten! Look how long its hair is! It's eyes are so blue!" Sarah's eyes filled with a tenderness which had not been there for a long time as she shyly stroked it, then hugged it closely.

"This stray kitten needs someone to care for her, and I thought you might be just the one to do it."

"Oh," breathed Sarah, "She's so tiny!" She held the wee ball of fur up next to her cheek and listened to it purr. "Do you know, when I was little I loved the kittens in the barn! I used to pet them and listen to them purr, then snuggle up to Mandy at night, by the fireplace, and try to purr like a kitten."

The kitten burrowed up against Sarah. Perhaps this was a long-sought answer to a great need. Jenny smiled as she watched the excitement in the girl's face. They looked at each other and began to laugh.

"Bring it down and let's see if we can get it to eat," suggested Jenny. They climbed down the ladder to the kitchen. Jenny warmed a small amount of milk and poured it into a saucer. Sarah brought the orphan kitten and touched its nose into the warm milk, then grinned as she stood and watched it lap the milk up hungrily. Richard and Mandy came in and they all gathered around and stood watching the tiny animal drink warm milk from a saucer.

From then on, the kitten went everywhere with Sarah. She laughed and played with it, and Jenny blessed the day she had seen the tiny, furry animal in Miriam's barn. Sarah named it Sunshine because it brought so much happiness to her and to the whole family. Everyone was pleased to see Sarah again finding some enjoyment in life.

Richard glanced up from his work one Saturday morning. Layers of thick clouds lay parallel to the distant horizon. Suddenly alert, he noted several mounted men riding toward him. As they approached, he recognized Jim Hansen and also fellow Mormon Lt. Colonel George M. Hinkle of the state militia. He held his breath, expecting the worst. The men exchanged hurried glances.

"Good morning, Brother Harris," Colonel Hinkle said.

Richard wondered how it could be a "good morning" with the grim looks on the faces of the visitors who had so rapidly approached. "What brings you here?" he asked with some apprehension. The air around him seemed tense and dry.

Colonel Hinkle shook his head. "Recent events have made it necessary to raise a group of men from among our people to protect our families," he said with a distinct note of urgency in his voice.

Richard raised his eyebrows. He felt a stillness in the air, as all attention turned toward him. He looked steadily at each of the men in turn. He noted the cold anger in the men's eyes and the anguish chiseled deep in their faces.

"A mob besieged Adam-ondi-Ahman, raiding our farms and settlements there. We have been authorized to raise a militia against the mobs," Hinkle continued.

Richard frowned and stood his shovel up beside the wall of the shed. "It's about time someone did something about these killers," he said vehemently. He knew the people in Far West and the surrounding settlements, like himself, felt defenseless and angry. Now, perhaps, they could at least protect themselves.

"The state militia was called out and the mob ordered to disperse, but one group thought DeWitt looked like a ripe plum, waiting to be plucked, so they moved down and cut off the approaches to that hapless settlement. They've been joined by others, and now they've sent to Jackson County for a cannon," Hinkle continued.

"Isn't the state militia doing anything to protect the settlements?" Richard asked, dismay in his voice.

"It doesn't seem they are. The mobbers gave our people in DeWitt an ultimatum, 'We'll give you until October first to get out of here. If you ain't gone by then, we'll come in and wipe you out and throw your goods into the river.' DeWitt is our only river port where goods and immigrants can be landed and Diahman is still in a great deal of trouble."

"Someone has to stop them," Richard cried. "They will destroy us all if we don't. I'd heard rumors of increasing mob activity in the outlying areas."

"However ungodly the rumors, they don't begin to describe what's actually happening," Hinkle responded.

"Will you join us?" Another man asked, sucking his breath through thin lips. "We need the help of every able-bodied man we can get."

"I'd be glad for a chance to help do something about these fiends," Richard answered fervently as he spat into the dust. "Let me get my rifle and I'll be right with you."

"I'll get your horse," said Jim, "while you say goodbye to the family."

Richard strode into the house and with a well-calloused hand reached for his gun. His gestures showed complete confidence in his decision. "I'm joining the militia and going to Diahman," he told Jenny. "Our friends there are in grave danger."

He saw Jenny stiffen beside him. "Oh, no!" she cried, concern showing in her deep green eyes. "Please be careful! We could never get along without you."

Richard wondered for a second if leaving his family unprotected while he ran off to try and stop a mob which greatly outnumbered those fighting against it could actually be the right thing to do. "I hate to leave you here alone, but we have to stop this mob. Death is not an enemy, but living in constant fear is," he added, though he knew the statement sounded oddly out of place to Jenny and would give her little comfort at this precarious time.

He could almost feel, as well as see, Jenny's quick frown before her mouth began to tighten. He held up his hand to stop any comment, then leaned over, put his arm around her and gave her a quick kiss. "Be careful and take good care of the place and of the twins," he said. He gave each of the wide-eyed girls, who still had jam from breakfast on their faces, a peck on the cheek. "I'll feel better knowing you are here to help Jenny," he told Mandy glancing at her soberly.

He had to get out of the house fast before the emotion he felt showed. He turned and strode out the door, shutting it promptly behind him, and joined the men in the front yard. Jim was bringing his horse. Jenny dashed out and handed him his coat. The girls and Mandy stood outside as the men turned to ride off.

"Help take care of Miriam and Mary, will you?" Jim called as they disappeared up the road in a cloud of dust.

Jenny caught her breath as she realized with a shock both she and Miriam had been left to their own devises. A sudden instinctive dread clutched at her heart as she experienced terror one feels when helpless and threatened by an invading army.

Mandy and Laura withdrew into the house. Jenny looked down at Sarah, standing as if rooted to the spot. Sarah's lip quivered as she struggled to hold back her tears, her face pasty white with the unfocused look of hurt in her eyes. Jenny knew she remembered the old pain as well as the new fear and helplessness for both herself and her friends. Sarah's breath caught in an involuntary, childish sob. Jenny gathered the girl into her arms.

"There, there," she soothed. "We must be strong, Sarah," she added from between white lips.

Jenny glanced down at Sarah's tear stained face. She took the girl's shaking shoulders in her hands and turned Sarah towards the light so she could look directly in her eyes. "I never had a daughter," she said, trying hard to keep the tears pushing against her lashes under control. "I always wanted one, and I think I would want her to be just like you."

Sarah lifted her face with an air of new determination. "Thanks, Aunt Jenny," she said. A fleeting smile made the corners of her lips turn up for an instant.

Jenny wiped the tears from the child's eyes and said, "Come now, we have lots to do." She lifted the latch and they entered the cabin. Jenny pulled the creaking door shut behind them.

CHAPTER FOURTEEN

Without Richard, the house seemed quiet and empty, but Jenny found little time for regrets or self-
pity. The present required action which took all of the wom-
en's available energy. The animals had to be taken care of and
the outside chores done as well as the usual inside tasks.

It seemed unsafe to hold school in this environment, and
with a heavy heart, Jenny closed the school, hoping conditions would soon improve. She thought back to what she had
accomplished with the children. The Rawlins family might
be poor but the children were extremely bright. They had
quickly learned to read and to feel the joy of accomplishment
and confidence born of being at the top of their class. Even
Ezra's reading and Isaac's spelling had improved.

The girls had made many things, including new dresses,
in the Saturday morning group. These young women were
developing a beauty of their own as they grew and matured.
Jenny hoped that beauty would not be damaged by wicked
men of the mob, constantly on the heels of the Mormons.
Richard still wanted to kill the man who had taken advantage
of poor little Sarah, and so did Jenny.

Richard and Jenny had always managed to see the poorer
families around them had wheat to make bread. The improved

nutrition showed in the faces of the children, especially the Wilson girls. Alice and Adeline Wilson had really blossomed. They looked so plain when Jenny first set eyes on them, but now they were beautiful young ladies. Widow Wilson's positive attitude about life had rubbed off on her children and though their lives remained hard, they radiated beauty from within. Young George Wilson had become a real favorite of Jenny's and she had noticed a bond growing between him and Laura.

Jenny thought about Lucy Clark and her eyes misted. Lucy had been an obnoxious, outspoken little girl, but she had begun to take on some polish. Lucy remained an impulsive child. Jenny just hoped Lucy didn't grow up to be as critical as her mother towards her neighbors. But lately, even Mrs. Clark had started showing some compassion to others.

Sam Hill had always been Jenny's favorite. He and Sarah had developed a close friendship. Jenny often wondered if Richard wasn't a lot like Sam when he was a boy. Though Sam had a fiery temper and strong will, he possessed that gentlemanly bearing which showed not only in actions, but in attitude—an attitude which came from emulating the example of parents whose good manners have been taught to children through the example of adults confident of their place in life.

In spite of being tired, Jenny had a hard time sleeping that night.

The next morning, she awakened to find Sarah standing beside her bed. "Don't get up, Aunt Jenny," she begged. "I want to get in with you." Jenny held out her arms and Sarah collapsed into them, shivering. Jenny tucked the covers around Sarah and held her more tightly in her arms, as if by doing so she could protect her against anything which might ever hurt her again. Sarah's tears began to flow—slowly at first, then in great streams. Jenny let her cry until she fell silent and seemed calm. When Sarah wiped her eyes, Jenny smiled reassuringly and suggested, "Don't you think we'd better get up and get busy?"

As they ate their breakfast, Mandy suggested, "I'd sho' feel better if Miz Miriam an' Mary come here wid us."

"You're right; that's a wonderful idea," said Jenny setting down her spoon and laying her hand to her cheek. "After breakfast will you hitch up the wagon, and we'll all go get them."

They piled into the wagon and headed toward Hansen's place. As they approached, Jenny could see Miriam's snow white washing hanging on the line and flapping in the breeze. "Goodness," she said, "It's Monday morning and we never even thought about doing the wash!"

"Some things is mo' important den washin'," said Mandy with conviction, "an dis is one o' dos things!"

When they arrived at Miriam's, she appeared, red-eyed but putting on a cheerful front. "We've come to get you," announced Sarah.

"Oh, I couldn't leave," said Miriam, leaning wearily against the door jam and shaking her head to dispel the tenseness she felt. "What about the animals?"

"Let's drive them over and put them in with our animals," suggested Jenny.

"It is terribly lonely and frightening here without Jim," Miriam admitted, dropping her hands in a sign of defeat. She hesitated and Jenny took her hesitation as a signal for action.

"Girls, round up all the animals and start them towards our place while we get the clothes off the line and pack what Miriam and Mary will need. Mandy will help you," Jenny instructed and Miriam nodded wearily.

Mary began opening gates and the twins shoed the cow, the horse, the pigs and the chickens down the road. Jenny brought in Miriam's washing and helped her get a few things together to take. Though only half-way to noon and the sun not that hot Jenny's face and lips felt dry and her throat parched.

Back at the Harris house that evening, when everyone had eaten supper, Jenny and Miriam both felt the strength of the other and felt glad they had combined their families to share these dangerous times. Jenny and Miriam sat beside the clay-daubed fireplace, Jenny darning one of Richard's coarse, gray socks over an egg and Miriam reading. Sarah sat cross-legged on the cord bed in the corner of the cabin working on embroidering a dish towel. Mary and Laura's occasional giggles drifted down from the loft.

Miriam looked up from reading her Bible. "I'm so glad you came over and got Mary and me. I just can't stand the loneliness and the waiting, for days on end, with Jim in some far-off place and no way to get word, or find out what's..." Her voice broke off as she reached up and brushed back her hair which hung softly around her face. Jenny noticed a touch of gray nestled in the pale brown strands.

At this outburst of sentiment, Jenny rose and put an arm impulsively around Miriam's shoulders. "Together we'll make it," she assured her friend.

"Yes, we'll make it," Miriam said, smiling a little shakily, though Jenny could see her thoughts held no comfort. "We always do, one way or another, but what will we lose this time?"

———————

The weather turned cold and the wind had a real bite to it. The sun disappeared and early snow began to fall. Some of the homeless families from Diahman arrived at Far West, having walked miles through the storm. They told stories of the depredations imposed upon them. Some brought their dead in wagons–those killed in the siege or who died along the way to Far West. None knew what had happened to friends and neighbors not in their party. Jenny and Miriam were unable to find out anything about Eliza and the Snow family or about Richard and Jim.

Three weeks later, Richard and Jim returned. When they first heard the horses Jenny and Miriam were frightened for fear it might be the mob, but when they saw who was coming they rushed out. Both women threw their arms around their men. "Oh, I'm so glad you're back. I've been worried sick!" exclaimed Jenny with tears in her eyes.

The two men handed their horses to Mandy and came inside. "What's happening in Diahman?" asked Jenny.

"When we arrived, homes were burning and livestock had been driven off. Then it snowed and the homeless had to walk miles through the storm to find shelter," declared Richard.

"How is Eliza?" asked Jenny and Sarah in unison. "And Mother Snow?" added Sarah.

"The Snow family is okay," said Jim. "They were among the lucky ones."

"I'm so glad. I've been so worried about them," Sarah exclaimed with a sigh of relief.

"Things are not good anywhere," confided Jim. "The citizens of DeWitt, seeing no hope, finally loaded their wagons and came here. They were promised payment for their land, but they'll never see it. Joseph has advised everyone in the outlying settlements to come to Far West. Refuges are filing into the city." "Many have come by here," said Jenny, "but nobody knew anything about you and Jim or about the Snow family."

"The militia, supposedly sent to protect us is raiding and looting our settlements," Richard noted, his voice an accusation.

"The militia men aren't all bad," said Jim. "General Atchison and General Doniphan of the state militia have been sympathetic to the Mormons. They appealed to Governor Boggs for help and were rebuked. He immediately sent superior officers who were anti-Mormon to place over them. General Atkinson resigned. General Doniphan became very angry, and he began to raise a group of men from among us Mormons to protect our people from the mobs."

"General Doniphan is a fair-minded man who believes we should be allowed to live as we wish," said Richard. "You know he's not only a general in the Missouri Militia but a lawyer also. He's befriended Joseph Smith in the past."

"Will there ever be any real peace for our people?" Jenny cried. "How can human beings treat each other this way?"

"I don't know," said Richard, stalking back and forth, his seething anger crackling, "But I'm afraid the trouble is far from over."

The cabin walls reflected the bright red of the fire burning in the fireplace and gave forth an eerie aura as Richard continued, "When our militia was called out to protect the Saints, the mob retreated. Then they found another way to try and drive us out. They set fire to some homes of the old settlers and said the Mormons had done it."

Miriam sucked in her breath, and Jenny could see cold beads of sweat on her brow. "They sent complaints to Governor Boggs saying we are breaking the law in many ways—stealing cattle, destroying property, and even trying to kill

peaceful citizens," added Jim. "Knowing Boggs, he will believe every one of their lies." Richard said, his upper lip pulling into a sneer which showed his dislike for the governor
more effectively than his words.

"Two of the apostles have joined the mob," said Jim sadly.
"Both Thomas Marsh and Orson Hyde have been excommu-
nicated. Brother Marsh was always a bit jealous of Joseph. In
anger, he went to Richmond and signed a statement saying
the Mormons planned to burn Richmond and Liberty, and he
convinced Brother Hyde to sign it also."

When Eliza and her family reached Far West, Eliza
stopped by to let her friends know they were safe. The girls
squealed as they ran to greet her, throwing their arms about
their friend. Eliza told how the former owner of the house,
which her father had paid for in full, had come and impu-
dently inquired how soon they should be out of it, as though
the man still owned the place. Her eyes held little warmth as
she recounted the experience.

A quick frown passed over her face. "My American blood
warmed to the temperature of an insulted, free-born American citizen as I looked at him and thought, poor man; you
little know with whom you have to deal—God lives."

Eliza's slight form stood straight and tall. Jenny instinctively reached out and grabbed her hand. Jenny marveled at
Eliza's strength of conviction. Eliza's faith never seemed to
waver. "Come inside and sit down for at least a few minutes,"
Jenny insisted.

Eliza gave a sad shake of her head and swept her hair
back with a swift gesture. I can't stay long, but I'll sit for
a moment. Jenny stepped back and slowly pushed the door

into the house open. She led Eliza to the rocker Jenny had brought from New York.

Eliza wearily continued, "It was hard to decide which was most to be dreaded, the Militia which was there to protect us, or the mob; no property was safe within the reach of either of them. She sighed and stopped for a moment.

"The temperature dropped to very cold when we left," Eliza continued, "and in order to warm my aching feet I started on foot and walked until the teams came up. About two miles out, I met one of the so-called militia who accosted me with 'Well, I think this will cure you of your faith.'

"Looking him squarely in the eye, I replied, 'No, Sir, it will take more than this to cure me of my faith.' His countenance dropped, and he responded, 'I must confess you are a better soldier than I am.' I passed on, thinking that unless he was above the average of his fellows in that section, I did not feel complimented by his confession."

Jenny looked intently at Sarah, who sat closely beside Eliza, holding her kitten tightly in her arms and hanging upon her every word. "I hate them all!" Sarah said angrily. Eliza's attention turned to Sarah. The child's intense concentration and her hands clenched together so tightly the knuckles were white told Eliza her account was fueling that memory hardest of all for the child to bear. She slowly stood up, put an arm around Sarah and said evenly, "Sarah, just remember, whatever happens to us here, our faith will remain strong, and no one can take that from us."

Aaron Hale was beginning to feel much better. The dull, heavy ache in his head, which he had begun to think would never subside, remained now as only a part-time companion. The fuzziness of vision was also beginning to clear. He felt anxious to get up and get on with his life, but his leg still throbbed miserably. He felt more cross and irritable every day.

Aaron was sitting up when Anna came into the room. "Don't get any ideas about getting out of that bed yet," she advised him firmly. "With a break like you had, most doctors would have cut off your leg. Any weight on it, and we may have to do that yet."

Aaron looked at her anxiously, then eased back onto the pillows with a frown. Here he lay in the household of a Mormon family—the religious group he hated with passion and from which he had come west to rescue his sister—afraid he was falling in love with one of them! If he didn't get out of here quickly, he'd be in a fine mess!

"Let me have a look at your leg," Anna commanded.

"Looking at it every five minutes isn't going to help anything," he complained. Then with a sigh of resignation, he pulled the covers back. As she bent over him, he felt light-headed again, just from her nearness. How he hated being helpless like this.

Each morning Anna brought a basin of warm water and bathed his leg, his feet and his back. Then she left him to bathe the rest of himself. Even that was difficult. He stretched to reach the back of his neck and his head began to throb. Why did anyone have to bathe every day anyway, he wondered. This woman had become fanatical on cleanliness, he decided. The next time she brought that basin, he would just pretend to wash.

Sunday morning Anna entered the room in a fancy dress. She looked absolutely stunning! She walked over to the table beside his bed, and set a book upon it.

"I'm sure you're well enough to get along by yourself for a while." she announced. "We'll be at church. I'll leave something you can read in case you get bored."

She exited the room, and he felt a pang of pain. It wasn't in his leg or his head, but in his heart. He always hated to see her go. It seemed so lonesome without her.

When she was gone, he reached over and picked up the book. It was a Book of Mormon. With a curse he threw it onto the floor. Anna didn't need think she could make a Mormon out of him just because he was temporarily helpless.

The hours dragged by slowly until Anna returned, accompanied by her father and an imposing man he had never seen before, but recognized immediately. It was the man in his dream who had been marrying him to this woman. He blinked and blinked again, but the man, impressive in his cutaway broadcloth suit, did not disappear.

Aaron felt all too conscious of the Book of Mormon he had tossed onto the floor. Anna noticed it immediately and picked it up without a word but with an accusing glance, put it back on the table.

"Aaron, there's someone I want you to meet," Mr. Morris said. "This is Joseph Smith."

"You're 'Old Joe Smith?'" Aaron blurted out, then felt embarrassed by his outburst.

Joseph laughed and came toward the bed with his hand outstretched. "Joseph Smith is the name I was given, but I don't know about the 'old'," he said with a smile.

Aaron winced. There was nothing to do but shake the man's hand. He couldn't be completely rude to the guest of those who had taken him in and were caring for him. As Joseph took his hand in a firm grasp, Aaron felt a shiver go down his spine—one he couldn't explain.

As they talked, Aaron began to feel an unwilling respect for this man nudge aside the preconceived opinions he had of the Mormon prophet. When Joseph left, Aaron realized he had actually enjoyed visiting with the man. He didn't look or act anything like what Aaron had expected. He had found himself asking Joseph to stop by again, but after he left, Aaron wondered if he, too, had been hoodwinked by the Mormons—he who had condemned Richard for being taken in by them. He would have to be more careful, he told himself.

The Book of Mormon on his bedside table was a constant irritant to Aaron. He wished Anna would move it, but she continued to leave it there beside his bed, where it sat all week. He was acutely aware of the book's position beside him, but he refused to acknowledge it or to read Mormon propaganda. Finally one day when Anna and her father left, he picked it up and opened the cover. He was so bored anything to read might be better than nothing. It wouldn't hurt to just read a few pages, he thought.

As Richard and Jim spent most of their time with the militia, the women tried to keep up with the extra work normally done by their men.

"I never realized quite how much Richard does around here," Jenny said, washing the dirt off her hands from working outside. "I find it almost impossible to keep things running smoothly without him."

"I know what you mean," said Miriam with a long, drawn out sigh. "I sure hope Jim comes home in time to slaughter the pigs before winter really sets in."

When they came home for brief periods of time—usually only an hour or two—the men seemed to have nothing on their minds but restraining the mob. Other settlements

suffered the same fate as Adam-ondi-Ahman when the bru-
tality of the mobs fell upon those in outlying areas. Many of
the men in the state militia, supposedly sent to protect the
settlements, became members of the mob.

"Those who fight against us know nothing of our real
character," Richard told Jenny one evening when he stopped
at home overnight. "General Parks, sent here recently, was
surprised to find the Mormons weren't anything like he had
heard. He asked me to make a copy for him of a letter he is
sending to Governor Boggs. He let me make an extra copy to
show Joseph. Listen to this:

> Whatever may have been the disposition of the
> people called Mormons before our arrival here,
> since we have made our appearance they have
> shown no disposition to resist the law or of hos-
> tile intentions...There has been so much preju-
> dice and exaggeration concerned in this matter,
> that I found things entirely different from what
> I was prepared to expect. It is true that a great
> excitement did prevail between the parties, and
> I am happy to say that my exertions, as well as
> those of Major General Atchison, and the officers
> and men under my command, have been crowned
> with success. When we arrived here, we found
> a large body of men from the counties adjoin-
> ing, armed and in the field, for the purpose, as
> I learned, of assisting the people of this county
> against the Mormons, without being called out
> by the proper authorities.

Richard and Jim weren't at home long. A messenger soon
came saying Methodist Reverend Samuel Bogart, a captain in

the state militia, had taken about forty men and gone to the homes of Mormons living outside of Far West threatening "to get their scalps" if they did not get out of the state. He said he was going to join another armed group at Crooked River and the next day they would visit Far West with "thunder and lightning." Now the mob had cannons, as well as guns, and Reverend Bogart said they would use them.

Colonel Hinkle called seventy-five Latter-day Saint volunteers under the command of David W. Patten, a captain in the local militia to meet this mob. Richard and Jim kissed their wives goodbye again and were off with Patten and the militia. Meeting these men head on seemed better than sitting home and letting them harass the Mormons without opposition, thought Richard, as he again felt qualms at leaving.

This clash between the Caldwell Mormon Militia and their enemies would become known as the "Battle of Crooked River." Casualties were suffered on both sides. A number of Mormon men were carried away as prisoners by the mob.

"They've captured some of our men. My mother wants to know if you've heard from Richard and Jim," young George Wilson came by and told the women.

The shock on Jenny and Miriam's faces showed they hadn't heard from their husbands. They both turned as white as the eggs laid by the white leghorn chickens in the basket sitting on the table. "I'm sure they're all right, or you would have heard," young George said quickly, trying to soothe the excited women and girls.

Reports soon circulated that Captain Bogart and all of his company had been massacred by the Mormons. The whole country was aroused by this false report.

New converts and Mormons from outlying areas continued to pour into Far West. A huge company of over five hundred Mormons, designated as "The Kirtland Camp," rolled in from Kirtland. Joseph asked the Saints to put up families in their homes or barns until they could be permanently settled. Many lived in their wagon boxes.

"You're welcome to stay in the barn," Jenny told two families who stopped.

"We'd be extremely grateful for the shelter," a thin, wiry man, whose small blond wife had static eyes and a tight mouth, told her. "We'll help care for the animals and keep an eye on them." he offered. "I hear the mobs are stealing cows, horses, and pigs whenever the opportunity arises." The couple stayed several days, then moved on.

Another large group with two hundred wagons came from Canada and the eastern states—some from a distance of fifteen hundred miles. As the numbers of Mormons increased, even the finest non-Mormon citizens became alarmed. Through that alarm, the lawless element of the frontier found an opportunity to plunder and ravage. Misunderstandings grew at a startling pace.

Caldwell County's Mormon Militia, under Col. Hinkle and Colonel Lyman Wight, never exceeded five hundred and they were greatly outnumbered by the State Militia harassing the Mormons. Richard, Jim and other Mormon Militia members tried valiantly to protect their families and property.

Six thousand armed men, many of them members of the mob, joined the State Militia. Gen. Parks and other officers interested in keeping the peace found they could not control the men. The Militia, sent to disperse the mobs, aided them instead. The frontier had become a seething mass of mobbers intent on killing an unarmed community.

As Richard and others had suspected, Governor Boggs did believe the false reports he had received about the Mormons. Without investigation, he issued an order to the

Commanding Officer in the field, General Clark, which would later be referred to as the "extermination order:"

> The Mormons must be treated as enemies, and must be exterminated or driven from the state if necessary for the public peace—their outrages are beyond all description.

On October 30, a mob-militia approached the town of Far West. Colonel Hinkle, who led the defenders of the city, requested an interview with General Samuel D. Lucas, commanding the State Militia.

"Perhaps they'll work something out," Richard told Jim, hopefully.

"It won't happen," said Jim with some contempt.

The next day, Colonel Hinkle and a few of his men went into Far West.

"I wonder what they're up to," Richard worried.

They were soon back with Joseph Smith, Hyrum Smith, Sidney Rigdon, Parley P. Pratt, George W. Robinson and Lyman Wight. They escorted the men to General Lucas' camp. Richard, Jim and others waited anxiously to see what would happen.

Rumors and wild accounts swept the camp. The men soon learned that Col. Hinkle had delivered their prophet and other leaders to General Lucas under the pretense of meeting with him, and without their knowledge of what was actually happening. Greatly outnumbered by anti-Mormon State Militia units, Richard, Jim, and other Mormon men knew they could do nothing to help their leaders.

"I thought we were delivering them to General Lucas's camp to meet with him, but when we got there Colonel

Hinkle told General Lucas, 'General, these are the prisoners I agreed to deliver up,'" one young Mormon militia man confided to his fellow soldiers that night. "They were surrounded and marched away. It was evident from the surprise on their faces, they had been tricked."

Richard was livid when he learned of the treachery of his commanding officer.

"I wonder whose side Hinkle is on?" Richard told Jim.

"I've never quite trusted the man," Jim confided. "I hear they're holding a court-martial tonight to decide the fate of Joseph and the other men."

At the court-martial, the prisoners were sentenced to be shot at sunrise on the public square of Far West, as an example to other Mormons. The Mormon troops felt enraged and bitter toward Hinkle. They had a difficult time keeping their emotions under control.

General Doniphan, ordered to carry out the execution, with great courage replied to his commanding officer, "It is cold-blooded murder...if you execute these men, I will hold you responsible before an earthly tribunal, so help me God."

The Mormon leaders were spared, but placed in a foul jail. General Lucas dismissed the greatest portion of the state militia and these men, still bearing arms, became looting mobs with license to kill.

CHAPTER FIFTEEN

Late one afternoon, Mandy came from the home of Isaac and Minnie Miller's mother, where she had assisted in another delivery. "It's a boy chile, an' a big 'un," she announced, "but heaven help the chile coming into dis world."

But the delivery wasn't the only news Mandy brought. "Oh, Marsa Harris," she said. "More den two hundred mob mens rode into Haun's Mill with guns an' shot down de Mormons. Little chillins were kilt an' mudders an' daughters abused."

"Oh, no," cried Jenny. Shocked by this terrible news, she sank into a kitchen chair. "Widow Wilson has a sister there!" she added, as she thought of her neighbor who had already had so much sorrow in her life.

"De mob shoot and shoot into de blacksmith shop where de people hidin', den tore open de doors and finish killin' eberybody."

"I must go over and see if Wilsons have heard and if their relatives there survived," Jenny said quickly. "Mandy, bring the horses and wagon." She ran her fingers through her hair, then brushed her hands against her apron. "And Mandy, she yelled out the door, throw a couple of sacks of wheat on the wagon."

"I'll take care of things here," Miriam said softly.

Widow Wilson had received the news. Her sister's two oldest sons had been killed. "I can't believe the inhumanity of these men," the widow told Jenny. "During the raid, one small boy lay hidden under the bellows in the blacksmith shop, hoping not to be seen. 'Nits make lice,' commented one of the mobbers as he shot the child in the head. Though shot through the hip, the child's brother lived to tell the story. At least seventeen Mormons were killed and twelve escaped into the woods severely wounded; some of the wounded will not make it."

"How dreadful," sighed Jenny

"There were not enough adults alive to bury the dead so the few survivors put all the bodies in an old well and covered them with dirt. All the wagons and horses were taken by the mob, but the next day five armed men rode into the village and told the sorrowing ones who remained to either deny their religion or get out of the state at once."

Jenny helped Widow Wilson the rest of the day, doing what she could to comfort her. Being around Widow Wilson made her feel so thankful to have Richard, even if he was gone most of the time now and acting more cross and irritable every day when at home. She vowed she would try harder to show Richard how much she appreciated him.

When Jenny left, she let the Wilsons borrow the wagon and horses so they could take the grain to the mill to be ground for making bread. Young George drove her home.

Jenny looked around her home critically. The woman had tried to harvest the corn and all the vegetables in the garden, but a few, not yet fully ripe, now hung heavy and frozen on the vines. The air smelled tangy as cider. A family of blue-birds nesting in the rafters of the barn had deserted their tattered nest and flown south.

The mobs were becoming more and more frightening. Jenny gathered all the women and girls in her household to-gether one evening and said, "We have to figure out a plan of action in case we need to protect ourselves."

"What do you mean?" asked Laura as she reached down and picked up Sarah's kitten which was rubbing against her ankles. "What could we do if the mob comes here?"

"Well, I've been thinking," said Jenny, "we're here all alone and we need to be able to do something to protect our-selves. We don't have guns or ammunition, but we do have two heavy cast iron frying pans. I think Mandy and I should each keep one of the frying pans beside our beds, and if we hear noises in the night, station ourselves beside the door, frying pans ready. We could probably knock out a couple of mobbers that way if they came inside the house."

For a moment they stood looking at each other in silence, then Laura smiled hesitantly. "That's a great idea," she said. "I'd love to see some of those old mobbers smacked silly. It would serve them right. I'd like to smack one myself."

Miriam smiled at Laura and pulled one of her braids. "Laura, you have a great throwing arm, and we could put that to use," she suggested. "I've seen you throw rocks at the hawks and other predators bothering the chickens. Jenny has two sad irons. We could keep them along the edge of the loft, and you girls could down a man or two with a flying iron. If there weren't too many, we might be able to protect ourselves."

"We might make a bucket o' lye water, like we does for soap, and somebody could throw dat on 'em," suggested Mandy. "If it got in der eyes, it might blind 'em."

"Why don't I take a frying pan, and you take the lye water, Mandy" suggested Miriam. "You would have the strength to throw it where it would do the most good."

"That's a good idea," said Jenny. "I'm afraid by now that some of the mobbers might realize there are only women in this house, as in many of our homes with our men off in the militia. Being here on the edge of town makes our lives even more dangerous."

"What will we do if they set the house on fire?" asked Sarah, her voice on a somber key. "They've burned many homes."

"If they set it on fire, that's a different story. We'd just have to run for our lives," admitted Jenny, but perhaps they wouldn't.

———————

Jenny slept better just knowing they had some plan to protect themselves. It helped her feel less unsettled, uncertain and helpless feelings becoming all too familiar during the long nights when they were alone with their thoughts and more questions than answers.

With a plan of action, Jenny noted a transformation of attitudes in everyone. They would refuse to go down without a fight, even though the main source of their security was gone.

The women's plan had to be implemented sooner than expected. A few nights later, Jenny awoke in the middle of the night and sat bold upright. She felt alarmed, but for a moment couldn't understand why she should feel that way.

Her attention sharpened and as she listened fearfully she realized it was the sound of approaching horses' hoofs that had awakened her.

Jenny felt a cold chill of fear and a big knot quickly forming in her stomach. Mandy had been called out to help with the birth of another baby; possibly it was her returning she told herself, trying to remain calm. But it didn't sound like a wagon, it was horsemen, and Mandy had been told not to come home until morning.

Jenny quickly woke the others and they silently took their places, hearts pounding. Sarah's nightmares, where she couldn't run fast enough, where she always got caught, came from the darkest reaches of her mind and she felt almost paralyzed with terror. "This is your chance to get even with these terrible men," she said softly to herself, and the thought gave her the impetus to do her part.

"Sarah," Jenny whispered. "Since Mandy isn't here, can you throw the lye water if we need it?" Sarah quietly took her place beside the pail.

Light from the full moon filtered in through the windows and their covering of lacy curtains Jenny had crocheted.

"What if it's Mandy or Uncle Richard and Jim?" whispered Sarah.

"We'll have to make sure before we do anything." said Miriam softly.

Soon they heard gruff voices and shouts of men obviously out for blood. "You get the animals, and we'll check out the house. I think we can have some fun here before we torch the place." The words were followed by muffled laughter.

Jenny shivered at the realization of what they had in mind. Her arm shook and she felt perspiration breaking out all over her body. Her throat was so tight she thought she would choke. She was glad Mandy had one of the wagons and teams and Widow Wilson and her family had borrowed the other to haul the wheat to the mill to be ground. At least they wouldn't get the teams and wagons.

They heard the crack of a whip and Rosie's resulting bellow. Laura softly sucked in her breath as she heard her favorite animal being mistreated, but she kept her head. They heard men running toward the house, then the heavy door creaked on its dry, leather hinges as it was pushed open. Jenny prayed that there wasn't many of them, and that their plan would work. As someone stepped inside, Jenny's frying pan came down hard on the first man's head and Miriam's pan on top of hers. The sound of iron hitting iron rang out into the night.

The first man fell just inside the door—out cold. The next one stumbled over him and caught Laura's flat iron right in the side of the head. He, too, fell in a heap.

"That's for Rosie and her calf," Laura said softly.

From outside, another man let out an oath and shot his gun into the darkness several times. He didn't hit anyone, and the women all remained quietly in their places, though it was suffocating torture to keep from running. Mary quietly picked up the other sad iron and handed it to Laura. Everyone knew Laura had stronger arms and was better at throwing than she and Sarah were. Laura had hit the mark with the first iron.

The man, holding his rifle in front of him, eased into the doorway. "Come out of there, or I'll kill you," he shouted.

The women hardly breathed. Laura took careful aim with her second iron. She knew if she hit Jenny or Miriam it might kill them, but she was confident of her own throwing ability and he was well silhouetted by the light of the full moon. She had flung many a rock at rodents in the corn patch and predators after the chickens, she told herself, and she usually hit her mark. The iron sailed through the air and the man let out a scream of terror as he fell outside the door.

The women could hear hoof beats of riders retreating, then all seemed quiet outside. They stayed rooted to their places until they felt sure the others had gone. Jenny felt sick; she wanted to cry. Then anger claimed her. These men had no right to do what they were doing. How dare they attack innocent people and ruin their lives. This was an act of vicious vengeance against peaceful, unsuspecting people who were only trying to find the freedom to worship in their own way.

Moonlight flooded in through the open doorway. Jenny's mind whirled as she wondered what to do next. Wiping angrily at her tears, her chin held high, she found the basket of rag rug strips. With controlled fury, she began to tie one of the unconscious men's hands behind him. Laura and Mary scurried down from the loft. "I didn't even get a chance to throw the lye water," Sarah said bleakly. Everyone helped tie the hands and feet of the mobbers firmly together.

"What will we do with them?" asked Miriam. "The others will probably return and burn the house when they realize these men are not coming."

"I don't know," said Jenny, "but let's drag them out of the house."

Dawn chased away the dark of night. Mandy came driving up in the wagon.

"We'll throw them in the wagon and haul them over to the Far West police," Jenny decided. "Everyone will have to go along; we need to stay together for protection."

"Lord a mercy," said Mandy.

When they returned the women took inventory. The chickens had been scattered, and were clucking in protest. Though the Harris horses had escaped being taken, Hansen's horse was gone. Rosie and her calf and the old sow and pigs and all of Miriam's other animals were gone.

"I guess we won't have to worry about killing the pigs this fall," Miriam said softly, sinking onto a kitchen chair.

Jenny dropped into her rocking chair feeling weak and spent. She didn't know how they would get along without Rosie's milk and the meat from the hogs. She hoped her neighbors were safe.

Jenny heard the hoofbeat of horses feet and peeked out. She fairly flew out the door before the group of men reached the yard. Richard swung down from his mount and dropped the reins, ground-tying the horse.

"Are you okay?" he asked quickly.

"We're okay." One look at his face and she knew something was terribly wrong. "What is it?" she asked as he gave her a quick peck on the cheek.

"We must get out of here," he said. "Joseph and others have been captured and jailed. A huge mob is on the way toward the city. Governor Boggs has issued an order to exterminate the Mormons, which will give the mobs complete license to kill."

Jenny was speechless with horror and her face went white. She stared at him with astonished eyes. "He plans to kill us all?" she finally asked, not believing what she was hearing. She threw up her hands in a gesture of despair. "Why?"

"We have only tried to defend ourselves, but the governor has used this as an excuse to issue an order of extermination saying that we must be treated as enemies, and must be exterminated or driven from the state if necessary for the public peace."

"But how can he do that to over fifteen thousand citizens of the state?"

"I don't know," said Richard, "but we haven't time to talk now. We must leave within the hour."

Jim was lifting Miriam up behind his saddle. "They took all our animals," Miriam told him sadly.

Jim stopped in his tracks. "That means we don't have another horse to hitch to the wagon."

A puzzled look crossed Richard's face. "Where's our other wagon?"

"Oh, in all the excitement I forgot. Widow Wilson borrowed it to take grain to the mill."

"I'll ride over and get the wagon and the Wilsons while you start packing," Richard decided. "On the way back I'll leave my horse at Jim's to help pull his wagon."

"Thanks," Jim breathed. "I don't know what we'd do without you. Can Mary stay here until we get back?"

"Of course," agreed Jenny, and the others galloped off at full speed. She turned to Richard with tears in her eyes. "What will happen to Aaron?"

Richard hesitated a moment. "We'll have to trust God and the Morris family to see to him; we don't have any time to spare." Then looking at Jenny's stricken face, he added, "I'm sorry, sweetheart."

"Food must be first priority," Richard instructed. We'll line the sides of one wagon bed with sacks of wheat. The kids can sit on the grain sacks. Widow Wilson won't have much foodstuff to bring, and they'll just have to leave most everything else.

Jenny thought about her friend. "She's lost so much lately," she sighed. "I don't know how she keeps on going."

"While I'm getting the Wilsons, you and the girls pack the absolute necessities into the trunks. Mandy, you hitch up the wagon that's here. Hansens and several other families are meeting here in one hour so we can travel together," Richard shouted as he rode off.

"Lord a mercy," said Mandy, "I can't believe my ears." She hurried to the barn as Jenny and the girls ran back into the cabin.

———————

Jenny glanced around her home, which had grown very dear to her. There were all her cooking pans and kettles hanging beside the chimney; the rocking chair she had brought from New York; her pine cupboard and the beds Richard had made; her bright rag carpet on the floor and small braided rugs; the quilts they had pieced. Heartache swelled up inside her breast as she thought of leaving her little home, but she did not hesitate for long before rolling up her sleeves and girding herself for the battle with trunks, and barrels.

Jenny quickly laid out the two large trunks. "Girls," she commanded, "go upstairs and get one good warm dress each, one change of underwear, and the heavy quilt off your bed." The finality in her voice sounded too convincing to argue against. They obeyed as if in a trance.

Jenny went into the school room and grabbed six New England Primers, two third readers, two spellers, and six slates. She placed them in the bottom of one trunk. She left her sewing basket, but tucked her thimble, needle case, some thread, crochet hooks and knitting needles into the trunk. She picked up the Bible, her English Prayer Book and the Book of Mormon from the kitchen table and placed them in the trunk, then on second thought rolled up the doily on the kitchen table and stuffed it into a corner for packing material. She knew there wouldn't be room for her linen tablecloths, which she had brought to Missouri. She gave them one sad, farewell look.

On top of the books, she folded and placed the coverlet from her bed, her two Paisley shawls, and her most serviceable dress. She added a heavy woolen shirt of Richard's, his new pair of homespun pants, and Mandy's extra dress. She looked at their Sunday clothing, and with a sigh refused the urge to try to pack it into the bulging trunk.

"Where are we going?" Sarah asked with fear filling her eyes as she handed Jenny their dresses.

"I wish I knew," said Jenny. She folded the dresses and put them into the trunk then snapped the lid shut, all the while feeling that she had forgotten something very important. "We'll just have to trust in God to lead us."

"Sure," said Sarah, "and hope he protects us better than he did me."

Jenny looked at the child with fear illuminating her eyes, and stopped a moment to place an arm around her. She felt so much responsibility for these two children she had begged God to let her have.

"Oh, Sarah, I'm so sorry. We'll just have to do what we have to do. Help me fold the small rugs into a pile beside the trunks," she added, hoping the work would keep Sarah too busy to do much thinking.

"Mary and Laura, bring all of the quilts We will keep these out to wrap around us," she said. "I'm afraid it will be awfully cold."

Laura brought the quilt from Mandy's bed and set it beside the others. "I wish we'd never come here," she said.

Jenny felt a tight lump squeezing her chest till it was difficult to breathe. "Oh, God," she prayed silently, "please protect us all."

"Get the bake oven and one frying pan," she told the girls, "and put them here beside the trunks." She picked up the rolling pin, five plates and cups, a few utensils from the cupboard and placed them in the other trunk. She looked about her trying to think what else she should pack. She put several bags of dried herbs into the trunk in case of illness, then all the food they had in the cupboard—the butter, jams, pickles, a pail of lard, and sacks of dried fruit. Whatever will we do without Rosie's milk, she wondered again.

The girls struggled with the bake oven, each carrying one side of the heavy pot, then Laura went for the frying pan. Jenny picked up a sad iron, wiped the blood from it and put it in the pile.

"Now," instructed Jenny, "bring all the coats, hats and mittens here. When you have finished that, go upstairs and put on all the extra clothing you can wear and still move about. Be sure you put on extra underwear." The girls scampered off and she wiped her forehead with her hand. The air felt cold, but she was sweating.

She heard the squeak of wagon wheels as Richard came into the yard with the Wilsons. Mandy pulled their largest wagon up beside the door and she and Richard hurried into the cabin.

"We'll have no room for furniture," Richard noted as his eyes went lingeringly from piece to piece—to the things he had made with his own hands. Jenny helped him carry out the largest trunk.

The wagon was already half full of tools, vegetables and grain. Some chickens in a cage were wired to the back of the load. Jenny quickly grabbed a shovel from the wagon and started digging up her precious lilac bush.

"What on earth are you doing?" asked Richard.

"Just load the wagon," she answered testily. It rankled her to have to stuff what she could into a couple of wagons and leave the rest of her belongings for her enemies.

He shook his head, and without further comment finished loading the wagon. There was barely room enough for it all to fit. Jim and Miriam were there before they finished.

The kids climbed up behind the seat onto the heavy sacks of grain, and Mandy bundled them under a quilt, then wearily climbed up beside Widow Wilson into the driver's seat of the other wagon. Jenny climbed up beside Richard as he slapped the gentle old horses vigorously with the lines. They clattered onto the road, as a couple of other wagons drove up and fell in behind them.

"Where are we going?" asked Jenny

"Brigham Young has told us to go across the border into Illinois as quickly as we can get there," said Richard.

"But that's such a long way!" exclaimed Jenny. "And what about our homes and property?" She looked back over her shoulder at the little log cabin which had been their home such a short time, and thought a home of her own—where no one could force her to move—would be the most wonderful possession in the world.

This little cabin, which she had considered ugly at first, had held so much love, had heard so much laughter and singing, and had become so much a part of her life. She pressed her hand hard against her eyes to stop the flow of tears, so near the surface, but they dripped through her fingers.

"I got my lilac," she said weakly.

Richard's face looked pale and a muscle twitched in his jaw. He put a gentle hand on her arm. "I know, Jenny, it's not fair that you have to give up everything a second time, but we will just have to trust in God." He raised his left hand to swipe at his hair, much longer now than he usually wore it. "All I want is a place to worship in peace—a place where happiness for you and Sarah and Laura can become a reality. But, I don't know where happiness lies, for anyone, just now in this troubled, crazy world." He shook his head sadly.

"The prophet is in jail along with Hyrum and many of our leaders. We have been denied any legal protection, and we have no choice but to do what Brigham Young has instructed," he continued. Richard had an uncomfortable feeling of being compressed into an ever-shrinking space between his family's despair and his own ever-growing anger with the situation. He knew this journey would be an ordeal all of the Mormons would have to go through and many were less prepared than his family. At least his family had wagons.

Jenny did not speak. She sighed and wrapped a quilt more closely about her. Bleakness hung in the air. It didn't take long, she thought, to have the entire world dissolve under one's feet, its music ended, its hope shattered, its beauty suddenly turned to ashes. All the homesickness of the past few years swelled up to choke her. Perhaps she dreamed of having too much out of life—a peaceful home, a good man's love, and children's laughter.

"We'll never be safe!" Laura wailed. "It just isn't fair." Jenny turned and wrinkled her nose at the twins, trying to give them assurance that things would be all right. Sarah, clutching her kitten in her arms seemed oblivious to everything around her. She held the kitten up to her face making up a little poem to it. It had been a long time since Jenny was that age herself, but she could still remember the adjustments, so difficult to make, yet so small compared to what the twins were going through now.

She looked into the next wagon and saw Miriam gasp as she lost her breath in a gust of wind. Jenny felt relieved they were not traveling alone. Miriam was always an inspiration to Jenny and had become her dearest friend. She looked over at the wagon bringing the Wilson family, with Mandy driving the team. Over Mrs. Wilson's shoulders, bony and slightly bent, hung a worn shawl and on her head a calico sunbonnet stiffened with ribs. She didn't look very prepared for the cold days and nights they would surely encounter. We are indeed a sorry plight, thought Jenny. She felt thankful to see the Wilson kids all wearing the hats and mittens she and Mandy had knitted for them.

Richard had often said that if there were no shadows, no contrast, they would not enjoy the perfection of beauty. "What would we know of daybreak if we never experienced dark? We would not have the splendor of the gorgeous sunsets if night were not coming on. We must have adversity in order to fully enjoy good times."

She looked at him now in worn-out pants, his hair blowing in the breeze. Maybe he could see the value in adversity, but Jenny felt she didn't want to enjoy anything if it involved any more suffering or persecution. She'd had enough adversity to last a lifetime. Richard hadn't an idea of what their future would hold when he'd made that statement. She looked lovingly, almost fearfully at each member of the family group.

Squinting against the bright red-orange glow of a sunset, Jenny turned to gaze around her. Although the sun had set, Some light still showed in the western sky. She gazed at the trees and thought them totally bereft of beauty. Oaks, Poplars, birches, and maples stood as ghosts, their bare branches now deserted, even by the birds. Flaming maple leaves scurried across the ground moved by a constant wind which blew every day, relentlessly battering the traveler's faces. She stared at the fallen leaves and thought of the beauties and joys of her own life that were past. When would the day again end in a comforting blanket of darkness without danger, fear, and terror? They had born trial enough for their devotion to the Gospel even before coming to Missouri. One loss after another, disappointment after disappointment! Was it possible that only a few years before she had been that happy, carefree girl in New York? The last two years had contained such an eternity of hard experiences. She rubbed her eyes wearily, as if it might improve what she saw.

The line of covered wagons lumbered heavily, clumsily, over rough, uneven ground. Jenny heard the rumble of slowly turning, creaking wheels; the dull thud of horse and oxen hoofs; the crack of whips and the vibration of raised voices. As dear to her heart as was her lovely little log home, when she had to make a choice, she realized she would cling to Richard and their religious convictions and meet whatever hazards and sacrifices this action might involve.

Jenny turned her face wearily toward Illinois. Perhaps there they would find peace and a chance to practice their religion without persecution. Perhaps there her family could live without fearing the future.

Chapter Sixteen

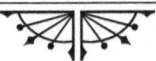

After a few days on the trail, Jenny tried to settle her family into some sort of routine. Unlike on their journey to Missouri, the weather remained beastly. First a cold, drizzling rain fell from dawn to dusk and everything turned drab, bleak and brown. Then the storm became vicious and the voice of the wind wailed high and thin. It became hard for drivers to see where to guide the horses with flakes of snow whirling madly about, seeming to come from every direction. There seemed little they could do except cling together for warmth.

Storms continued to bear down upon them as they huddled in the wagon, feet and fingers red and cold–so cold they lost their feeling. Jenny looked back at the girls and felt glad she had knitted their mittens to come high up on their wrists. It was so cold that even with mittens on, they had to put their hands securely under their armpits to keep their fingers warm.

Jenny climbed back by the girls and took off their shoes, one at a time, then rubbed their feet, hoping no one would end up like Miriam, having to have a foot or hand amputated because of the cold freezing weather. The lashing wind stung any exposed flesh. Jenny wondered how much of the chill up her spine was from the weather and how much came from the terror inside her. She caught a whipping strand of red hair away from the wind, and tucked it under her hat.

They slept close together without taking off any of their clothes. As each night came, Jenny felt so tired she could hardly move. She often wondered how she would have the energy to get up the next morning. Her back ached, but she told herself she had better get used to this life, backache and all—it was what they would have for a while.

When the storms quieted, the sun rose on a cold, white earth. The air, which brought color to their cheeks, bore a pleasant tang, but could also chill them through and through. The girls squirmed impatiently. On long afternoons they sang gospel songs as they rolled along, or spent a few hours changing places with others and enjoying a visit with their friends. Laura wanted to ride in Mary's wagon or with the Widow Wilson's children more than in their own. She seemed to enjoy the company of young George Wilson.

George, the same age as the twins, now took almost as much responsibility as a man. He spelled Mandy off on driving the team and helped his mother with the other children.

"My father told me before he died that I was now the man of the house and had to take care of our family," he confided to Laura one day when she was riding beside him while Alice and Adeline rode with Mary.

Laura's forehead puckered in thought. Her breath caught in her throat. "I never knew my mother," she finally said. "It's probably harder to lose a parent when you've known them and learned to love them, but at least you knew your father. I've often wondered what it would be like if my mother had lived." She sighed, "Since coming with Aunt Jenny and Uncle

Richard, I feel like I've stepped into another world, not a very nice one lately."

George looked into her upturned face, always so serious, and of late, so angry with the world. "I'm glad you're here with us now," he said softly.

Laura's nose wrinkled as a smile parted her lips for an instant. That was one of the little, endearing things, George liked about Laura—the way her nose wrinkled when she smiled.

"That's better," said George. "It doesn't help things a bit to be bitter. My mother says all the hard things that happen to us are only stepping stones to make us stronger, and that if we could see the whole picture, we'd realize that."

Laura blushed. She knew she had been terribly angry and bitter lately. She wondered how George could have such an amazing attitude after all his family had suffered. The more she was around this young man the more she wanted to be near him. She vowed to herself that she would try hard to look at things in a different way in the future and try to put her trust in God like George always did.

"I wonder what Illinois will be like," Laura mused. "Living in Missouri is so different from living in Virginia in my father's home. We used to have big rooms with high ceilings and beautiful furniture. A big curved staircase led to the second story and our bedroom. It was grand there!"

"Are you sorry you left?" asked George looking at her intently.

"I don't know," said Laura thoughtfully. "I would be if it wasn't for being here with you. For a long time I missed Sully and Greene, but I've made new friends here. I just wonder what will happen to us all."

————————

Even on good days, night came early and settled with cold and foggy darkness so thick it seemed you might reach out and touch it. No matter how heavily they all dressed, little fingers of cold penetrated their wraps. Jenny's weariness of soul seemed heightened by the clay and mud which stuck to their wagon wheels and the dreariness of the world. They were all covered with mud and grime, which seemed to get into everything. Mud covered the lower half of all the men's trousers.

Again sorrow entered unannounced. Young John Wilson developed a terrible cough. Jenny took one of her quilts over to Widow Wilson's wagon. Her icy fingers fumbled as she helped the mother wrap it around her sick child.

"He's terribly hot," said Mrs. Wilson, her voice breaking.

Alice and Adeline Wilson peered from the wagon with hollow eyes. Usually a great comfort and help to their mother, they now looked as if they felt every last shred of hope blowing away on the cold wind.

"Let me watch him for a few hours while you sleep," insisted Jenny. "You all look totally exhausted. It has been a long day."

Mrs. Wilson felt grateful for a chance to sleep awhile. "I'm really getting worried about him," she confided to Jenny. "He's never been very strong."

In spite of their prayers in his behalf, the illness continued sapping the boy's life away. By morning, his face had taken on a deathly pallor. Widow Wilson had anxiety written all over her face and her eyes looked red and moist.

"His father wanted so much to reach Zion and join the Saints and make a home there for his family, but God willed it otherwise. How can we go on this way being driven from one place to another, leaving our loved ones beneath the sod of strange places?"

Jenny had no answer; she knew Widow Wilson did not expect one, and she felt unable to produce words of comfort. She pulled in a deep breath and wondered how they could come to terms with bleakness and death, and go through life without flinching.

It was a bitter morning, cold and windy, when little John's breath refused to come from his congested lungs. They did not dare stop, even to bury the child. Widow Wilson wrapped his body in the quilt Jenny had brought her and carried it along with them until they could put more distance between themselves and the mobs. Young George sat beside his brother's body trying to protect it from the elements. Laura and Mary took turns riding beside him.

A couple of days later, when Hansen's double tree broke, they stopped while the men made a new one from a heavy bough. George and the women took turns digging until they had a grave suitably deep to bury little John.

Mrs. Wilson held the child close to her bosom and drew in a long, quivering sigh. She laid him in the center of the quilt and brushed the boy's long hair back out of his eyes and kissed his hard cheek. A soft sob escaped her lips, white and thin from trying to hold back her grief.

Jenny's eyes filled with tears and her throat was tight as she looked over at Laura standing beside young George, whose face was set in sorrow as he watched his mother. Not willing to let tears flow, he was trying so hard to be a man.

Jenny knew little of the crushing sorrow, the stark tragedy through which Mrs. Wilson had struggled. She sensed that day after day Widow Wilson had missed the lovely things she so much desired to enjoy, because life demanded her to perform the hard, necessary tasks. Jenny detected a hope-lessness in the widow's eyes which she had not seen there before.

Jenny had often gained strength from the example of Widow Wilson. She marveled at how close she now felt to the other women. In Missouri the Saints had been forced to share alike in joys and sorrows. They had to help each other. Through this sharing they developed closeness and strength of character. The persecution they were experiencing forced these women into close bonds of sisterhood which would never be broken. Jenny sensed the ache in Widow Wilson and wished that some way she could ease the burden and the weight of sorrow in her friend's heart. She wished she had been more mindful of her in Far West and had taken time to run down the street once in a while and visit her.

Holding the corners of the quilt they lowered young John's body into the grave and slowly laid him to rest. All of the quilts were needed to keep the living warm, but they could not increase Widow Wilson's grief by taking away the only protection for her son's body. They covered him with the edges of the quilt and slowly shoveled the dirt back into the grave.

Mrs. Wilson dropped to her knees beside the mound of fresh dirt, her face drained of all hope it ever held. Young George walked over and put an arm around his mother's shoulders. Jenny put a protecting arm around Alice and Adeline Wilson who seemed almost in a trance. Sarah and Laura's hands were clasped together in the act of sharing strength with each other. The setting sun tinged the whole landscape with a wash of rose colored light as Richard said a prayer over the boy's grave.

Even in sorrow duty wrapped at Widow Wilson's door daily, holding her to the task of caring for her brood of living children. She arose and went on. They prepared to travel another few miles before darkness obliterated their way.

Most of the 15,000 Mormons, anxious to escape the Missouri Mobs headed straight east toward Western Illinois. Church leaders lacked time to plan a new location for their membership. They left the responsibility of directing the people in the hands of Brigham Young and Heber C. Kimball. Joseph and other leaders languished in jail for five months while fifteen thousand Church members, denied any legal protection, were driven from their Missouri homes. They left property valued at between a million and a half and three million dollars. Painfully making their way toward Illinois, many died from exposure and illness during the winter of 1838-39.

Scattered membership temporarily abandoned the attempt to live together as a community. Non-Mormons believed this was the end of Mormonism, but soon the remarkable ability of Brigham Young became apparent. Brigham Young was born at Whittingham, Vermont on June 1, 1801. This young man, with blue-gray eyes under thick, light-colored hair had large, broad shoulders. Now in his mid-thirties, though an excellent carpenter, cabinet maker, painter and glazier, he lacked pretension. His mother had taught him to read; his formal schooling consisted of eleven days under a traveling schoolmaster, but his memory proved amazing. A copy of the Book of Mormon had come into his hands in New York State and after months of study he wanted to be baptized. He converted all his brothers and sisters, his aged father, and his wife. A few weeks later his wife died.

Brigham Young took his children and went to Kirtland, where he was thrown into the maelstrom of rapidly moving events, and suddenly forced into a role of leadership. After several missions, a one thousand mile foot march with Zion's Camp and supervising the carpenter work on the Kirtland temple, in 1835 he was chosen as an apostle.

Now, under his direction a written covenant circulated, in the first two days, signed by two hundred eighty men. It bound them to consider not only their own needs, but to help all of the poor remove from Missouri.

Brigham Young sent agents down the Missouri River to make caches of corn for use of the Mormons while exiting the state and to arrange for ferries and other necessities. When mob leaders realized the role he played in the Church, he was forced to flee for his life, but due to his efforts a long line of covered wagons trailed eastward.

Old and young, sick and feeble, women and children abandoned their homes and fled. Most had little food or clothing. Many had no horses or wagons and were compelled to walk. The animals driven off by the mobs were now sorely missed.

"Jenny," Richard said one evening as they neared the Illinois border, "I hate to tell you this, but as soon as I can get you settled in Illinois, I must return to Far West."

"Return to Far West!" Jenny echoed, not believing what she was hearing. "But why? The things we have left behind are not worth risking your life for. We have each other, the girls and Mandy. That's all that counts."

"I know, I know, and I wouldn't return for any material consideration, but there are thousands of our people who need assistance. Jim and I have both signed a covenant saying we will help until everyone is out of the state and out of danger from Governor Boggs's extermination order." He reached over and took her hand. She pulled it away and set it in her lap. Richard's eyes narrowed and his mouth formed a grim line. He leaned forward and spoke sharply, "You know I don't like leaving you here, but we must work together until every person who is suffering the persecution of the mob is out of the state. Our wagons can mean a great deal to those who have none. Brigham Young has asked all of the men who have wagons to return and help the poor, who have no means of travel but their own two feet. Do you think we should leave them to be killed by the mobs?" He instantly regretted his tone.

The color drained from Jenny's face, and she did not speak for a few minutes. When she did, her voice came clear and firm, "You have to do what you have agreed to do," she replied. She silently wondered how long it would be before her family could be reunited. And Aaron? What had happened to him and the Morris family who had befriended him?

Eastward, in a direct line with the flight of the Mormons sat the town of Quincy, Illinois. Quincy Bay afforded a natural harbor for river craft and boasted ferriage facilities. Jenny looked at the small town located on a limestone bluff about one hundred and twenty-five feet above the river on the east bank of the Mississippi, and wondered what would become of them there. She had at least expected to have Richard with her at this difficult time. How could she and the girls survive with him just dumping them off and leaving them in this strange place?

Richard observed her face which was noncommittal, and wondered what she was thinking. "It isn't much, but it's a touch of civilization," he said. "I hear it was laid out in 1825, but did not become a town until three or four years ago."

Jenny looked at the river and shuddered. She hated boats and rivers, but there was no alternate course to take. This late in the season, they were lucky to get there while they could still cross the Mississippi.

The ferry boat operator was a Mr. Thomas. He took three wagons at a time—Richard's two and Jim's on the first trip. They unhitched the stock and secured the wagons.

"I can't see a people in free America being driven from their homes and expelled from one of the states of the American union because of their religion," Mr. Thomas said. "What do you plan to do in Quincy?"

Jenny, whose head reeled from the rocking of the boat, spoke up quickly. "I am hoping to find a teaching position, and the girls and I are seamstresses. Surely there will be some work in Quincy."

The ferryman pointed out a little log cabin near the cliffs. "Check with my wife," he said. "She might be able to help you."

Mrs. Thomas, a pert, grandmotherly little woman with a ready smile, welcomed them. "Pull the wagons up into the yard, and we'll see what we can do," she said when they explained their plight. "Lawsy me, I can't imagine people being treated that way!"

Jenny took a quick liking to the woman." Don't worry, Dearie, we can find work for you," she told Jenny. "It seems I heard they needed a teacher in one of the schools in town. There's a real shortage of schools around here and so many children that need some learnin'. You might want to start your own school. I'm sure we could find a place."

As twilight arrived, they heard a cow mooing in a nearby pasture and a woman trudged by with a milk bucket. Laura's eyes filled with tears, and Jenny knew what she was feeling. Rosie had been not only a source of milk, but a special friend to Laura and the rest of the family as well.

A dog barked somewhere along the river bank. Twilight deepened and a lone star appeared in the night sky. They were safely across the river and into Illinois. It was a wonderful feeling to know that at last they were out of reach of Governor Boggs' order. Quincy seemed like a friendly little town.

As Richard led them in family prayer that night, he thanked God for their safe arrival. Jenny felt a stab of sorrow as she thought of Widow Wilson and the loss she had suffered along the way. As Jenny lay beside Richard in the wagon bed that night, she watched the rhythmic rise and fall of his chest and realized how much she loved this man. She felt a stab of guilt and vowed she would try to be a more understanding wife and companion.

Richard's brown eyes looked tired these days and his face stern. He seemed enveloped in both physical and spiritual weariness. He found it hard to deal with the fact that the prophet Joseph and his brother, Hyrum, were still incarcerated. Jenny knew the events of the past few months had made him feel helpless. He tried hard to deal with this feeling, so foreign to him. It was difficult now for him to have to ask help from strangers. If only she knew how to help him find peace, she thought as she gave a long sigh and stretched her legs, trying to get the kinks out of them so she could go to sleep.

The next day, Mrs. Thomas took Jenny to see about a teaching position. The school consisted of a one-room log cabin, with two windows and split log benches. The schoolmaster they hired that fall had run off with one of the patron's wives. The parents, whose children attended there, gathered and grilled Jenny with questions.

"I don't like the idea of hiring a Mormon!" one tall, whiskered man with long legs and a lined face exclaimed.

"Because they've been persecuted in Missouri, you think we should persecute them here too?" asked a short, blonde woman with a baby straddling her hip.

Finally, they decided to meet and discuss the question the next day. A tall woman walked over to Jenny. "My name is Rebecca Johnson," she said with a broad smile. "We'll let you know what the parents decide by tomorrow evening."

Mrs. Thomas seemed determined to help the Harris family. The next day she found dressmaking work for Laura, Alice and Adeline. Mandy, dark eyes almost ready to overflow, went to work as a servant for the most well-to-do family in the town. George Wilson hired out to help at the general store. Mrs. Wilson and Mary found temporary field work.

Mrs. Johnson brought word the school had decided to hire Jenny, though the man who had voiced his objection the day before had withdrawn his children.

Sarah looked lost. "Don't worry a minute, dearie, Mrs. Thomas insisted. I need a little help, myself. It won't pay a lot, but it will pay room and board and a little cash."

On November 29th Richard brought home a newspaper. "Listen to this address to the state legislature by M. Arthur, Esq.," He said to Jenny. "At least someone has the facts." Richard began to read parts out loud:

> Respected friends—Humanity to an injured people prompts me at present to address you this. You were aware of the treatment (to some extent before you left home) received by that unfortunate race of beings called the Mormons...not being satisfied with the relinquishments of all their rights as citizens and human beings in the treaty forced upon them by General Lucas, by giving

up their arms, and throwing themselves upon the mercy of the state, and their fellow citizens generally, hoping thereby protection of their lives and property, are now receiving treatment from those demons that make humanity shudder, and the cold chills run over any man not entirely destitute of any feeling of humanity. Those demons are now constantly strolling up and down Caldwell County, in small companies armed, insulting the women in any and every way, and plundering the poor devils of all their means of subsistence left them and driving off their horses, cattle, hogs, etc....leaving the Mormons in starving and poor condition. These are facts I have from authority that cannot be questioned, and can be substantiated at any time.

The men packed the little remaining food, clothing, bedding and supplies into Richard's largest wagon to leave for the women and children and prepared to return to Far West. The wagon box would have to serve as a home for Jenny, Miriam, Mary, the twins and the Wilsons until they could find better accommodations.

With dry eyes, Miriam and Jenny watched their men go. They felt like they had cried so many tears, they had none left.

"There's a lot of things in this life that are mighty hard to take, but we have to learn to take them," Widow Wilson commented as the men and wagons boarded the ferry to return to Missouri.

Residents of Quincy and Western Illinois gave a kindly reception to the exiled Saints and encouraged Brigham Young to settle his people there. Soon, thousands lined the shores of the Mississippi on both the Iowa and Illinois sides, living in wagon beds, tents or dugouts.

The weather grew colder. It seemed impossible to stay warm at night in the wagon. "Let's dig a dugout into the bank of the rise above the river," suggested Miriam. "It would give us some protection from the wind and weather. Young George is strong enough to help us a lot, and we can all do some digging."

Jenny felt thankful they had brought the shovels. Soon the young ones were taking turns and the hole in the river bank grew until it was almost the size of a room in one of their cabins, though not nearly as high. It had to be large enough to hold the Harris, Hansen and Wilson families—at least for sleeping.

"Be careful not to dig too close to the top, or it might cave in," young George cautioned the others.

Many Mormons slept on the ground, and lived chiefly on corn. Sickness and disease took a heavy toll. Graves were opened daily as the refugees laid loved ones to rest in Quincy. The spectacle of all these people being driven from Missouri aroused the indignation and sympathy of the people of Illinois and other states.

Richard and Jim returned for a few days. Jenny could feel the chasm between her and Richard growing as they were forced into separate ways. They never had an opportunity to be alone together, and it was impossible to talk about anything personal. Misunderstandings thrived on the many quirks of circumstance, things they could probably handle one at a time, but were quite overwhelming all together—the hard work, the persecution, Sarah's rape, being driven from their home, the lack of necessities, the loneliness. These things had all caused bitter disillusionment to them both.

Again the men left to help the destitute. Food became even more scarce than it had been and everyone ate sparingly as they rationed supplies. Many people were running out of corn, which had been their only food, and suffering from starvation. The small amount of food that Jenny's students occasionally brought helped sustain life for the Harris, Hansen and Wilson families. Jenny knew her family was luckier than most of the Mormon refugees.

Sister Drusilla Hendricks and her invalid husband James were in a nearby dugout. Drusilla told Jenny how they had been on the verge of starvation. "I had only one spoonful of sugar and a saucer full of cornmeal. I made mush out of it for James and the children, stretching it as far as I could make it go. When it was eaten, I prayed for strength, then washed everything, cleaned the dugout, and quietly waited to die."

"How awful!" Jenny sympathized. "So many of our people are starving. I wish I had known; I'm sure we could have found a little food to share with you and James. If things ever get that bad again, promise you'll let me know."

Drusilla continued, "Before long, the sound of a wagon brought me to my feet. It was our neighbor, Ruben Allred. He said he had a feeling we were out of food, so on his way into town, he'd taken a sack of grain to be ground into meal for us. I knew my prayers had been heard and answered."

"Your prayers were surely heard and answered," agreed Jenny. "Mine have been many times also."

"But that wasn't all," continued Drusilla. "A short time later, Alexander Williams arrived with two bushels of meal on his shoulders. He told me that he'd been extremely busy but the Spirit whispered to him 'Brother Hendricks's family is suffering,' so he dropped everything and came with help."

Jenny pondered Drusilla's story in her heart and knew God was answering their prayers. Days dragged into weeks. Everyone's strength was almost gone. They were growing thin and haggard. It was hard to teach school on an empty stomach. Jenny inquired daily of new arrivals, looking for word of Richard, Jim or Aaron. No one had seen or heard anything of them. She knew her brother Aaron was at a disadvantage, being unable to walk on his leg, and a feeling of despair enveloped her when she thought about him.

Jenny was thankful the twins were getting enough work that they were seldom forced to stay in the dugout, though they stopped by often. She couldn't bear to think of the girls suffering any more than they already had.

When Sarah stopped by she told the others, "I heard today that Isaac Barlow went into Iowa Territory up the Des Moines River a ways. When he told the people there of the persecution and how we were fleeing from Missouri, local families gave him not only food and clothing, but letters of introduction to several people. These included Dr. Isaac Galland, who Mrs. Thomas says is a gentleman of some influence, living on the banks of the Mississippi in a small settlement north of Quincy called Commerce."

"Yes," said Mandy, who had managed to get away for a brief visit. "I'se heared that too. Dr. Galland owns lots o' land in Commerce and lots in Iowa.

"He wrote, telling the Mormons here that several farms could be rented there," continued Sarah, "and that maybe fifty families could be taken care of at Commerce. He also offered his land in Iowa to the Mormons for two dollars an acre, to be paid in twenty yearly payments—without interest.

The Church leaders are holding a conference in February to consider his offer."

The women went to the conference and voted to accept Dr. Galland's offer, but the majority of the Saints voted not to locate lands at that time. In March Church leaders called another meeting. This time they appointed a committee to examine the lands of Dr. Galland and others.

Richard and Jim returned. They attended a public meeting in town that night. Richard reported to the family, "Leading men throughout the state are lending support to the Mormons, including Governor Carlin, Stephen A. Douglas and Dr. Isaac Galland. The Democratic Association of Quincy passed a resolution saying that the Latter-day Saints are in a situation requiring the aid of the people of Quincy, and they want us to 'state our condition, so they can lend us aid.'"

"The people of Quincy have been very kind," said Jenny, but how can such a small town help so many of us?"

"We're doing all we can to help ourselves, Richard said, except for a few who have given up." He added sadly, "Not all Mormons moved from Missouri. I can't believe that David Whitmer, and Martin Harris have left the Church."

Jenny shook her head. She couldn't blame anyone for giving up at this point.

CHAPTER SEVENTEEN

On the 24th of April, Jenny returned from school to find Richard whistling as he sorted through their few belongings.

"You seem to be in a good mood," she said.

"Guess who escaped from Missouri and joined us here today?" he said with a grin.

"Joseph! Are you sure he's here?"

Richard looked down and laughed at the surprise still obvious on Jenny's face. "I saw him with my own eyes. He told us how the prisoners at Liberty Jail were removed for Grand Jury trial, first to Daviess County, and later to Boone County. While enroute, it was hinted to them that it would please the authorities if they were to escape and they were allowed to purchase two horses. The guards conveniently went to sleep, except one who helped the weakened prisoners mount their horses and get away."

The Saints gathered to hear their prophet with hope beginning to swell again in their hearts. "We cannot stay here," he told them. "There are too many of us and our needs are too great; we must have a place of our own, where the Saints can gather. There is much work left for us to perform."

A few days later, Richard announced, "I'm going with Joseph Smith, Newel Knight, and Alanson Ripley to Commerce to try and locate a home there for us." He paused and looked into her eyes, but saw only a guarded reserve—a wariness he hadn't seen there before.

Jenny gave a slight wave of her hand, "So we can be chased out again?" she asked wearily.

"I hope not," said Richard.

Jenny watched him as he walked off. She had to admit it was good to see him showing some enthusiasm for a change. She had watched him retreat further and further inside himself these last few months. He was doing what he could to help those less fortunate than themselves, but as he did, his outrage toward the situation increased. She could often see the cold fury in his eyes.

The swampy, mosquito infested area mockingly designated as Commerce lay covered with underbrush and scattered trees. Some places were hard for a footman and impossible for a horse to cross without sinking. Bounded on three sides— in a mighty horseshoe-like sweep—by the muddy waters of the Mississippi, it consisted of half a dozen stone and log houses squatted along the river bank. Richard was surprised when Joseph said this was the place where his people should locate. Most of the more desirable land, available in Iowa, required cash money for its purchase.

Church leaders gave a total sum of $14,000 in promissory notes to Dr. Galland and Hugh White for the initial tracts of land in Commerce. With faith in what it might become, Joseph renamed the place Nauvoo—meaning "City Beautiful."

On the tenth of May, Joseph moved his family into a small log house on the bank of the river, a mile south of Commerce. Others were allotted lands according to their needs as many of those who had previously gone to Quincy filed into Nauvoo.

———————

Tom picked up the New York Times. It was a treat to get a New York paper, even if it was over a month old. He had become quite interested in reading articles by young Horace Greeley, who was making a name for himself as a brilliant New York editor. Tom's eyes fell upon one of Greeley's articles and it immediately caught his attention.

> It is a burning disgrace to civilization and humanity that the outrages which the poor 'Mormons' were the victims were committed, but a far deeper disgrace that those enormities have not to this day been made the subject of any judicial investigation. The grand juries and prosecuting attorneys of the counties adjacent to the scenes of horror are grossly culpable; but what shall we say of a governor (L. W. Boggs) who officially countenanced the murder of a people whom he was bound to protect? Missouri, until the blood is washed from her garments, is a disgrace to the Union.

Tom's face turned white and he put down the paper. He hadn't heard from his family for a long time. Were they all murdered? He had let the twins go to Missouri with Richard and Jenny thinking it would be the best thing for them. He had been so absorbed in his own grief that he had given no time to his daughters. Was it now too late? How could he ever forgive himself for his selfishness?

He and Ruth's courtship had quickly become serious. They were planning an autumn wedding. He had wanted to contact the girls and see if they would like to return to Virginia and the plantation now that he had a companion to teach them the niceties women needed to know. What a fool he had been!

––––––––––––

The June sun beat down on the men, and Richard was glad it wasn't any later in the year. As he stopped to look at the cabin going up, he had a feeling of deja vu. Counting their trek from New York to join the Mormons in Missouri, this was the third time they had been displaced since joining this new religion. They had left their beautiful home in New York; been driven by the mobs from their home in Jackson County, Missouri, to Quincy; and now to rebuild in Nauvoo. As Richard looked at the house, he wondered what life in this new home would bring for his family, or if they would be willing to join him here. He hadn't even talked to them for over a month, and Jenny seemed pretty distant when he saw her last. He took a slow, deep breath. Jenny and the girls had made a place for themselves in Quincy, and seemed to be doing fine without him.

His family deserved security they had not found previously, and he hoped they would find it here. He hoped this would be the last move they would have to make. Jenny had been forced to move enough, and she had become all too familiar with the sorrow and pain of persecution, but now they would build a home where they could stay. Surely this time they would find peace from their enemies. He had heard rumors that eventually the Saints would move to the West, but this seemed a much better solution.

He quietly shook his head as he suddenly realized how unfair he had been to Jenny the past few months. He had enjoyed the girls as much as she had, but was too proud to admit, even to himself, that he loved them as though they were his own, and appreciated having them as part of his family. He should never have accused Jenny of being responsible for what had happened to Sarah because she had insisted on bringing the girls to Missouri. He should not have withheld his love from her these last few months. Quiet tears rolled down his cheeks as he told himself he would make it up to her if she would be willing to give him the chance.

Richard swatted the pesky mosquito sucking blood from the back of his neck, then turned and glanced out over the swamp land surrounding him. Much of it was now being drained, with homes going up as fast as the land was dry enough and as building materials could be procured. Richard wondered if the city they were now laying out could live up to the new name Joseph had given it—Nauvoo, the city beautiful. Before building began, Joseph had some of the brethren survey the area and lay out broad, straight streets with right angles.

"We will build a temple on that small hill overlooking the Mississippi River," Joseph had confided to Richard. Richard had heard stories of the great sacrifices the people had made to build the temple in Kirtland. The women had even given their china dishes to break up and put in the outside plaster so the building would have an indescribable sheen to it. Richard wondered how people, so lacking in worldly goods, could manage to build another temple, but he knew if the prophet asked, they would rally to do what was required of them.

One difference in this house-raising from that in Missouri was now Richard knew most of the brethren. He took out his handkerchief, wiped his face and blew his nose, as Daniel H. Wells, a tall, long nosed man with sharp brow walked over to join him. Richard hoped Daniel would think he was just suffering from the abominable heat and moisture.

"It's looking good!" Daniel said, appraising the house with a critical eye.

"Yes," agreed Richard. "I can't believe how fast it's going up—thanks to all of the help I'm getting." He looked at Daniel with thoughtful eyes. Daniel was not a Mormon, but had lived in the area before the Mormons purchased the land, and had been friendly to them. He had been especially friendly to Richard, helping arrange for this choice piece of land, showing him how to drain the swampy area and always being there when help was needed.

"You've done a good job," said Daniel. "You won't have water seeping up through the floor in this spot. Even your crop land is beginning to dry out nicely. I wouldn't be surprised if you could plant corn next week."

Richard's eyes swept the acre he had drained and cleared and he felt a great lump of gratitude to this man swelling up in his throat. These people had been wonderful—all of them. Lucius Scovil, working on the back corner of the house was a prominent man. He had come to Missouri with Kirtland Camp in 1838 bringing his wife and two children. He was anxious to open a bakery and confectionery, but had taken time out from his busy schedule to help Richard raise his home. Shadrack Roundy, on the other side, had furnished shelter to the prophet in his home in Far West in 1833 and was now a member of Joseph's bodyguard. John E. Page, notching out the last log, had been ordained a member of the Council of Twelve Apostles of the Church in Far West.

He had previously served several important missions for the Church and in 1835 had converted 600 people in Canada and brought them to join the Kirtland Camp.

Each of the men, busy and active in many areas of the work, had taken out time to help Richard. "We must get your home up so Jenny can get her school opened again and get on with the business of educating the children," John said, slapping him on the back. "You know education has always been a top priority amongst the Mormons, young and old alike." Richard didn't tell these men he and his wife were practically estranged. He looked at the men, giving of their time to help him and Jenny. Actually, he thought to himself, I'm in the dark as much as you are concerning what will happen with Jenny and my family. He took a slow, deep breath and told himself to think positive.

"What are your plans for tomorrow?" asked Lucius. "It looks like we'll have the roof finished today. I'm sure the wife and kids would be glad to come over and help chink the logs if you can use them."

The women would mix wet clay with dried grasses and chink the cabin, filling the mixture into the spaces between the logs to keep out weather, flies and the incessant swarms of mosquitoes which raised red welts all over the body as they persistently tried to eat one alive. Building fires to smoke them out helped some, as did long-sleeved, heavy clothing, but Richard was always plastered with the red, itching welts resulting from their attacks.

Richard looked up at the clear sky. "It looks like the weather may stay good for a while. I think I'll go to Quincy and get Jenny and the girls. If the ladies would be willing to work on chinking the cabin, that would be great."

He hoped Jenny would be willing to join him in Nauvoo. Now that the land was dry and he had a cabin to cover their heads he found himself anxious to bring his family to their new home.

The next morning Richard opened his eyes before the crack of dawn. Lucius had been right, they had finished the roof the previous evening just as dusk invaded the land and made further work impractical. The timing couldn't have been better. He crawled out from beneath his blanket and rubbed his aching limbs which attested to the strenuous nature of house raising, even with lots of help. His muscles, though already hard from manual labor, ached and he was thankful for the assistance of his friends.

He rummaged in his packs and found a loaf of bread, then broke off a large chunk and cut slices from a block of cheese with his penknife. This he washed down with a mug of milk he poured from a small pail of fresh milk one of Daniel's children had brought over for him the night before.

When his quick meal was over, he rounded up Daisy and Doll, threw the harnesses over their broad backs and buckled them on. He led the team to the wagon, backed them up, and hitched them to it. By the time the bright pink streaks of light in the eastern sky reflected in the water of the river, he was on his way to Quincy.

When Richard arrived at the empty dugout in Quincy, he waited impatiently, then finally picked up the hammer and started working on the wagon box. He looked up, his hammer raised, and saw Jenny approaching. She was worn and sparse-looking, but still a beautiful woman, he noted with satisfaction. As she came closer, he lowered the hammer, dropped it and held out his arms.

Instinctively she ran into them. "Darling," he said, holding her close, "it has been so lonely without you. Can you ever forgive me for being such a brute these last few months?"

This simple little act did what tragedy had failed to do. Jenny felt their feet were back on solid ground. Together they could endure whatever might befall them. She felt warmth as Richard bent his head and laid his cheek against her hair. It seemed the barrier between them had begun to come down.

Her lips began to tremble and soon she was crying softly. Forgive? Was there something to forgive? She could not remember. There was much to forget, but together they could do it.

"Let's gather up our family, and go home," Richard suggested. He held his breath for a moment, then let it out slowly and silently.

"Home? And where might that be" Jenny asked. "We haven't had a place to call home for so long I can hardly remember what the word means," she added, pushing back a few strands of wispy hair that fell down about her ears and tickled her face. "I get all excited just thinking about a home, but thoughts are all I have," she added, staring him straight in the eye. They were so intent, no one even blinked.

Richard eyed Jenny speculatively, then answered in a soft, even tone, "I've built us a cabin in Nauvoo."

Jenny gasped. That was exactly what she wanted, the family together again at last, and ahead of them a new and hopefully better life in Nauvoo.

Richard lifted his head. Jenny looked up and saw a mischievous twinkle in his deep brown, almost liquid eyes. She hadn't seen that look for so long. She smiled, but studied his face for unspoken, hidden messages. She saw only the pride of having accomplished the unexpected. Jenny laughed weakly. "You're talking in riddles," she said, "but if you've built us a home, what on earth are we doing in this old dugout? This is probably like old clothes to you by now, but I get all excited just thinking about having a home again."

Richard chuckled softly at her enthusiasm, and held her tightly in his arms, savoring her nearness as long as he could. He blinked hard, not wanting Jenny to see his tears. "I love you, Jenny," he whispered. They held the embrace tightly; neither saw fit to waste breath explaining what the other one already knew.

Richard turned at the sound of Laura's voice, "Uncle Richard! What are you doing here?"

Things, once again, seemed almost perfect, Jenny thought, if only she knew what had happened to Aaron, but she had heard nothing of him and felt sure he had been killed by the mob in Missouri. It was strange, she mused, that Aaron, who had come to Missouri to kill Richard, would end up losing his own life at the hands of the mob.

"That's the way life is, filled with the unexpected," she said softly.

"What did you say?" asked Richard.

"Nothing," said Jenny. "I was just mumbling to myself. Let's go get Sarah and Mandy, then get the wagon loaded so we'll be ready to leave in the morning. I'm sure Miriam will be willing to take over the school until she and Jim have other plans."

Jenny looked at the little log cabin with a plank roof and thought it looked much like the one in Missouri when it was first built. It would take a lot of work to make it into a home. Laura looked around. There was no ceiling, nothing between the rafters and the floor but a few poles going across. "Where are we going to sleep?" she asked.

"We haven't got the loft done yet, but we soon will," Richard said. "I was just so anxious to bring you all here that I couldn't wait."

"Oh!" the twins exclaimed in unison, looking at each other.

The women and girls were soon mixing clay and dry grasses to finish chinking the logs. Lucius's family had already done much of the work.

"I'm tired of doing this," Sarah complained.

"It's a yearly ritual with the Mormons," said Laura, "a new home each spring."

The home was barely livable when illness struck the family with a vengeance. Richard took to his bed with chills and fever.

"Most o' Nauvoo's sufferin' from de fever." Mandy announced after helping deliver a neighbor's baby. "Joseph and Emma's house is filled with de sick and so is tents all over der yard. Many mo' is jus' lying on quilts on de grass. Sister Emma, she's been gon' from one to another, but now de's all sick, even Emma and Joseph! De's all laid low."

That afternoon both of the girls looked peaked and felt hot to the touch. The next day Jenny and Mandy joined them. It was all Jenny could do to get the family a few bites to eat before collapsing onto her bed. She could not get back up.

Widow Wilson came from Quincy to help feed and care for the family. Joseph had already arranged a piece of land in Nauvoo for the Wilsons. One morning she rushed in with a strange story. "This morning Joseph arose and began to bless the sick. He went from one to another healing those in his own home and yard, and then to those on the river bank in other homes and yards. He and some of the other Church leaders he healed crossed the river to Montrose and healed the sick there, including Brigham Young. I've never heard or seen anything like it," she said, her eyes large with wonder.

That afternoon Joseph came to their home and blessed each family member. Jenny had little life left in her body, but after his blessing she arose and attended to the needs of her family. Everyone rose from their beds and Richard accompanied the Prophet as he went to bless and heal other families in Nauvoo. Even the twins and Mandy marveled at this manifestation of the power of God.

It was miserably hot in the kitchen with the wash water heating on top of the wood stove. Mandy had used the horses and wagon to bring barrels of water from the river early that morning. She filled the wash tub until the water came about half-way up the side, then lifted the tub into the kitchen and onto the new cook stove to heat before sorting the wash.

While the water heated, she gathered up the week's washing and sorted into three piles: whites, light coloreds, and darks. She held up Richard's coveralls and grimaced at the amount of dirt covering them. They would almost stand up by themselves. "Glory be, he's brought half o' de swamp home on his coveralls," she exclaimed.

When the water was warm, she lifted the tub outside and set the washboard into it, its legs against the far bottom of the opposite side and the top leaning against the side nearest her. She filled a metal boiler with water and put it on the stove to heat before she picked up the first white piece—Jenny's high-necked white blouse. She checked the blouse for soiled spots which might need a little extra scrubbing, then dropped it into the tub.

The temperature outside already felt uncomfortably warm, she thought as she reached for the bar of homemade lye soap. Pulling the blouse onto the washboard, she rubbed it with the cake of soap. She set the soap onto the shelf-like ridge near the washboard, then grasped the top of the blouse in both hands rubbing it up and down several times along the metal ridges of the board. With each upward stroke she pulled a little more of the garment into her large hands, and scrubbed a new section of the blouse.

When the blouse was finished, she rinsed it, wrung out the excess water and dropped it into a large copper kettle. She took a deep breath and reached for another white piece. Before the whites were all done she felt like she'd been in a steam bath, as rivulets of sweat ran down her face and between her breasts. She dragged her soapy arms from the wash tub and dumped the whites into the boiler on the kitchen stove, sending clouds of steam into the air, then stuffed them down with the wash stick. The stick was a peeled hickory limb, about two inches in diameter and eighteen inches long, made smooth, especially at the ends, to keep from snagging any of the clothing.

She washed all of the light coloreds, then the darks, rinsed them and hung them out on the line to dry. The light breeze cooled Mandy and made the wash flutter in the wind. She dumped the dirty water and drew clean rinse water.

By now the whites were boiling. She dipped the wash stick into the water, hooked each piece of clothing and dropped it into the large kettle. She dumped them all back into the wash tub of clean water for a few rubs up and down the board and a good rinse before ringing out as much water as she could and hanging them out to dry.

While Mandy hung the whites onto the line she looked up and saw someone approaching. As he came closer, she could see it was Brother Joseph and waved at him. He had a smile as big as a little boy with a freshly baked cookie.

"Mandy," he called, "you're just the person I was looking for!"

"Yassuh," Mandy said looking at Joseph with surprise in her eyes, "what might yo' want me fo'?"

Joseph's eyes twinkled, "Mandy, I have the biggest surprise for you. Some of your own people—free Negroes—arrived at my home today. What an example of faith," he said rubbing his hands together with excitement. "I wish more of our people had half the devotion of this little band of wonderful Saints."

Mandy couldn't believe her ears. There were a few men of her own race in Nauvoo at that time. They had a glimpse of one another at church meetings, socials or a nod in passing, but she knew of no other women. She stared at Joseph, her mouth wide open and absolutely speechless.

"Miss Jane Manning is the head of the little group and she has brought her young son, her mother, sisters, brothers and in-laws on an 800 mile trek from Buffalo, New York." He paused and smiled again at Mandy. "You'll just have to hear the experiences of their travels for yourself. You won't believe all they went through to get here. If it had been most people, I fear they should have backed out and returned to their homes."

"Lord a mercy," Mandy exclaimed, wonder in her voice as she wiped her hands again on her apron.

"I want you and the Harris family to come over this evening with some of the other brothers and sisters to hear their experiences for yourself," Joseph said. He paused rubbing his chin into the palm of his hand.

"Yassuh, Brother Joseph," Mandy said, almost too overcome to talk.

"Is Jenny in the school room?" Joseph asked.

"Yassuh."

Joseph disappeared around the back of the cabin to the entrance of the school room. Mandy stood in confusion for a moment, her big, black eyes filling with tears. There were so many times when she ached to find another woman of her own kind to share her private thoughts, her feelings. She scooped up the last of the clothes and hung them on the line.

Chapter Eighteen

That evening Joseph and Emma had placed chairs all around their big room so everyone could sit. Richard, Jenny, Mandy and the girls all listened, spell-bound, as Jane Elizabeth Manning told of the experiences of her family. She told of being forbidden to listen to the Mormon missionaries by her Presbyterian minister under penalty of losing her soul, then sneaking out to hear Brother Wandall, the missionary, and being fully convinced in one sermon that he was presenting the true Gospel.

Mandy had listened to many sermons and found the things presented to make sense, but she still had doubts and hesitated to accept baptism. Jane had known immediately, and Mandy felt a tinge of envy at her strong convictions. Jane had been baptized the following Sunday after her first encounter with the missionary, and one year later, after converting her whole family, started with them for Nauvoo.

Mandy looked at Eliza Manning, Jane's mother, who was about her age, and felt an immediate kinship with the woman. As their eyes met she felt she had found the friend she had always hoped for. Here at Nauvoo she had freedom to come and go and would be able to develop a true friendship.

Jane continued telling about their trip, how they had made arrangements at Willon, Connecticut, for passage on a boat, for which they would pay when they arrived at Columbus, Ohio. But the canal boat captain demanded the full fee at Buffalo, New York, and when they could not raise the amount put them off the boat. "We started on foot to walk over 800 miles. We walked 'til our shoes were worn out and our feet cracked open and bled; 'til you could see the whole print of our feet with blood on the ground!"

Her voice shook slightly as she remembered the terrible ordeal, then came full and strong as she continued, "We stopped an' united in prayer to the Lord. We asked God the Eternal Father to heal our feet. Our prayers were answered and our feet were healed."

The Smith family's guests looked at each other with tears in their eyes, then nodded their heads in approval, marveling at the great faith of these people. They had seen the healing power of the priesthood in their lives, and if these Saints had that much faith, miracles might happen to them also. Joseph and Emma seemed to accept them without reservation.

"When we arrived at Peoria, Illinois, the police stopped us an' ask to see our 'free papers.' We didn't know what they meant for we'd never been slaves. After lots o' questions, they finally let us go." Jane dabbed her eyes with her handkerchief.

"We went on 'till we come to a river. There was no bridge, so we walked right into the stream. In the middle the water was up to our necks, but we got safely across. It got so dark we could hardly see our hands in front o' us. We saw a light in the distance, so we went toward it and fond an ol' log cabin, where we spent the night."

Jane looked at the others in the "little band" as Joseph had called them, and they nodded their heads in approval of her rendition of the trek. "The next night we was out in the forest, out in the open air. We started early, walkin' through the frost with our bare feet. Frost fell so heavy, like light snow till the sun rose an' melted it away."

Mandy looked at Jenny who shivered instinctively. She hated being out in the cold. Jane's voice continued, "But we went on the way, rejoicin', singin' hymns, and thankin' God for his goodness and mercy to us, an' blessin' us as He had, protectin' us from harm, answerin' our prayers an' healin' our feet." She paused a moment as she mentally relived their trek, "we had to keep to the woods, eatin' berries, sleepin' in the thickets with the rabbits."

Yes, Brother Joseph was right, thought Mandy. Many people would have turned around and gone home before they went through half of what the James family had. Jane concluded her remarks: "We have now arrived at our destined haven of rest, the beautiful Nauvoo! Here, too, we went through all kinds of hardship, trial and rebuff, but we at last found brother Orson Spencer and he directed us to the Prophet Joseph Smith's home. When we found it, there was Sister Emma standin' in de door, and she kindly says, 'Come in, come in!'" Tears swelled up in Jane's eyes.

"And you are among friends now," concluded Joseph.

Richard and Jenny wondered what was going on in Buffalo, and were anxious to talk with the Manning family about their previous home. At first they passed pleasantries back and forth, and as they became more comfortable with each other, asked many things they wanted to know. After plying them with continuous questions until it grew quite late and the talk died down, they left, feeling an echo of happiness within themselves. But Mandy, the happiest, knew that though she would always miss Sully, her little granddaughter, much of her loneliness would be ended now that she again had friends of her own race.

It was good to get back to living as a family instead of using all of their energy for bare survival, thought Jenny. After all the ugly, dehumanizing things which had happened to them, action had become a substitute for expression of feelings, and it seemed they had to learn to talk to one another all over again.

Sarah still questioned why, if there were a God, he would put them through such persecution. Richard knew she continued to have feelings of guilt and unworthiness, though heaven only knew why. He sat down with her and tried to answer the questions expressed only in her haunted eyes—to pare away the scars of pain, rejection and suffering and find the confident girl that once resided there. He searched for words that would help her.

"God's people must be strong and must have a lot of faith. Those who do not will be weeded out, as will those who joined the Church for the wrong reasons. That is already happening," he sighed. "Many of our problems have been caused by those of our own people who do not have the faith to live the Gospel."

He paused and shifted uncomfortably. "I couldn't see that for a long time; I became very angry and wondered why God would let so many awful things happen." He looked into her half-wondering, half-wanting-to-believe eyes. "Brother Joseph says strength comes from adversity and now I can see that is true."

"Lucy says I must be a bad person, or terribly bad things wouldn't have happened to me." Tears formed in Sarah's eyes. "I'm not bad, Uncle Richard, I'm really not bad!"

Richard paused and looked down at her upturned face, noting her pain and vulnerability. She desperately needed his approval. His brown eyes filled with fresh anger as he took a quick breath and tried to keep his voice even. "Lucy is wrong, dead wrong. Just last September Brother Joseph received a revelation about that. He was told the righteous would suffer along with the wicked and it was wrong to say someone had transgressed because they had bad things happen to them. He reminded us we were not to judge others."

"Do you think that revelation could have been especially for me?" Sarah asked quietly as she brushed her dark hair back out of her eyes.

"I think it was especially for you and all those who had awful things happen in their lives in Missouri," he answered, putting an arm around her. She tried to smile, but anger, embarrassment and hurt kept the corners of her mouth from turning the right direction.

Richard was sure Lucy's sentiments had come from her mother who he felt had a mean attitude and an acid tongue. He knew she was disgruntled, disillusioned and disappointed in the way things had been going, but how dare she imply what had happened to Sarah was the child's own fault. The things they had suffered had forever altered everyone's world. The Saints had experienced hunger, pain, the loss of loved ones. They had survived, though their clothing was worn, dirty and tattered—and some of their dreams almost as ragged. Through their sorrow and persecution, some became bitter and disillusioned, others thanked God for the things they did have and grew stronger from their experiences.

———

Nauvoo grew rapidly as exiles from Missouri gathered and converts continued to arrive from both the eastern states and foreign lands. The Mormons prospered in Nauvoo.

As they drained the swamps and built a city, the malaria carrying mosquito all but disappeared.

Joseph, with the help of some of the men, drew up an unusual city charter, granting broad powers to the city council–consisting of a mayor, four aldermen and nine councilors elected by the voters. A militia, known as the Nauvoo Legion, would be equipped by the state and officered by the citizens of Nauvoo. The municipal court was independent of any but the State Supreme Court.

Those from both political parties sought the Mormon vote, and the charter was passed by the state legislature. The charter, accepted by the state, the city became independent of all other agencies in the state. Nauvoo was practically a city-state. The charter would protect the people from mobs, illegal court proceedings and passing whims of higher government agencies–indignities they had suffered from in Missouri.

Joseph told Richard and others, "I concocted it for the salvation of the Church, and on principles so broad that every honest man might dwell secure under its protecting influence, without distinction of sect or party."

As they sat around the dinner table, Richard explained to his family, "Because of the lessons we learned in Missouri, Joseph says we shall not attempt to isolate ourselves from others. A proclamation by the First Presidency invites people of all religious denominations to live with us in Nauvoo."

"Do you think many will?" Jenny asked, wiping her mouth with her clean white cloth napkin before draping it beside her plate.

"We have a sprinkling of several religions here now, and the city council just passed an ordinance protecting all people in the practice of their different religions."

"It would be so nice if we could all live together in peace," Jenny said wistfully.

"The city is growing unbelievably fast. Hastily constructed cabins and shacks are being replaced by beautiful frame and brick dwellings," Richard remarked. "Many of the homes are being built of brick. Nauvoo's kilns are kept busy turning out mellow, tawny red bricks." Richard noted. "In two years' time the city has grown from thirty buildings to over twelve hundred, with hundreds of others in various stages of construction."

Many new converts brought their skills to the community as artisans and craftsmen. Carpenters, cabinet makers, masons, brick layers, tinsmiths and iron workers, professional people and common laborers came to Nauvoo. Shoulder to shoulder they toiled, establishing a bond between them. For entertainment on summer evenings, friends sat together on porches, enjoyed one another's company, and sometimes ate together.

There was nothing haphazard about the growth of the city. The wide city streets—running north and south—were dotted with residences, set back a uniform distance and bordered with white picket fences. Homes each had their own individual style, though most of the important buildings exhibited modified Georgian architecture, known as Federal. The homes exemplified not only refinement and good taste, but also the courage, and determination of a people rich in faith in the face of great adversity.

The Harris family moved into a home that far excelled the one they had left in Buffalo, New York. Finely upholstered sofas and chairs replaced the hand-made furniture of earlier times. Paintings hung on the walls. Their home again knew harmony and contentment, love and laughter.

Lilac bushes started from that first lilac root Jenny had brought from Buffalo bloomed in profusion, filling the air with their scent. Jenny had placed each shrub carefully in its designated space and tended all the plants until their feet were finally rooted deeply in the soil.

Jenny's school and teaching methods were as modern as any of the day. New pupils, with different names but the same expectant faces, learned to read and to write, to cipher and to spell. Mandy, Sarah, and Laura were her helpers in a class much larger than Jenny had ever taught before.

The whole country, under cultivation for many miles around, produced corn, wheat, potatoes and all kinds of produce. Except for an immense garden, Richard had given up farming and was back in the shipping business. With the Mississippi River practically at their doorstep, opportunities in shipping were abundant.

Sarah's cat, Sunshine, lay in a little bed Sarah had made for her. Three helpless baby kittens snuggled close beside her. Sunshine was a mother! Sarah and Laura doted over the kittens.

"Joseph has drawn up a charter for a municipal university—the first in the nation," Richard told Jenny one evening at supper. "The city council is drawing up plans for an educational system which will include all grades from elementary to university classes and plans to build schools for them all. Joseph told me he plans to see all of our people educated—young and old."

Jenny looked alarmed for a moment. "What will happen to our little school?" she asked, leveling a disbelieving stare. Richard reached out and gently took her hand, a short squeeze, nothing more. She looked so much healthier now. Lines under her eyes weren't deep and dark as they had been before. It was especially gratifying to Richard to see Jenny happy and healthy again.

"Nothing for now," Richard mused. "These plans are highly ambitious and will take a lot of time and planning before any changes are made. Eventually you may find yourself teaching in a modern building with a lot of advantages you don't have here. How would you like that?"

"I'm not sure," Jenny answered honestly, smoothing out the wrinkles in the tablecloth Richard had been able to ship in from the East.

One summer evening in 1841, Richard brought home a copy of the St. Louis Atlas. "Look what it says about Nauvoo," he insisted.

Jenny, sitting in her new rocker, picked up the paper and read aloud:

> The population of Nauvoo is between 8,000 and 9,000 and of course the largest town in the State of Illinois. How long the Latter-day Saints will hold together and exhibit their present aspect, is not for us to say. At this moment they present the appearance of an enterprising, industrious, sober and thrifty population, such a population indeed, as in the respects just mentioned, have no rivals east and we rather guess, not even west of the Mississippi.

Jenny folded the paper and handed it back to Richard. "Well, they've sure changed their mind about us, haven't they," she said.

Saturday dawned as a beautiful sunny day. Both girls were dressed in their new white dimity dresses with wide pink sashes. Mandy combed Laura's hair while Jenny did Sarah's. Sarah flinched and pulled a face as Jenny combed through the snarls. "I'm trying to be careful. I didn't mean to hurt you, but you're so tender headed," said Jenny biting her tongue so she wouldn't scold her wiggly niece. "You're going to look beautiful. Your father will be so surprised!"

It had been Richard's idea to have a likeness of the girls taken to send to their father. He had made the appointment with Brother Maudsley, the portrait painter.

"Father won't recognize us now," said Laura. "It's been years since he's seen us." She looked over at Sarah and continued, "I haven't changed much, but my sister is a completely new woman."

They all laughed. Laura was starting to develop quite a sense of humor. It was so nice to see her former bitterness disappearing, though she still showed apparent awkwardness around the men of the settlement.

"Laura, you're such a caution," said Mandy. "I don't know how we put up with you."

Jenny studied the girl for a moment. She was small and dark with even classic features. Her skin remained untanned as though it seldom saw the sun. Her wide blue eyes showed her emotions so plainly. While she and Sarah still looked strikingly alike, anyone close to the twins didn't have any trouble telling them apart. Their personalities differed so greatly.

"We'd better hurry," said Jenny, straightening Laura's sash bow. "Your uncle will be here with the wagon before we're ready to go." She sighed, "And you know how impatient Richard gets when he wants to go somewhere and has to wait."

Richard pulled up in the wagon as she spoke. They all rushed out the door. He reached out a hand to Jenny and helped her up beside him on the driver's seat. Richard was jubilant. When he latched onto an idea, he acted upon it, and this was one of the best ideas he had come up with in a long time. Jenny noted that he was so proud to be sending Tom a portrait of the twins. His brown eyes were surrounded by smile lines as he glanced proudly back at the girls, then over at Jenny.

Mandy stopped at the post office, and the postmaster recognized her immediately. "I'm glad you stopped. We have a letter for Brother Harris."

"Is der anything else fo' dem?" Mandy asked. Jenny had sent her to see if the mail order she had sent for school supplies had arrived.

"That's all," the jovial man said, handing her the letter.

Mandy looked at the postmark; it was from Virginia, and it looked like Massa Tom's writing. She fairly burst with excitement by the time she reached home.

Laura sat by the window reading the Book of Mormon, which she had started reading again since they moved to Nauvoo and seemed to be enjoying doing so. Jenny busily dusted what little furniture they had. "You know, Aunt Jenny, these people had awful things happen to them, like we did in Missouri."

"Yes," Jenny said. "Joseph says their story was written for us in this time, because we need to learn the same lessons they..."

"It's a letter from Massa Tom," Mandy announced as she burst into the room and handed the thick envelope to Jenny. The girls were instantly at her side.

Jenny looked at the thick envelope curiously, then rose and moved to the table, setting her mending in the center. She pulled out a chair and sat down. "Let's see what your father has to say," she said smiling at the expectant faces of Sarah and Laura.

Mandy stood behind Laura looking almost as excited as the girls.

"Bring me the letter opener, Mandy," Jenny directed, but Mandy, anticipating her request, had already fetched it, and held it out to her.

Jenny opened the envelope carefully. The folded letter protected a bank draft. It was made out to Richard for the amount of one hundred dollars. Jenny couldn't believe her eyes.

Money was scarce in Nauvoo, even in their recently found prosperity. While the people were prospering in Nauvoo, most still had little cash money. School was still paid for by a few eggs here, some milk or butter there, jerked venison, a side of bacon, beans, wheat or meal. Receiving a hundred dollars was like becoming rich overnight. Jenny set the bank draft carefully on the table beside the envelope and began to read the letter:

> My Dearest Family,
>
> You have no idea how welcome the likenesses of the girls were to my eyes. I longed to see their countenances.
>
> From what I had read in the newspapers, I was afraid that you had all been killed.

The girls have changed so much I hardly recognized them. I still thought of them as little girls, but they have become young ladies. I had no idea when they left how much I would miss them and Mandy.

When you left the house was so quiet I was forced to find company elsewhere, and to my pleasure discovered Miss Ruth Kearns who was visiting her brother on the adjoining Kearns plantation. I wish you could have all come to the wedding.

I'm sending some money, which I hope will help with the care of the girls, and I want them to know they are always welcome if they ever want to come home.

Love, Tom

"Hurry with those dinner dishes, girls," said Jenny, "or we'll be late."

"Where's Uncle Richard?" asked Laura as she finished washing a plate and set it in the rinse pan.

"He's down on the flat helping the police make preparations for the show," said Jenny. "He'll be here any minute."

"Won't he have to eat before we go?" asked Sarah.

"No," said Jenny, "I sent him a lunch so it wouldn't be such a rush."

Jenny grabbed a dish towel and started helping Sarah dry the dishes. The wild animal show had been advertised all over town for weeks, and it seemed the whole town was excited about seeing the act.

Jenny was just drying the last bowl when they heard the new buggy on the street outside. The girls dashed out the door leaving Jenny to hang the dishtowels and wipe off a few drops of water spilled on the table.

Mandy, who had been cleaning the school room, asked, "Is der anything I can do t' help yo'."

"No, Mandy, you and the girls just get in the buggy and I'll be right out. I'm all finished here," she said as she untied her white apron and hung it on a peg on the kitchen wall.

As she went out the door a gust of wind blew dust into her face and her eyes smarted. She glanced at the sky. "I do hope the weather stays nice," she told Richard as he helped her into the carriage.

Richard's eyes narrowed as he scanned the sky. The wind was starting to blow and a few clouds were rolling in. It didn't look too promising. He flicked the reins and the buggy started to roll down the street.

Several other families had carriages, buggies, or wagons at their doors, and the street was beginning to become crowded with others on their way to this event.

Jenny waved at Widow Wilson, then at Eliza Snow and her parents as they passed. The wind was getting stronger fast. Gusts were starting to sway carriages. Just as they arrived at the flats, a tremendous burst of wind blew down the canvas which had been raised to protect the crowd from the sun during the performance. Empty carriages and wagons clashed into each other, horses snorted and shied and general bedlam erupted. The girls squealed, Mandy was mumbling a prayer, and Jenny, with white knuckles, clung to the side of the buggy. Richard had his hands full trying to control the team.

Jenny thought they had started early, but half the city seemed to already be there. People were crowding onto the blown down canvass and obstructing the efforts of the exhibition people to do anything to get things righted so the show could begin. The animals added their voices to the confusion.

Police Chief Hosea Stout called the Nauvoo Police together to restore order, but the crowd was out of control. One policeman, then another started swinging their clubs, and several people were knocked down before order was restored.

The Harris family, still in their wagon their team now under control, looked horrified at the turn of events. It began to rain, not softly but in great torrents. The wind blew the rain into the carriage. Rain pelted down on Jenny's dress and it clung to her bosom. The force of the rain stung her arms, and wet hair was falling into her face. The girls and Mandy, in the back were a little more protected, but still getting wet. Jenny couldn't help but notice the crest fallen look on their faces.

"Are we going to just sit here all day and get soaked," asked Sarah, her voice sharp, "or are we going to do something?"

"Maybe we ought to go home," said Richard.

"No! No!" chorused the girls. "I've never seen an elephant, and I want to stay for the show!" Laura pleaded.

"Well, I'll drop you women off at the Seventies Hall," Richard decided. "I'll take care of the horses and carriage and meet you later."

By the time they were in the Seventies Hall many others had crowded into the building until there was barely standing room. "Where's Sarah?" Jenny asked as she tried unsuccessfully to keep everyone together.

"She's back there by the door," said Laura, "talking to Sam Hill. His family just moved to Nauvoo, and boy has he changed! You should see how handsome he is now…and he still seems to like Sarah!"

Jenny looked at Laura, bubbling over with excitement, and thought what a constant delight the twins had been in her and Richard's lives. They were a source of perpetual amazement—at times, heart-tugging pathos and at others, sheer delight.

A clamor of voices made a continuous din. Stricken with indignation, a large woman with a loud voice standing behind Jenny was saying, "Did you see the way the police just went over there and started knocking people down? They ought to be knocked down themselves."

A short, thin fellow with a straggly beard challenged, "If people would act like they had some respect for order and decency, they wouldn't have to call in the police. People were crowding onto the canvass so the show men couldn't do anything."

The woman turned on him angrily, "I'll bet you're one of them."

In spite of wind and rain people, anxious to see the show, did not leave. The street, as well as the Seventies Hall, remained filled with people. The winds began to subside and the show men, with the help of the police arranged the wagons to make a barrier from the weather, got the canvass back up, and announced the show was ready to begin. People filed out of the Seventies Hall and congregated under the canvass. By now George Wilson had joined them and was talking to Laura.

Rain continued to fall, but it failed to dampen the enthusiasm of the people of Nauvoo for the trained elephant and other exotic animals performing. There were two camels, a cage of monkeys, and a mountain lion. A thick odor permeated the area and hung over the crowd, but Jenny noted it didn't seem to bother anyone. Sarah and Sam who had also joined the family, seemed as spellbound as Laura. Mandy didn't take her eyes off the performance.

The show was impressive, but Jenny, still uneasy about what happened preceding the show, felt relieved when they headed back towards the buggy. "I know the police had to do something," she told Richard, "but I can't quite believe they needed to get that rough."

Richard looked thoughtful. "If we're going to thrive as a people, we have to learn to respect law and order." His eyes narrowed, "That crowd was almost as out of control as a mob. We'll get no respite from our enemies if we act just like them."

Jenny looked up in surprise. She hadn't thought about it that way.

"On the other hand," Richard continued, "men have a tendency to abuse power when they have too much…"

All of a sudden Jenny stopped dead still. There coming toward her was Aaron and Anna Morris. She let out a glad little cry and ran towards them and soon had Aaron in a bear hug.

With a smile on his tanned face, Aaron held out his hand to Richard. "I hope you'll forgive me for the things I said the last time I saw you," he said. "I realize now I was wrong." He looked at his sister with a twinkle in his eye. "Jenny was right; I was the one who needed to be rescued."

"There's nothing to forgive," said Richard, grabbing his hand enthusiastically. "I'm just glad to see you up and walking and safely here in Nauvoo."

"I'm sure you remember Anna," Aaron said with a grin. "She was such a good nurse that I'm trying to convince her to become my wife."

Richard looked at Anna and a small smile creased the corner of his mouth. "You mean to tell me you've fallen in love with this scoundrel and Mormon hater?"

"Okay, Richard, rub it in," said Aaron. "Seriously though, that accident was the best thing that ever happened to me. Because of it I met the girl of my dreams. I watched her family and soon decided that if they were any example of Mormonism, the things I had heard about the religion were completely false."

"Oh, Aaron, I'm so happy for you," exclaimed Jenny.

"Time went so slow when I was confined to bed, and Anna here set the Book of Mormon just close enough so I could reach it. At last my curiosity got the best of me and I began to read. I'm planning to be baptized next Sunday."

"You are?" exclaimed Jenny and the others in unison. "What a wonderful surprise! Are we invited?" Jenny asked.

"You surely are, and we'll be offended if you aren't there," spoke up Anna, who seemed delighted with this unexpected turn of events. "Aaron is building a house on the northeast corner of the first street in Kimball's Addition."

"I can't believe you're in Nauvoo and we didn't know it," said Jenny. "Nauvoo is getting to be so large people know only their neighbors."

———————

On the way home, everyone chattered at once. Richard hadn't seen Jenny so radiant for a long time. It was good they had found Aaron; Jenny had been so worried about his safety, and had lost all hope that he might still be alive.

In the back, Mandy thought about the laundry this outing had generated. "Lawsy me, girls, I'll never get dos dresses of yo's clean. You both look like yo' had a bath in a mud puddle."

Jenny looked at the city with new insight as they drove towards their home. Many spectacular homes and impressive buildings, of brick, lumber and stone, graced the wide streets of the city patterned after the Zion, which was first envisioned to be in Jackson County, Missouri. On the brow of the hill, up from the river, where the city joined the prairie, a temple site had been chosen and construction begun. The temple was to cost a million dollars—more than ten times the amount spent on the Kirtland Temple.

While the Church had seemed at a low ebb to the casual observer during the Missouri crisis, the strength within had become greater than anyone realized. The zeal which now characterized the Mormons had never been paralleled in modern history. A penniless people was becoming the most prosperous in Illinois. Missionaries continued to carry the gospel to many lands, and the Church was growing.

In an unbelievably short time their city had become the envy of many earlier settled communities. Perhaps here in Nauvoo they would find the peace and freedom to work towards a nobler way of life, and brotherhood with all men. Nauvoo was truly living up to its name—"City Beautiful."

Persecution had solidified the Church. Jenny realized that her experiences and those of others had increased her strength to walk the road ahead—through the darkness and despair to see the light of the Gospel burning steady and true. The things they had suffered had been stepping stones to stronger faith and greater conviction.

That night in her bed, Jenny thought about her family and her eyes filled with tears. Aaron had been "brought back from the dead" as far as she was concerned. His leg had healed, leaving him with only a slight limp. The girls had brought a dimension into her and Richard's lives that they could never have enjoyed without them. They were both so wrapped up in excitement of friends and young love. They were immature, but each had the heart of a woman. Even Mandy glowed with happiness as she mingled with her new found friends.

Jenny and Richard again enjoyed a closeness that had been missing from their lives for a long time. She slid into Richard's arms, and they closed tenderly around her as she melted into his embrace. She felt thankful their relationship was again bringing love and fulfillment into their lives. She felt a swift happiness within; once again there was joy in the Harris home. With calm assurance, the Harris family looked toward the future, whatever it might bring.